From *The Cigarette Girl*

'I don't know,' I said. 'I think the road signs are getting harder to read. I just turned twenty-eight and feel like I'm making the same mistakes over and over. I've got to try making new mistakes.'

I've never understood the connotations of the phrase 'Just for sex'. Just for sex is a lot – if the sex is good. It's no small thing to be getting fabulous sex.

'Can't turn friends into lovers,' I explained to Mimi. 'Don't know how to do that.' 'Oh, it's easy,' she said, somewhat exasperated by my ineptness. 'Just have a couple of drinks and ****.'

Let me go on record right here and say I never have been and never will be a Rules girl. I refuse to turn my life into a strategic arms agreement. If their advice is don't sleep with him for the first four dates, my advice is don't sleep with him for the first four hours.

I've always thought that someone should do a study on the relationship women have with shoes. It defies logic. Forget sending flowers, guys. That's sweet and everything, but the way to a girl's heart just might be through her feet.

Carol Wolper

The Cigarette Girl

PAN BOOKS

First published 1999 by Riverhead Books,
a member of Penguin Putnam Inc., New York

This edition published 2000 by Pan Books
an imprint of Macmillan Publishers Ltd
25 Eccleston Place, London SW1W 9NF
Basingstoke and Oxford
Associated companies throughout the world
www.macmillan.co.uk

ISBN 0 330 39074 0

3 5 7 9 8 6 4 2

A CIP catalogue record for this book is available from
the British Library.

Typeset by SetSystems Ltd, Saffron Walden, Essex
Printed and bound in Great Britain by
Mackays of Chatham plc, Chatham, Kent

FOR 'SIDNEY'

'Why don't you fuck the bimbo
and have the cigarette with me?'

CARRIE FISHER,
Postcards from the Edge

Many thanks to Angela Janklow Harrington and my editor Julie Grau. Without them this book would not exist.

Also thanks to those friends who always encourage me to say it the way I see it.

Sean Macpherson. Gina Gershon. Eric and Lisa Eisner. Tom Hedley. Stacey Sher. Stephen Hopkins. Stephanie and Dewey Nicks. Chloe King. Daphna Kastner. Susan Campos. Tony Drazan. Lisa Specht. Marcia Strassman. And, of course, the late, great Don Simpson.

One

My boyfriend wanted to visit me on location, but his parole officer wouldn't let him. That phone call was the beginning of the end of our relationship. Not because he couldn't make the trip. Of course he couldn't make it. He'd been in prison for drugs, and I was working in *Miami*. It was the beginning of the end because of the conversation that followed. 'I'm really bummed,' he said.

'It's probably better,' I replied. 'I'm working sixteen hours a day rewriting an action movie *while it's shooting*. I only operate on two modes. Insecure and exhausted.'

'No, no, no,' he interrupted. 'I'm bummed 'cause it would have been good for me. Being on the set would have been good for my career.'

Something about the way he said 'on the set' – as if he'd been hanging out on one for years – stopped me cold. Six weeks out after doing two years in prison and already he was talking the talk. I had to proceed cautiously here, fearing that the next sign on this highway to unhappiness would be a large one. A large neon one, warning there'd be no food, gas, or lodging for the next five hundred miles.

'Which career?' I asked gently.

'Acting,' he said as if he were stating the obvious.

There it was, the giant, flashing, neon sign that foretold a future filled with acting classes, head shots, more classes, more head shots. None of which he could afford. And the truth is, he wasn't even a good enough actor to convince me he was in love with me. If he had been, I probably would have gladly paid for all those classes and photos, which I couldn't afford either. But he wasn't, and I wouldn't, and the unraveling of our brief relationship began with that phone call.

It was not a pretty picture. My search for Mr. Maybe had led me to an ex-con actor wannabe. This is not where I thought I'd be at twenty-eight.

*

I never thought I'd be the kind of woman who searched for a guy. I always thought it would just happen. And it always did. But things change when you move into the zone – that seven-year period between the ages of twenty-eight and thirty-five when women feel the pressure to resolve the marriage and baby issues.

Before my twenty-eighth birthday hit, I was perfectly happy to live my single life. Work. Work out. And sex. That's all I needed. Maybe that's a little on the shallow side, but I live in Los Angeles. Shallow is politically correct here. Besides, Southern California is all about velocity and optimism, which has everything to do with its two most glaring characteristics: freeways and sunshine. They do something to you. You start believing that 'it,' whatever 'it' is, will all work out. That is, until you hit the zone. Then it doesn't matter how fast you're moving or how beautiful the day, you start believing that whatever 'it' is, it'll never work out and you were crazy to believe in 'it' in the first place.

The zone changes everything. It confuses everything. Sometimes you can talk yourself into believing something's on track until you're so far into it that the realization that it isn't can't stop the runaway train.

*

Hollywood abounds with runaway trains. No one wants to be a fantasy buster in fantasyland. Example. My friend Marcy. She used to be a real party girl. She literally danced on tables. And chairs. And – occasionally – laps. She loved hanging out at clubs and being up on any info that had to do with hot guys, hot gossip, and shoe sales at Barneys. She could always be counted on for key info – like the name of a bikini waxer who would take it all off.

'You'll love this woman,' she told me. 'She'll wax the whole thing. I brought her a photo from a porno magazine and said, "Can you make my pussy look like that?" And she said, "No problem, hon." She even makes you get on your hands and knees so she can deliver the full porno wax job. Rumor is, a Warner Brothers executive was so pleased with his wife's new look, he went out the very next day and bought her an emerald ring and sent the waxer flowers. Orchids.'

That was typical Marcy – until she hit the zone and left her wild-girl ways behind to become engaged to a humorless corporate lawyer. Their marriage was a serious WASP event, breaking tradition only briefly when the minister quoted from Kahlil Gibran. I wasn't buying the new Marcy and her zone-inspired conservatism. None of her friends did. But we all made toasts to the happy couple, drank a lot of champagne, and left thinking, Okay, it'll last a year or two . . . which by L.A. standards is a respectable length of time.

What I didn't expect was a call from Marcy the next morning at nine A.M., just seventeen hours after saying 'I do.' She was phoning from the bathroom of their honeymoon suite at the Hotel Bel-Air.

'I don't know about this marriage business,' she said, using the same tone she used to use when she was about to shift her allegiance from one club to the next new thing. 'I don't knoooow,' she repeated, dragging out the word so there was no mistaking her meaning. Her 'knoooow' was a 'no.' Sometimes even the zone isn't powerful enough to squash a killer attack of Oh my God, what have I done?

★

Personally, I had few illusions about married life, and my heart was still with the wild girls, yet there was a part of me . . . call it female instinct or millions of years of DNA memory, that felt a tug toward – if not yet motherhood – some kind of couplehood. Clearly I was ambivalent though, fighting it all the way. You don't hook up with an ex-con if you're seriously looking for a partner. Someone 'fresh out' has to go through reentry. He has to reacclimate. He has to find a job. That said, he was not a bad guy. I thought of him as a cross between Spicoli (Sean Penn) in *Fast Times at Ridgemont High* and McMurphy (Jack Nicholson) in *One Flew Over the Cuckoo's Nest*. What can I say? I've always been a sucker for someone who fights the system. Plus, he was good-looking in that bad-boy kind of way. And the first time I met him – at the gym (of course) – he came up with the kind of provocative line that jumpstarts my hormones.

5

He was supposed to be selling me on the idea of hiring him as my trainer. He was giving me a free workout to demonstrate his method.

'Let's start off with two sets of lunges,' he suggested.

'Hmmm,' I replied, not moving an inch. 'I don't do lunges.'

'You don't *do* lunges? What's the problem? Knees? Hamstring pull?'

'Nope. Just don't like them.'

He took a moment to compute that. 'Okay.' He nodded. 'Then let's start with squats.'

'I don't do squats.'

'You don't *do* squats?' He looked at me like I was an alien creature.

'Nope. I hate them.'

He took a few moments to assess the situation, took another gulp of his Power Blast protein drink. 'Uh, I don't know you very well,' he said calmly, 'so this might sound weird. But you might want to consider the concept of surrender.'

Loved that line. It put a big smile on my face. Okay, now it was getting interesting. I didn't do the lunges or the squats and never worked out with him again. But I did invite him to lunch.

*

We went to a trendy place on La Brea. One of those restaurants known for salads made from ingredients that should never be put in the same bowl. Feta and beans. Fennel and tangerines. Walnuts and zucchini. We sat outside and talked about sex. I had to ask him the question anyone would ask a guy who'd just gotten out of prison.

'Two years. No sex?'

He didn't seem at all put off by my bluntness. 'I was in prison for one year, eleven months, and six days,' he said. 'I didn't have sex for one year, eleven months, and twenty-one days.'

'So,' I continued, 'what was that like? The first time after almost two years?'

He put down his fork. 'Well, to be honest, when I was done with her, she didn't know if she wanted to call the cops or marry me.'

I have to admit it. Hearing that intrigued me even more. But then again, I've always been a curious girl.

At first it was pretty great. And though I never contemplated marrying him after one of our sex-capades, I did for a moment consider having his teeth marks tattooed on my shoulder. But thankfully I didn't, and a few weeks later I left for Miami.

★

I tell you all this as a way of introducing myself. I guess I should also tell you my name: Elizabeth West. I'm a writer – obviously – but this Miami job was the first significant action movie I'd ever worked on. I'd been brought in to rewrite part of the script that had already been written and rewritten by eight other writers. The big news was I wasn't there just to do chick dialogue. I got to do the scenes leading up to and including the big shoot-out finale. Not that my other script assignments have called for a gentler touch. You want *Little Women* or *Waiting to Exhale*, don't hire me. Estrogen movies, I call them. All emotion, no edge. Not my thing.

Of course one of the reasons I like working in action is I meet a lot of cute guys. Cute actors. Cute stunt men. Cute special-effects dudes. So you see, in spite of my testosterone-heavy résumé, I'm all girl.

Even though I can sit in a story meeting and sound like one of the boys – 'Guys, in this scene, I think we need to see some MP5 semiautomatic carbines' – nothing proves I'm more of a girl than my relationship to the telephone. And it is a relationship. I'm very attached, and it's very emotional.

There are times when I'm so frustrated (call after call, and not one from the right guy) that I want to throw the phone out the window. Other times (when the right guy finally checks in) it becomes my lust link. My pit stop to pleasure. The instrument of my seduction.

But that afternoon, with my relationship with the ex-con approaching splitsville, I had every reason to expect the next call would be some work-related headache – the worst case scenario being writer number ten already en route from Hollywood to replace me. When the phone finally did ring and I reluctantly answered, it was more heartache than headache.

'What are you doing?' he asked. It was the way he often opened a conversation. 'He' was Jake, the forty-year-old director of the movie and the guy who hired me or, more accurately, forced me down the studio's throat. He was my boss. My mentor. My buddy. He was also for a long time a level-one crush.

Level-one crushes are crushes that are so strong they wipe out any preexisting or potential crushes. When in the throes of a level-one crush, Brad Pitt could hit on you at some bar and you wouldn't care. You might not even mention it to your girlfriends. Someone you once obsessed over could ask out a girl you despise and you'd be sincerely happy for her. When you have a level-one crush, your object of desire is the only guy on the map. Life is very simple. It's all about him.

The thing is, I can sustain a level-one crush only if

the crushee is available. If, as in Jake's case, he starts dating somone, then he becomes a level-two crush. Level-two crushes are still great, but you don't automatically blow off Brad Pitt, or anyone else.

And Jake was always dating someone else, usually someone under twenty-five who could be called a bimbo, but not by Jake. He really believed that Ashley (or Lacy or Cyndi) was smart. He'd boast that she was studying archaeology or something like that at UCLA. I always wanted to pull one of them aside and say, 'Uh . . . Ashley? Pop quiz. Spell archaeology.'

'What am I doing?' I echoed his question to stall for time. Whenever he started off a conversation like that, I felt the pressure to say something smart and funny or at least interesting. But I never did because even a level-two crush can throw me off my game.

'Want to meet me for a drink downstairs?' he asked. 'I'm hating this city. I can't get laid here. I need a martini.'

'I'm sure you can get laid wherever you want,' I said. 'Besides, what happened to Berri?'

'Barri. Her name is Barri. She hurt her ankle Rollerblading.'

'There are lots of things you can still do with a hurt ankle,' I reminded him.

'Not as many as you might think.' He laughed. 'At least not with Barri. Anyway, it's not happening,' he concluded, which is as much as he ever says about the end of any of his affairs. 'I'll see you downstairs in ten,' he said and hung up.

★

When I arrived at the hotel bar, Jake was already there. His martini half drunk, he was snacking out of a bowl of mixed nuts.

'Answer this,' he said. 'How come it's impossible, and I mean fucking impossible, to get a decent curried chicken salad from room service?'

Before I could reply, he had the waiter at our table.

'Get her a . . .?' Jake looked at me.

I drew a blank. I was still trying to come up with a clever response to the curry chicken line. 'A . . . whatever he's having,' I stammered.

The waiter scurried away.

'I think you scare him.' I smiled.

'Good. People need to be scared.'

I laughed. That's Jake. He loves his rep as a tough guy. A wild guy. A guy who understands the bottom line and the one below that. But anyone who spends any significant time around him knows he's a real teddy bear. He even looks a little bit like one, though he'd hate me for saying that. Less so now than when I first met him, seven years ago. Back then he was sporting a beard and a bit of a belly and on that particular night was even wearing a soft, fuzzy sweater. Since then he's shaved the beard, gotten rid of the excess bulge with the help of a twenty-four hour on-call trainer and is now seen only in dark-colored clothing by Italian or Japanese designers.

The event seven years ago was a Christmas party. I knew Jake was one of the town's legendary bad boys. His rep was intimidating, but he also had a way of looking at a girl that made her (me) feel as if there were no one else in the room. His stare might have made me feel special but I was smart enough to *know* that I was probably nothing more than a blip on his radar screen.

He was standing off in a corner talking to a couple who looked like their idea of having an edge was to occasionally tune in to a rap station while cruising in their Range Rover. I hung out within hearing distance while they discussed some girl Jake was seeing. The wife seemed excited by the update.

'So you're still seeing Linda? That's great.'

'Yeah,' Jake said. 'It's great.'

'She's a great girl,' the husband chimed in. 'Always liked Linda. How long have you two been going out?'

'Let me see,' Jake mused. 'About four months?'

'Four months!' The wife cheered. 'I'm so happy for you.'

'Yeah,' Jake said again, finishing off his drink.

'It's really working out great.' He paused. A slight, mischievous smile crossed his face. 'I would have brought her tonight . . . but you know, she *is* living with someone.'

I burst out laughing. That was the moment I decided I had to meet him. I had to work with him. Any guy who could embrace ambiguity like that had something to teach me. Although when I later mentioned it to my friend Mimi, she said, 'What the fuck are you talking about? He's just another loser terrified of commitment.'

I disagreed with her then and still do. Okay, I admit Jake might have a little problem with emotional intimacy, but a loser? Never. To me he's one of the coolest, smartest guys around, but don't ask me to define cool. The best I can come up with is that I think it has something to do with honesty. And as crazy as Jake is, he has no secret agenda. Plus, he's also the only guy I've ever called on a Saturday night who was home reading a biography of Thomas Jefferson — and not because he was thinking of turning it into a movie. He'd hate for that story to get around. He'd prefer I'd spread stories about his decadent Palm Springs weekends with one of his Ashleys.

'So what are you doing for sex these days?' he asked as the nervous waiter brought over my martini.

Now I truly was tongue-tied. Was he asking me

to see if I was available, or was he just asking? Was it bait or fake bait?

'I just broke up with my boyfriend, but he doesn't know it yet. Well, he suspects, but I haven't come right out and said it's over.'

'Should never have to,' Jake shrugged. 'If someone can't read the road signs, fuck 'em.'

'I don't know,' I said. 'I think the road signs are getting harder to read. I just turned twenty-eight, and I feel like I'm making the same mistakes over and over. I've got to try making new mistakes.'

'New mistakes? I like that.' He chuckled. Then he leaned in closer. 'You know what my philosophy is? My philosophy is: It's all math. Problem/solution. If the total is zero, it's zero. Get some new numbers. Let your mantra be "next."'

'Guys are good at that,' I said. 'That's what makes them guys. Girls get into things like, Well, maybe the total isn't zero. Maybe I just added wrong.'

Suddenly he got this look in his eyes. The kind he sometimes got on the set when he had figured out how to get a particularly difficult actor to do the scene his way. He reached for his cell phone and punched in a number. I could hear a voice-mail message click on at the other end.

'David, where the fuck are you?' Jake barked. 'I'm sitting here with your next wife. She's going to be back in L.A. in two weeks. You've got to call her.

Although if you had any balls you'd be on the next plane to Miami.' He hung up, laughing.

'Next wife? How many has he had?' I asked, not really caring. Did I feel flattered that Jake was trying to fix me up with a friend of his? No, I felt like a reject because he wasn't trying to fix me up with himself.

'He's the perfect guy for you,' Jake said earnestly.

'What makes him so perfect?' I sounded less than enthusiastic. In fact I was sulking, but he didn't notice.

'Trust me. Uncle Jake knows.'

'Uncle Jake' was what he sometimes called himself when he was playing the role of my personal adviser. He thought it was cute. I hated it. It made me feel small and prepubescent, like a cute, cuddly stuffed animal. Not like the fuckable babe I wanted to be.

I finished off my martini. 'There are some things Uncle Jake doesn't know.' I was trying to be provocative, but he was already on to the next thing.

'I know this,' he exclaimed. He was on a roll. Putting his phone back in his pocket, he pulled out a few script pages. 'These lines you wrote for the heist scene are great. I love this.'

JOE
I don't deal with dickbrains.

LESTER
Funny thing about that word, 'dick.' If you're gonna
use it, you better have one.

He read them in character, really getting into it, as
if he were auditioning. Not hard to see he harbored
a not-so-secret desire to be Mel Gibson. Probably
Mel Gibson of the first *Lethal Weapon*.

He went on to the next page. 'And this scene with
Karin. When Joe says "I'd love to be with a girl just like
you but ten years younger." Her response is genius.'

KARIN
Really.
(twirling a piece of her hair)
And I'd love to be with a guy just like you . . .
(pause . . . smile)
but ten times smarter.

Now he had reached the final page. 'But this is
my favorite. When Karin looks in the mirror in the
party scene and says . . .'

KARIN
All dressed up and no one to blow.

'That's really my friend Shane's line,' I confessed.
'He gave it to me. You know we do that. Writers
give each other lines from time to time.'

Jake playfully punched my shoulder. 'Never admit that. It's in a script with your name on it. What's he going to do, sue you? Besides, there are probably people stealing your lines as we speak. Writers in pitch meetings spewing out your words as theirs. Not to mention the studio execs who passed on your pitch but used your ideas to sound smart at their weekly staff meeting.'

I was about to argue against his cynicism when a girl walked in. Not just a girl. An Ashley. A Miami Ashley, except her name was Blaze. She was wearing tight white pants against sun-kissed skin, and a little black top that exposed a stomach that looked like it had never been fed anything more than a few celery sticks a day. Her blonde hair was pulled back in a perky ponytail.

'Hi there,' she said as she sidled up to Jake and gave him a kiss. 'Am I late?'

He enthusiastically pulled over a chair. 'Sit down. Want a drink?'

'Just water.' She smiled at the waiter, who was instantly charmed. His first good moment of the night, and he was grateful.

'Want lemon or lime with that?' he asked.

She looked at him with awe, as if he'd inspired an epiphany. 'What a great idea. Uh . . . lemon. No, lime. No, lemon.'

'Blaze is studying art at the University of Miami,'

Jake said proudly. Only then did she look at me, and I swear I could see her adding up the numbers. This one's no threat. Not a model. Not a celebrity. Not a problem.

'Hi,' she said, her ponytail bobbing. Her attention then swung right back to Jake and, a moment later, to the pages in front of him.

'Is this part of your script?' she asked, picking them up.

'What do you think of it?' He smiled.

She reached into her Gucci bag and pulled out a pair of black-rimmed serious glasses. More than anything I wanted to try them on, convinced they had clear lenses. Glasses like that are usually a prop for girls like her. As if thick frames equal IQ points.

The waiter briefly interrupted her concentration when he brought over what can only be described as a family-sized side order of lemons. 'Thank you soooo much,' she cooed as Jake glared at the waiter, once again sending him scurrying to the other side of the room.

Blaze read the pages carefully, intently, her brow furrowed cutely. Finally, she took off her glasses and put them back in her bag.

Damn. If she'd put them on the table I would have gone for it. I would have grabbed them to check whether the lenses were as transparent as her ambition.

'That's really good,' she said. 'Who's playing Karin?'

'They are good pages, aren't they?' Jake beamed.

I couldn't remain silent any longer. I needed to bring the competition back around to a game I knew I could win. The mental game.

'Oh great,' I said, looking right at Jake. 'Use my words to seduce another woman. What am I, Cyrano?'

'Now that's a good line,' he said. 'Too smart for an action movie, but a good line.'

'Who's playing Karin?' Blaze repeated, predictably ignoring me and my smart line. She tugged on Jake's shoulder. Then she whispered something in his ear that made him roar with laughter. I would have given a week's salary to know what it was.

My martini glass was empty, and clearly there wasn't going to be a second round. I felt like I was simply the warm-up act for Jake's main attraction. Being Cyrano was bad enough; now I was turning into Ed McMahon.

As I watched them leave together, Blaze leaned into Jake, her hand lightly touching his lower back. She knew how to work it. She knew how to offer the promise of whatever it is guys like Jake think they want.

Two

L.A. can be a tough place to come home to even if you've lived here all your life. The drive from the airport always makes me feel like a first-time visitor. Who are these people? What's the deal with all these ugly strip malls? Where's the city's fucking pulse? Even when the cab heads north on La Cienega and then east to my neighborhood, known for its quaint bungalows and sycamore (not palm) trees, I still don't feel like I'm on familiar ground. It's not until I'm back in my car, a four-wheel-drive 4Runner that'll never be put into four-wheel-drive, that I start to feel my emotional alignment return.

And I do mean return. Being in Miami taught me that my alignment doesn't travel. When in L.A., I feel reasonably confident I can handle anything. That confidence didn't make it to Florida – a fact made clear when I found myself sitting in a production meeting biting my lip so hard it bled. But now I was back on terra firma. Putting on my Nikes and heading for the gym made me happy. And on my first morning back, the phone, my favorite means of torture and pleasure, didn't stop ringing.

Andrew called. He's one of my best friends. Make that best friend. Best male friend, anyway. He's a guy you can talk to about the big stuff. 'So how are you *really*?' he'll ask when I'm being especially glib. And here's the thing. He really wants to know.

Andrew looks like he should be in a J.Crew catalog. He even has a dog that looks like it should be in a J.Crew catalog. But he hasn't had a J.Crew life. A wild child in New York in the eighties, he crashed, burned, and through a Herculean effort, resurrected himself. Wait a minute. Maybe that *is* a typical J.Crew scenario. Preppie bad boy gone good. Anyway, at thirty-four, he's got a small art gallery and a big heart. Need proof? One day when I was being painfully self-deprecating, he interrupted me to say, 'Elizabeth, since you clearly have no self-esteem today, I'm going to have self-esteem for you.' That's a friend.

Mimi was my next call. She thinks Andrew and I should go out, but I can't do it. There was a moment when it could have happened. The first time I met Andrew I thought, He's so cute and sexy and smart . . . and *not* an actor. We immediately liked each other, but the next day he was off to New York for two weeks, and when he got back I was away. And when I got back he had a girlfriend, and when they broke up I had a boyfriend. That's the thing about L.A., there's always a lot of moving around. It's easy to miss your window of opportunity. Before you know it, you've become friends, which for me is an anti-aphrodisiac.

'Can't turn friends into lovers.' I explained to Mimi. 'Don't know how to do that.'

'Oh, it's easy,' she said, somewhat exasperated by my ineptness. 'Just have a couple of drinks and fuck.'

I'm sure Mimi finds me as mystifying as I find her. She has no patience for my analytical nature, and I consider her the most self-obsessed person I know – and that's saying a lot when you've grown up around actresses. She owns a small clothing store, and no customer spends more time in front of the mirror than Mimi. Her name says it all: me-me. But I prefer that kind of narcissism to the 'Why me?' variety. Mimi will never wallow in victimhood. She's a get-on-with-it kind of girl. And often getting on with it simply entails checking herself out in a new Nicole Miller mini. She wishes I'd talk less and shop more, and I don't blame her. I do overthink everything, and my standard uniform of jeans, T-shirt, and motorcycle boots is getting tired. 'Getting?' I can imagine Mimi shouting. 'It is *so* tired. Tired and *over*.' But we didn't even discuss my tired look this time around because our conversation was cut short by call waiting. My call. Had to take it.

'Elizabeth, this is David. Jake's friend.'

It took me a second before it clicked. 'Oh, David, the perfect guy.'

'Is that what Jake told you?' he replied smoothly. Right away there was something about his voice that I liked. As Mimi always says, a good voice and good shoes are a must for a guy. Non-negotiable.

'Jake's a great advance man for you,' I said coyly.

'Well, he told me you're pretty special, which is why I'm calling.' He paused. 'Uh . . . this is going to sound a little strange, but I'm calling to say I've started seeing someone. So I won't be able to get together with you.'

'What?' I shrieked, and I never shriek. 'You're calling to tell me what?'

'That I've started to see someone . . .'

'No, no, no,' I interrupted. 'I get that part. I heard the words. What I can't believe is I'm being rejected by someone I've never even met. Whoa, that's a first.'

He laughed. 'I know it's a little unusual, but Jake said you were waiting for my call, so I figured I should . . .'

'That you should what?' I jumped in again. 'Call, introduce yourself, and dump me?'

'Dump you?' That smooth voice of his developed the hint of an edge. 'I don't think you can call this dumping.'

'Well,' I conceded, 'it's a conceptual dumping, because never having met me, you just have a conception of who I might be and that's what you're rejecting.'

'I'm not rejecting you at all,' he stated adamantly. 'I told Jake I'd love to meet you, but a couple of weeks ago I met this girl, so it doesn't seem like this is the right time to start up with someone else.'

I felt the need to switch gears, to get into my hmmm mode. 'Hmmm, I understand.' I softened. 'It's kind of sweet. Almost old-fashioned. Just curious, though. How old is this girl?'

He hesitated. 'Twenty-one, but she's really very mature and sophisticated.'

'An actress?'

'Yes, but New York-trained.'

I saw a path opening up in front of me. A way out of this conceptual rejection, which felt too much like the real thing.

'Well, all right,' I purred. 'Here's what I have to say. If things with the twenty-one-year-old, sophisticated, mature, New York-trained actress don't work out, give me a call.' I paused, drumroll to the finale. 'Preferably after midnight.'

With that I hung up. I know a good exit line when I hear one. I get paid to come up with lines like that. Two minutes later the phone rang.

I picked it up to hear that smooth voice in a more

playful mood. 'How about drinks at Jones? Do you know that restaurant?'

'Sounds good,' I said.

'Seven o'clock?'

'I'll be there.' Then it hit me. 'Wait, what do you look like?'

'Don't worry,' David said. 'I'll find you.'

★

I think I should stop right here and say I know this is not what I'm supposed to do. I'm not supposed to be so aggressive with men. How many books out there advise women that the way to a man's heart is through withholding? So many they should devote a whole section to them in bookstores. Next to the fiction and nonfiction sections could be the withholding section. That's where these books belong. They pretend to be talking about real love, but they're really talking about real cash. They pretend to be talking about the wonderful world of marriage and how to get there, but they're really talking about the wonderful world of financial security and how to close the deal. A more accurate title for one of those books would be *How to Land the Big One Using the Lure of Sex for Ante*.

Sometimes I wonder. Did I do a Rip Van Winkle in reverse? Did I awake after decades of sleeping to find we've drifted back to the fifties? Let me go on record right here and say I never have been and never will be a *Rules* girl. Zone or no zone, I refuse to turn my love life into a strategic arms agreement. If their advice is don't fuck him for the first four dates, my advice is don't fuck him for the first four hours.

And magazines are as bad as these silly books. I've read countless articles about dating that sound as if everyone they've interviewed is or soon will be sexaphobic. The other day I was reading one of those articles, I think it was in *Marie Claire*. They quoted a guy saying, 'If a girl calls me up the same day we've met, I think she probably sleeps with everyone. I'll go out with her maybe once, have sex with her once or twice, but it'll never be a relationship.'

This is what I say to that guy: If what you want is a woman who though wanting to call you represses her natural and harmless instinct to do so because strategically it's a bad move, then you deserve all the alimony payments in your future.

I have no trouble acting on my instincts, and I don't care what the guy thinks of that. I'll say what I want. Do what I want. I'll be as provocative as I want. Until we actually sleep together.

Sex changes everything except the sex. The initial erotic connection remains intact, but what it inspires is at the very least a terminal case of free-floating anxiety. It's the 'Does he like me or like me not?'

syndrome. All my preorgasm bravado dissipates, and I become yet another neurotic female waiting for the phone to ring. But not having slept with David, or even met him, it was easy to sound 'cocksure.'

★

Jones is a restaurant that inspires trouble. The good kind. No windows. Dark wood and comfortable booths. It's the sort of place where you drink, eat, drink some more, and end up engaging in public displays of affection. I've never been at Jones when there hasn't been at least one couple kissing as if they're surgically attached.

When I checked in with the hostess, a beautiful girl named Marika who looked like she too could be a twenty-one-year-old New York-trained actress, she immediately led me over to my date.

'You get points for being on time,' I said as I slid into the side of the booth opposite him.

'You lose points for keeping points,' David teased.

That whole exchange took five seconds, and that's all it took for me to decide Jake was right. This could be the guy. Right age (thirty-six). Smart (he had to be if he was Jake's friend). Accomplished (ditto). Sexy (that smile of his). A bad boy who had enough of an edge to excite me but not so much I'd end up over some cliff. Adventure and security. Isn't that the ultimate Mr. Maybe?

He looked a little like Denis Leary, which had me fantasizing his whole bio. A working-class Irish Catholic smart-ass who was too ambitious for his factory town. A quick study with great survival skills who'd come to L.A. by way of New York.

'That's okay,' I flirted. 'I like being the underdog.'

'Yeah, well, we all do,' he said, 'as long as we cross the finish line first.'

'And what would crossing the finish line be in this case?' I asked.

'This case? Right here? Right now?'

'Yeah.'

'Hard to say.'

I looked at him and smiled. 'Hmm, not that hard.'

*

There are certain times when you have to drink to get through a night, and there are other times when your balance is so precarious you have to make sure you don't drink to get through the night. After my first drink I knew I had to put the brakes on. There we were, getting along great, no mention of his new girl. But he did admit to a former wife. A quick post-college union that lasted a year. And even though he didn't have a Denis Leary bio (grew up in an upscale neighborhood in Dallas), it didn't matter.

What *did* matter and had me ordering an espresso was that this guy wasn't just trouble, he was danger-

ous. As dangerous as they get. He was an SCU – a
self-contained unit. He was one of those guys who
might look and talk like he wanted a relationship,
might even talk about marriage and babies, but my
gut intinct told me he was a solo act. He liked not
needing anyone. His idea of commitment was probably a three-day weekend. What was it about him
that made me come to this conclusion? Again,
instinct, but also the fact that he'd been living in a
hotel for the last two years – and loving it. 'Only
until I find a house or a piece of land I want to buy,'
he explained. 'Plus, I'm getting a really good rate.'

Yeah. Sure. *Make note*, I told myself. *This guy can't
even commit to an address.* The espresso was definitely
the right choice. It kept me from operating with my
two feet firmly planted in midair. I had resigned
myself to the fact that this would be a drinks date and
nothing more. But then a funny thing happened.
Suddenly everything going on seemed to conspire to
make us fall in lust. The songs playing on the
restaurant's CD jukebox. The electricity that comes
from witnessing random acts of lunacy. We both
happened to be glancing over at the next booth when
a guy who had been carrying on for the last hour,
the life of his party, literally fell asleep while talking.
That provoked uncontrollable laughter from us and
an order for another round of drinks. Fuck the brakes
– I ordered a martini. We discovered we both loved

29

early Elvis Costello and Norman Mailer. He quoted from *An American Dream*, I offered my favorite bit of wisdom from *The Deer Park*. We both thought Paris and East Hampton were alike in that they were two of the most beautiful spots inhabited by some of the worst people. We also loved college basketball, the idea of surfing but not actually surfing, and talking about sex,

The sex talk put me right smack in the middle of the intersection of danger and trouble. What was I going to do?

'Let's get out of here,' David said. 'Want to follow me?'

I looked at my watch. I'd known him for four hours and twenty-five minutes. 'Sure,' I said. 'I love following someone when I have no idea where I'm going.'

'Oh, you know where you're going.' He smiled.

I wasn't exactly sure what he meant, but I liked the sound of it.

*

On the way out to Santa Monica, I thought about Jake. Would sleeping with his good friend make it more or less likely I might someday sleep with him? It was a thought, not a debate, because as I said before, I'm not a big believer in strategizing my way into a relationship, or even a one-night stand. I also don't intend to put my life on hold because Jake is a constant level-one (or -two) crush in my life. I'm all for worshipping my number-one lust object, but I'm not about to become a burnt offering.

During the drive, I also kept thinking . . . it takes half an hour to get to David's place from mine. Maybe longer at rush hour, unless I take Robertson to Lincoln. I contemplated this as if I'd be making the trip often. *Stop it*, I scolded myself. *What are you, eleven?* I was acting like I did in fifth grade, when I'd write down my first name and the last name of my latest crush and stare at the paper as if I were staring at my future. Except now I wasn't leaping ahead to a future china pattern but to a future traffic pattern. *Why am I even doing this?* I asked myself. *Why am I on this road and not even looking at the road signs?* Easy answer. Because sex with a smart, funny, attractive guy who comes highly recommended, knows a lot of the same people you do, but is still a stranger . . . is hot.

*

His hotel room, on the other hand, was cold. Like a blank canvas, an empty stage – perfect for any fantasy – with a built-in soundtrack, the ocean outside his window.

Not that I had doubted it, but he definitely had it going. He knew the moves. The way he opened the champagne. The way he pushed me up against the wall, and of course the way he kissed. Mimi says the first kiss is her favorite part of an affair. And though not my favorite part, it can be pretty amazing. If he's a good kisser, you can pretty much trust that it's going to be a fun ride. Great lift-off, no turbulence. My kind of flight.

And true to that first kiss, he proved to be a great fuck. The night was part fairy tale, part porno movie. He also passed the Goldilocks test – not too big, not too small. And he didn't fall asleep after coming.

*

At three A.M., wearing just a white terrycloth robe, he walked me to the elevator. *Don't say it,* I was thinking. *Don't say, 'I'll call you,' because if you say it, I'll believe it and then I'll spend every waking minute waiting for the phone to ring.* And even if he meant it, there was no telling when he'd call. Tomorrow? Next week? When his twenty-one-year-old sophisticated, mature, New York-trained actress was out of town? None of this ruled out the possibility that I would call him. I do stuff like that all the time. I could handle calling him first, and I could handle never hearing from him again. What I'm not good at is being set up just to fail. *Don't say it, don't say it, don't say it, I prayed . . . unless you mean it.* Of course I kept this pleading to myself.

We played out the good-bye moment as if it were scripted.

INT: ELEVATOR DOORS: NIGHT

David kisses Elizabeth as the elevator doors open.

> DAVID
> We'll talk.

> ELIZABETH
> (confident)
> I'm sure we will.

She steps inside the elevator.

> ELIZABETH (cont'd)
> Or not.

He looks confused.

> ELIZABETH (cont'd)
> Did anyone ever tell you you can eat a girl
> into a coma?

She laughs flirtatiously, hits the elevator button. The doors close.

> CUT TO:

As I waited for the hotel valets to bring my car around, I analyzed the implications of 'We'll talk.' It

33

could mean anything. It could mean this is a 'to be continued.' Or it could mean that we'll cross paths again sometime, somewhere, and when we do, we'll say hi. By the time I was halfway home I was convinced David was exactly the kind of guy girls in the zone should avoid. I decided he was a Mr. Never disguised as a Mr. Maybe. He was alluring enough, but he was a friend of Jake's. If that's not an advertisement for commitmentphobia, nothing is. Every bit of experience and wisdom I'd earned over twenty-eight years told me that unless I was in it just for fun, this was a hopeless situation. And even if I'd settle for fun, it didn't mean I shouldn't book extra sessions with my shrink right now.

*

By the time I hit Sunset and turned left up into the hills, I was overcome by depression. Suddenly this experience and my whole dating life felt like a romantic version of Outward Bound. Was this survival training for the emotionally challenged? Would I be a better, stronger person for spending a great night with a guy I could never really have? And then suddenly as I turned into my driveway, the depression almost miraculously lifted. One thought changed everything: *Nothing else has ever turned out the way I thought it would, so why should this?* I could probably count on the fact that whatever I thought would happen wouldn't happen. Imagining the worst was actually my insurance against the worst happening. Feeling much better, I pulled into the garage and hurried inside the house to check my voice mail in the hope that David had already called.

Three

'What does David do?' Mimi asked between bites of her toasted (no butter) bagel. We were having lunch at the restaurant at Barneys, Mimi's favorite store. Mimi's idea of a healthy life is lunching out on the terrace amid at least a few famous faces, followed by stops in the lingerie department on three and the shoe department on one. She adheres to the philosophy that the right G-string and the right pair of stilettos will do more for your self-esteem than a decade of therapy.

'He's an architect,' I said.

Mimi gave me that look, the one that says *This bears further investigation.* 'He's an architect? And he lives in a hotel? Why isn't he living in some fab house he designed?'

'Maybe he's looking for the perfect spot,' I countered.

'Oh, no, he's not one of *those*?' Mimi asked with mock horror. 'One of those guys who is forever looking for the perfect spot, the perfect girlfriend, the perfect wife.' She nodded in the direction of an older man, two tables away – an aging playboy who was lunching with a pretty young blonde with Sharon Stone's haircut and Pamela Anderson's *Playboy*-era tits. 'Guys like that are still looking when they're fifty.' She waved her hand as if she were sweeping away a particularly irksome mosquito. 'You know what they say about guys like that? "The wheel may be turning, but the hamster's dead."'

'Maybe he doesn't have the money to buy the perfect spot.' I could feel myself getting defensive. I was going to stand up for my man no matter what. It was a perfect example of my theory that once there's been penetration there's no such thing as objectivity. And I do mean once. The act hadn't been repeated. But because I still had hope that it would be, I was hormonally predisposed to defend David and his lifestyle.

'How much money do architects make?' Mimi asked aggressively. 'And what has he built that I know?'

'I don't know, Mimi, and I didn't ask.'

'You didn't *ask*?' Her decibel level doubled. 'Well, call up Jake and get the whole story.'

'I don't want the whole story. Not having the whole story is what makes it exciting.'

Mimi backed off and picked at the lettuce on her plate. My version of excitement was her idea of

CAROL WOLPER

boredom. She scanned the terrace, looking for something to pounce on, but it was a quiet day. There
wasn't even a second-rate TV star in the crowd. Just
junior agents and a few producers, none successful
enough to be known to Mimi. She pushed her bagel
and salad away.

'Where's Julie? If she blows us off without even
calling, I'm going to be pissed.'

'She said she'd stop by if she could.'

'What does that mean, "if she could"? What's she
doing?'

'I don't know,' I replied calmly. 'And I didn't ask.'

Mimi crossed her arms and sat back in her chair.
'Elizabeth, let me give you some advice. We live in
the information age. You've got to start asking!' Then
she laughed. 'Don't you love when I start giving out
advice?'

Actually what I loved was that Mimi punctuates
her bad moods with exclamation points and then gets
on with it. Instantly she switched gears, moods, and
plates, moving on to a fruit tart and a new topic.
'Last time I was here, I saw Harrison Ford. He's on
the list,' she proclaimed.

'You can't put someone on the list you haven't
actually met,' I reminded her. 'How do we know
what Harrison Ford is really like?'

I was being hard-line about this because the list is
sacred to me. Though I had to admit I'd be surprised

if Harrison Ford didn't end up on it. But still, just because someone looks a certain way and talks a certain way doesn't mean he *is* that way. 'Separate the message from the messenger,' was the only good advice my mother ever gave me. Getting on the list required more than a good message. I guess I should explain.

Julie and I once spent an entire flight to New York in a conversation that resulted in the creation of the list. It started with the question 'What makes a guy really sexy?' Once we got into how sexy integrity is, we veered off into our theory. It goes like this. There are two grand American myths. One is the American dream, that inalienable right to go from humble beginnings to the Oval Office. Though why someone would want to be president these days, I have no idea. Then there's the Hollywood version of the American dream. The right to go from a job as a production assistant who has to pick up the boss's dry cleaning to becoming the boss who never has to pick up anything ever again. Drop a pencil, watch your PA dive for it. But the people who make it onto the list, though successful, are not egomaniacal leverage abusers. This is where the second myth comes in. The myth that says Americans have independent spirit. We're mavericks and free thinkers. We threw tea in Boston Harbor. We just say no to whatever we feel like saying no to. We march to our own beat. We value vitality, and worship any manifestation of the life force. Yeah. Sure. What no one mentions is that ninety-five percent of the time, you have to sell out your American spirit to get the American dream. The five percent who don't are the ones who are on the list.

'Do you think David is on the list?' I asked.

Mimi smiled. 'Well, if you'd asked more questions, we'd know, wouldn't we?' Then with her characteristic habit of being too honest for *my* own good, she added, 'I really doubt it. I mean he's in his mid thirties, dating a twenty-one-year-old sophisticated, mature, New York-trained actress – and cheating on her.'

I didn't have time to argue the point – not that I had a ready argument anyway, because Julie's appearance with a Prada shopping bag captured Mimi's attention.

'What did you get?' she asked with an odd mix of excitement and panic in her voice.

Julie plopped herself and her shopping bag down. 'Just some shoes.'

Mimi was already digging in the bag. 'Which ones?' She pulled out a black leather clunky two-inch-high heel and let out a sigh of disappointment. 'I was going to get these.'

'So get them,' Julie said, smiling. Julie and I both enjoyed Mimi's glee when it came to shopping.

Unmitigated glee is in short supply in Hollywood – maybe everywhere – so I appreciate it wherever I find it, even if it's triggered by a pair of overpriced shoes.

I've always thought that someone should do a study on the relationship women have with shoes. It defies logic. I know women who get a rush from simply trying on a pair of Manolo Blahniks. I have girlfriends who in spite of not having their rent money would, without hesitation, splurge on a four-hundred-dollar pair of Stephane Kelian suede ankle boots. I've often thought that men should pay more attention to this powerful attraction women have to shoes. Forget sending flowers, guys. That's sweet and everything, but the way to a girl's heart just might be through her feet. I know of only one guy who got it right. He sent a girl he was dating a pair of sexy Versace sandals with a note that read 'I worship the ground you walk on.' Not only did she marry him, they've been together for eight years, which is practically forever.

Mimi was definitely a girl susceptible to seduction via shoes. She held on to Julie's new Prada purchase as if it were some kind of religious icon. But before Mimi could get too lost in her reverie, Julie provided a distraction. Reaching inside a much smaller shopping bag, she emptied its contents, about twenty-five makeup samples, on the table. 'From my friend who works for Prescriptives,' she explained. 'Take whatever you want.'

If Mimi and I looked like two sane young women enjoying a girls' lunch, that image was smashed by this unexpected bonanza. Like sugar-crazed five-years-olds checking out the goodies in a trick-or-treat bag, we started grabbing lipstick samples. 'Does this mauve come in matte? Is there a lip liner to match?'

Julie laughed and ordered an iced tea. Of the three of us, she is the most likely to stay relaxed no matter what. This is especially true when it comes to men and dating, but then Julie is a seasoned player, having already been married once. Her ex is a news anchor at a local L.A. TV station. 'A talking head who reads the TelePrompTer' is how she often describes him. It was not a friendly split-up. By the end, she became so turned off to him, she even turned off to working in news, which is how they had met. She switched to a job as an entertainment reporter for a cable network. It didn't have the cachet of hard news, but as Julie put it, 'You try sticking a mike in the face of a grieving widow.' Now she sticks mikes in the faces of people who grieve only if their movie opens to a mediocre box office.

At the moment she was giving herself a break from any zone pressure. She'd been divorced for only six months and was claiming the next six as a time to regroup. I jokingly told her that since she was cleansing her palette, we could refer to this as her sorbet period.

'I'm definitely between courses,' she agreed. 'Done with the salad and gearing up for the entrée. Just want to have a little fun first.'

Translated, this meant she was dating a lot of guys she'd never consider marrying. Some she'd never consider being seen with in daylight. But her cavalier attitude didn't mean she didn't have feelings. Coming up with a variation on a classic Bob Dylan lyric, she liked to say, 'I date just like a man, but break just like a little girl.' In the meantime she was the number-one cheerleader for any of her girlfriends' romantic misadventures.

'So how's the guy?' she asked. Of course she meant David.

'He's an asshole,' Mimi offered. 'He hasn't called.'

'It's only been a few days,' I said, doing my best to sound casual.

'A few days?' Julie asked. 'Since you fucked him? Or since he last called?' She was in her journalist mode.

'Since I slept with him,' I said, still doing my best to sound like it was no big deal. 'You know, it's guy time versus girl time. Three days is no big deal for them.'

'Any guy who doesn't call the next day is a skank,' Mimi declared as she sampled an under-eye cream.

'Oh please,' I argued. 'I've had skanky guys call the next day. Just because they call doesn't mean they're not a skank.'

'That's a whole other topic,' Julie intervened. 'The closet skank.'

'Thing is,' I continued, 'it could just be a jonesing situation.'

'Jonesing,' though a theory that was actually conceived by my friend Gina while eating dinner at Jones, has nothing to do with the restaurant. It's jonesing in the drug sense. Some guys need three, four, five days before they start jonesing for a girl. Girls usually need less than twenty-four hours. Hence the problem. If a girl gives in to the ache for a fix and calls the guy before he's reached his full jonesing state, he never develops a real hard-on for her.

'No way,' Mimi declared, while opening a small sample compact. 'The jonesing theory doesn't apply here. The phone call after the first fuck is a separate issue.'

I looked to Julie for support and saw in a glance that though she'd never come right out and say it, she too saw this as a separate issue. Or maybe her journalistic training had made her better at connecting the dots. But I didn't want to connect the dots. What's the point of connecting dots if all you get is a line sloping in the downward direction?

A silence followed, which was Julie's way of punctuating the conversation, but Mimi opted for another exclamation point. 'Oooh, I love this eye shadow, and I don't even wear eye shadow!'

Looking back on it now, I know if Mimi hadn't been so obsessed with trying to decide whether she liked the teal or the taupe, she would have warned me about what was happening. After all, her chair was facing the restaurant's entrance. She would have seen him walk in. She would have sounded the alarm. But instead I was ambushed. One minute I was sitting there and everything was fine, and the next minute those hands of his were on my shoulders.

'So is this one of those scary girl lunches,' he joked. He stepped around so he was facing me, a big grin on his face. That's Nigel's most seductive characteristic. That grin that makes him seem sexy and amusing. A court jester with testosterone.

'Yeah, we're really scary,' Mimi struck back. She made no effort to hide her contempt. You fuck with my friend, you fuck with me was her not so subtle subtext. Nigel ignored the attack but did remove his hands from my shoulders and thrust them into the pockets of his leather jacket.

Julie was more civil. 'What are you doing here?' she asked with the sweetness of a journalist softening up prey for the kill.

'I'm meeting a friend.' He took a cursory look

around the terrace before focusing on me again. 'I've been thinking about you.'

'You have? Hmmm. What brought that on?'

He continued grinning, as if this chilly reception he was getting was just a charade and he was in on the joke.

'Don't you think about me from time to time?'

The truth was, as little as possible but more than I'd like. The Nigel chapter in my life was not one I cared to revisit. Most of the time I didn't even refer to him by name. He was simply 'the Brit.' We'd seen each other, in an erratic fashion, for eight months. You couldn't call it a relationship. He certainly didn't. The fact that we slept together had no impact on how he related to me out of bed. He always introduced me simply as 'my friend.' He was so casual and vague about his connection to me that six months into this thing, which I took to calling 'friends-plus,' even his best buddy had no idea we were lovers. I learned that when the buddy got my number from Nigel and called to ask me out on a date.

But it wasn't Nigel's reluctance to acknowledge me as even a part-time girlfriend that had me trying to delete his image from my personal history; it was what happened at my twenty-eighth birthday dinner, three months earlier. There were ten of us at the table, including Julie and Mimi. Okay, maybe that third glass of champagne was a bad idea. Maybe I shouldn't have affectionately touched Nigel's arm in such a public setting. But he didn't have to bring up his ex-girlfriend Stephanie. We'd all heard enough about Stephanie, the love of his life. Nigel had told me everything about their two-year melodrama. He couldn't mention her name without getting into how beautiful she was, even if she was crazy. How passionate. How smart. How talented. Mimi and Julie glared at him in disbelief. Partially out of loyalty to me and partially because it was so fucking rude and boring. If it hadn't been my birthday, Mimi would have come right out and said, 'Nigel, snap the fuck out of it. Stephanie was and is an aging cocaine addict with a low-level job at a second-rate magazine.' But Mimi was on her best behavior, and Nigel kept going.

I did my best to ignore Nigel's tribute to his ex until he said the thing that made it impossible for me to sit there quietly. He practically looked teary when, in his most sincere voice, he said he didn't think he'd ever get over her until he fell in love with someone else.

That did it. If this had been a forties movie and I was a melodramatic actress, I would have thrown that third glass of champagne in his face. But this was real life and I'm a cautious and caustic writer, so instead I simply looked at him and said, 'Nigel, I have a little tip for you. Save this conversation and have it with someone you haven't fucked. Do not have this conversation with me.'

Since that finale, anything remotely British makes me cringe. Call a sweater a jumper and I want to scream. End a phone conversation with 'Big kiss, lots of love,' and I'm likely to rip your card out of my Rolodex. Use 'quite' in every other sentence and watch the American rebel in me emerge. 'No, I don't think it's *quite* lovely or any *other* variation of lovely.' I'm not proud of my behavior and await the day I can purge myself of this Britaphobia and go back to appreciating Brits again. Just not Nigel.

Not that he seemed to notice my disgust now, standing there with that grin of his.

'Can I call you?' he said.

'Can you call me? Why would you want to do that?'

He put one hand back on my shoulder. 'Because it'd be lovely to see you.'

At least he didn't say 'quite lovely.' I was also beginning to feel a little bad for him, the target of three women's wrath. Call me a chump, but I said, 'If you want.'

After Nigel walked away, Mimi repeated incredulously, ' "*If you want*"? I can't believe you. I've been hating this guy for three months on your behalf, and now you say "*if you want*"?'

'I know, I know,' I apologized. 'I don't know what happened. I choked.'

'I get it,' Julie said. 'Even when a guy's been a dick but the sex was good, he always has a chance at getting back in. And the sex was good, wasn't it?'

'We had some fun.'

Mimi sighed deeply. 'Do I have to be the one in charge of common sense at this table? A guy's got to bring more to the party than an orgasm. Christ, any four-ninety-eight vibrator can deliver that.'

'Vibrators can't deliver the kind of fun I'm talking about,' I said.

'There's still no substitute for the real thing,' Julie added.

Mimi perked up. 'Speaking of the real thing, Evan's coming to town next weekend.'

Evan was Mimi's best hope for Mr. Maybe, and though he didn't appear to have a drop of rock 'n' roll in his soul, who knows what wildness he could deliver in bed? Something was putting that naughty smile on her face.

We spent the next half hour talking about sex. Julie declared that a woman of the nineties makes good money and gives great blow jobs. Sounded right to me. Lounging there on that restaurant terrace with the sun shining it was easy to temporarily forget that I was in the zone. By the time we paid the check and headed out, we were all flush with a sense of our independence and how entertaining we were – at least to one another.

But as we turned a corner to the elevators, we were immediately sobered by the sight of a couple having one of those lovey romantic moments that looked like something out of a perfume ad, back when perfume ads tried to hook you with hokey romantic images instead of androgynous teen junkies.

'Is that Lydia?' Julie asked, loud enough that the woman turned and looked over at us.

'Is that Julie?' the woman replied excitedly.

It was then that I noticed that this Lydia was at least six months pregnant. But this was not the way I imagined I'd look at six months pregnant. I pictured myself with swollen ankles supporting my excess weight, and a face registering the stress that comes from worrying about everything that could go wrong between the point of conception and delivery. But Lydia was one of those girls who seemingly hadn't changed at all except for that cute little basketball in her stomach. If anything, she might have gotten more beautiful, with those slightly flushed cheeks and that glow that up until then I thought was just a lie you told pregnant women to make them feel better about not being beautiful.

'Julie, you know my husband, James, don't you?' Lydia asked, still holding on to her hunk's arm.

James smiled. 'We met at a party in Brentwood,'

he reminded Julie. 'Lydia and I had just gotten engaged.'

It was as if their engagement was the defining moment in his life. Calendar year one.

Mimi, of course, noticed that slung over Lydia's shoulder was a large Barneys shopping bag, the kind you get in the shoe department.

'What'd you buy?' she asked.

Lydia giggled. 'I can't believe I did this.' She reached inside the bag and opened the shoebox. Carefully, she pulled out a three-inch-high heel, to-the-knee, brown suede boot. 'I don't think pregnant women are supposed to wear things like this,' she said. 'But I just had to have them.'

'She looks so sexy in them,' James added.

'Well, I don't know about that,' Lydia replied, gesturing to her stomach. 'I probably shouldn't even be walking around in heels like this. I could trip or something.'

That's when James looked over at her as if she was his most prized treasure in the world. Putting his arm around her, he said, 'Don't worry, I'm never going to let you fall.'

Mimi, Julie, and I were rendered catatonic by that statement. We were still in shock after the perfect couple got into the elevator and the doors closed. Heavy silence ensued.

There it was. Like some cruel joke, we'd gone

from a hundred to zero. In a flash, we'd gone from happily single to miserably single. All because we had the misfortune of seeing two people whose actions suggested that they were experiencing everything we were brought up to believe we should have, didn't yet have, and might never get.

By the time we got to the store's main floor, I found myself thinking about how Nigel's hand felt on my shoulder. My good mood had been ambushed by a glimpse of a happily married pregnant woman, and now I sought solace in the thought that maybe Nigel really did miss me. I asked myself, *Is Nigel the kind of guy who wouldn't let me fall?* Hmmm. Not exactly. Nigel was the kind of guy who wouldn't even notice my fall. He'd be too busy saying 'Big kiss, lots of love' to some complete stranger.

Mimi led the way as we silently headed toward the exit. Predictably, she slowed down in the shoe department. There on display were the very boots Lydia had bought. Really beautiful. Especially in black. I tried them on. They made me feel like a video vixen in a shoot styled by Gucci. Can't hate that. But I didn't buy them. And the reason I didn't was that the zone was fucking with my shopping high. Used to be, boots like this were a mood enhancer – at least for a few hours. But I knew nothing would get me out of this state except a spiritual awakening or a guy. Hadn't done enough homework to inspire the former, so I was left longing for the latter.

'What are you going to say when Mr. "Big kiss, lots of bullshit" calls?' Mimi asked.

'I don't know,' I replied, thinking how the zone is an impossible place to be. At the same time that it forces you to see what a waste guys like Nigel are it makes you so vulnerable and insecure that you crave male attention and reassurance, no matter whom it comes from.

'Promise me you won't call him,' Julie said as we waited for the valets to bring our cars around.

'I promise.'

What I didn't say was that I wouldn't refuse his call. I guess I'm just a semi-tough girl in a totally tough town.

Four

There's always a point early on in an action movie, at least the ones I write, when the good guys are completely lost.

POLICE CAPTAIN
(to detectives)
What do you mean no one can tell me how 20 million
in CONFISCATED stolen jewels was STOLEN out of
the PD lockup?

The detectives have no answer. How did this happen? These tough veterans look momentarily sheepish. It was their evidence. Their fuck–up. Finally one of them speaks.

DETECTIVE
Guess we should pay Vinny a call.

There's always a Vinny or a Manny or a Paulie in these scenarios. Some guy who is their contact out there on the street. A guy who hears stuff, knows stuff, but doesn't always spill what he knows. He'll drop a few hints but never for free. What's in it for me? he'll want to know. What's the payback? And even if he does come up with something, the info isn't always worth the price. But here's the frustrating part for the detectives. Vinny/Manny/Paulie is their only lead. He might be a dead end, but he's their only beginning.

That's how I felt about Nigel. He might not have been the best candidate when it came to my search for Mr. Maybe, but at the moment he was my only lead. David had assumed MIA status, and Jake was rumored to be seeing another one of his 'Ashleys.' Nigel was my Vinny.

'I'm not buying it,' Andrew said.

Andrew's role as my best guy friend was to keep me from getting too girly. I could confide in him as I would in a girlfriend, but his advice always steered me away from being a bitch (which Mimi and Julie encouraged) or a doormat (my own natural tendency).

He was smiling when he said this, in part because he didn't take it too seriously. We were wandering through a small gallery owned by one of Andrew's biggest competitors. You wouldn't know it though. Andrew wasn't one to wear his competitiveness on his sleeve. It's one of the things I loved about him.

He was ambitious without being a pit bull. And unlike many in Hollywood, he wasn't acting. So what if his rival had just scored one of the hottest new artists on the West Coast? Andrew strolled around the place as if he didn't have a jealous bone in his body. He certainly didn't when it came to Nigel.

'Why are you smiling?' I asked. 'Do you think this is funny?'

'Come on. This is Nigel we're talking about. *Nigel!* A guy who has never dated a girl who wasn't a parasite looking for a host. Not that he's interested in being the host. He just knows girls like that are the closest thing a non-rock star can get to groupies.'

'Oh thanks, Andrew. So now I'm a groupie?'

'You didn't date him. You slept with him a few times.'

'Eight times. Over eight months,' I pointed out defensively.

'That's not dating. That's occasionally sharing a parking spot.' He put his arm around me and led me over to a painting. 'Look at that.'

We were in front of a large canvas that at first glance seemed to be nothing more than an intoxicatingly beautiful abstract entitled *Green Light*.

'It's the green flash created when the setting sun hits the ocean,' Andrew explained.

'It is? How come I've never noticed that?'

'It's out there,' he said.

Just then, like a parody of superficiality, my cell phone rang.

'Hello.'

'Are you on your way?'

No mistaking that voice. That accent. That seductive tone that made the listener feel so very wanted.

'Oh hi, Nigel. Uh . . . I'm fifteen minutes away.'

'Lovely,' he replied, suddenly sounding very boyfriendlike. 'I think this'll be fun, don't you?'

'Yeah. I'm really looking forward to it.'

'So see you in fifteen, love. Big kiss.'

When I shut off the phone, Andrew was no longer smiling.

'What are you going to have to give Vinny/Manny/Paulie in exchange for his info?'

'Oh, the usual,' I said. 'A blow job or two.'

*

Fifteen minutes later I was in Malibu, in front of the trendy beach restaurant that Nigel owned. And before I get into the details of what became a nightmare road trip, I should explain that I don't, haven't, and won't ever exchange blow jobs for information – or for anything else. In my book, sex and commerce don't mix. In fact, one of the reasons I never seriously considered being an actress – and almost everyone who grows up in L.A. considers it at one time or another – is because I can't imagine having to kiss somebody I don't passionately ache to kiss. To me, kissing is like taking some great mind-expanding drug. I can't open that 'door of perception' with just anyone. And certainly not just because some script calls for it. Which is a long, roundabout way of saying that those eight times Nigel and I slept together were good times. Being in bed together was always fun. Our problems started, as Ava Gardner reputedly once said of her relationship with Frank Sinatra, 'on the way to the bidet.'

As I turned in to the restaurant's parking lot, I was actually optimistic. It was that L.A. weather thing again. When the sun is beaming down on you, it's like getting a mental massage. You can feel all the angst and anxiety dissipating. Even the most cynical can find themselves expressing sentiments worthy of a Carpenters song. 'We've only just begun' can actually seem like a reasonable conclusion. And with the beach right there and everybody looking like they could qualify for the U.S. volleyball team, it's a Carpenters song for a Pepsi commercial. 'Generation next' following in the mellow footsteps of their parents.

As I parked, locked my car, and transferred my stuff into the backseat of Nigel's Mustang convertible, I was approaching my version of mellow – which means I let myself entertain the possibility that dating doesn't always have to suck. This flight of fancy would never happen in New York. It could be a perfect New York day, but my edge would still be there. It'd have to be. Turn a corner in Manhattan, and the sun is blocked by a thirty-story building. Two seconds ago, life was golden. Now it's back to being gray and harsh. Not to mention that in New York any sign of mellowness is perceived as a lack of intelligence. Only someone intellectually impaired would be stupid enough to drop their guard anywhere but in their shrink's office. But this was L.A., a place where shrinks play volleyball and buildings are rarely tall enough to scrape the sky. So my guard was not only down, it was in early retirement.

When my cell phone rang, I answered with a cheery hello.

'What are you so happy about?' It was Jake.

I laughed. 'If I told you, you'd lose all respect for me.'

He let that comment slide. 'I'm calling to say have a good weekend.'

'You are?' I never knew how to read Jake's road signs. Was he calling as a friend? A boss? A mentor? A potential lover? 'That's so sweet.'

'You've been working hard; you need a break.'

'That's it? That's all you called to say?'

'We'll get into the work stuff next week.'

'What work stuff?' I imagined the worst. I

imagined Jake watching the edited film and thinking how badly the dialogue sucked.

'We'll get into it next week. Don't worry about it.'

I decided to follow his advice and – for the moment – not worry. 'Should I call you Monday morning?'

'Yeah. And one more thing. I hate being called sweet,' he said. 'Got to go. Another call.'

What do I make of this? I thought. Jake's a very busy guy. Very busy directors don't usually call up their writers to say have a nice weekend. And then this thought hit me with all the force of a second-act plot point. Is he calling because he feels bad about the fact that David, his good friend, 'the perfect guy,' never called me? I could have dwelled on that possibility for hours, but just then Nigel exited the back door with 'The Draper.'

The Draper is one of Nigel's steady customers. And though all girls drape themselves around a guy from time to time, this one was a habitual draper. She did it to the point where you'd want to say, Doesn't that girl know how to stand on her own? My god, is something wrong with her legs? Get her a cane. Get her a crutch. Get her a handicapped parking pass for her car. Eventually it hits you. This is her way of flirting, and boy, does it work. Men not only don't mind her hanging all over them, it often inspires a goofy smile, like the one Nigel was sporting as he walked toward me. Had I not been so mellow, I might have thrown enough attitude to make him think twice about lugging The Draper over to me for small talk. Had I not been so mellow, the writer in me would have been screaming *foreshadowing*. This act-one setup will deliver act-three drama.

You see, this particular Draper isn't just a girl who gets a little too physical. And she isn't a simple bimbo looking for a guy to give her a life. It's more complicated than that. This Draper is also a Feeder. Her ego demands she get as much male attention as possible. It doesn't matter if she lusts after the guy. All that matters is that she can feed off his lust for her and then move on. An insatiable Venus flytrap with no shortage of volunteer flies.

And like all Draper/Feeders, she's not a girl's girl. She's about playing to the boys. And to that end wears her hair tousled and her clothes in disarray, always looking like she's just gotten out of bed and can't wait for the right guy to lead her back in. Everything about her says *sex, sex, sex*. And if you try to nail her on her life outside the bedroom, she'll say something about how she just got back from or is just about to leave for Paris. Though it's never clear why she's going or what she does while she's there. Guys are too mesmerized by the draping to care whether she's talking about Paris, France, or Paris, Texas. And I was too mellow to bust her on any of this, so I simply smiled.

'You two know each other, don't you?' Nigel asked, as if we were all one happy family.

'Yeah, hi,' I said.

'Hi,' The Draper replied brightly, then turned back to Nigel and gave him a quick kiss. 'Bye-bye.' She undraped herself and sauntered away. 'Have fun, you two,' she said, tossing the line off over her shoulder like she knew something I didn't. All I knew for sure was that up until that moment it had seemed like a perfect day for a road trip.

The plan was to spend a couple of days in Palm Springs. Nigel was interested in checking out a location for a new restaurant and since that would take an hour at most, I imagined the rest of the weekend would be dedicated to rest and relaxation. Or, more to my thinking, rest and recreation. With that in mind, I'd brought along my best La Perla underwear. This was my version of a truce. There'd be no mention of past hurts. No guilt. No blame. In an act of faithfulness or foolery, I would reset the clock and wipe all grievances from the slate. After all, Nigel, at least on paper, was a contender for Mr. Maybe. He was the right age. He had a job. More than that – a real business. And he actually had a life – not an examined one, but a life nonetheless. My goal was to be open-minded, to wear SPF15 sunblock during the day, and never to drink more than one glass per meal of the three bottles of Domaine Ott that Nigel had brought along. I interpreted the wine to be his version of La Perla. It was as if we'd both picked up our pens and signed a peace accord. The war is over. Let the celebration begin.

*

The drive to Palm Springs is not a pretty one, at least not for the first hour. A freeway tour of fast-food joints and car dealerships. But that's okay. I don't need great scenery if the conversation's good. Problem is, there was no conversation. No amusing anecdotes were exchanged. No meaningful innuendos. No sexual subtext. Not even any inane chitchat, because Nigel insisted on keeping the top down and it's impossible to hear a word when you're zipping along the freeway at seventy miles per hour with two-ton eight-wheelers passing you every fifteen seconds.

I thought about asking him to put the top up, but I decided that was such a lame thing to do. A chick thing. I could live without conversation. I tried to get into a cruising-down-the-highway spirit. Problem is, my hair was flying all around, working its way into tangles that already felt Rastafarian. I opened the glove compartment, hoping to find a rubber band or something to tie it back with. There was nothing in there but the car's user manual, a garage-door clicker, and a lipstick. Hmmm. Nars' 'Viva Las Vegas.' My favorite shade. Had conversation been an option, I might have said something about it. Instead, I made a mental note that it existed, tossed it back in the glove compartment, and pulled down the visor to check out my tangles. Let me just say right here that top-down, natural lighting is not a woman's best friend and runs second only to fluorescent lighting for sabotaging your self-esteem. Over eighteen and undermoisturized is not a pretty sight. I quickly put the visor back up. Nigel looked at me and smiled. It was exactly the same smile he'd flashed six or seven times since we hit the freeway. And I mean exactly. Not one variable in that smile. Which made me think the smile meant nothing other than *You're looking at me, so here's my return of serve*. And though it was a pretty weak return, it did keep the game going.

I tried to remain upbeat while I surrendered to looking bad. What else could I do? Usually I can regain a little confidence by saying something witty. And if I really get on a roll, the guy could be so amused he might forget about my dry skin and the giant knot that used to be my hair. Sometimes humor proves to be even more attention-grabbing than the sexiest La Perla. Let's face it. It's easy to make a guy hard. It's hard to make a guy laugh.

But because Nigel had the fucking top down and couldn't hear one of my best jokes even if I shouted it, I had no fallback position. If Mimi had been in this situation, she'd have had that top up before Nigel left Malibu. But that wasn't my style. First of all, Nigel was loving the drive and I didn't want to diminish his good mood. And second, I didn't believe in being a ballbuster. It seems to me that even if you win, you lose. Because at the end of the day, you're the one who's getting into bed with a guy with busted balls.

★

La Quinta is one of those upscale Palm Springs hideaways. Gated entrance. Private bungalows, each with its own Jacuzzi. To tell the truth, we could have been at Motel 6 and it wouldn't have really mattered. For me it was all about the company and all about the bed – or beds.

That was the shocker. The suite contained two beds, separated by a night table. What is the etiquette here? I thought. Do I suggest rearranging the furniture? Lose the table and push the beds together? Or does it even matter? What's wrong with fucking in one bed and sleeping in two? I can handle that. I'm not a horizontal Draper. I don't need to hang all over a guy all night. Nigel seemed to have no problem with the setup. He was already busy unpacking and uncorking.

He poured me a glass of the Domaine Ott.

'That's dangerous stuff,' I said.

'This?' he replied innocently.

I took a sip. 'I think of it as a combination of liquid Ecstasy and a truth serum.'

He poured himself a glass. 'I never do "Ex" and I always tell the truth.'

I laughed, thinking he was kidding.

'I'm serious.' He smiled.

'I'm just warning you,' I teased. 'Two glasses of this stuff and you start revealing your secrets. After three, you could fall in love.'

'I had three the other night,' he confessed.

'And?'

He stopped smiling. 'Got a killer hangover.' He reached for a cigarette. 'I could go for a steak tonight. What about you, love?'

I've got to say this for Nigel. He knows his restaurants. Dinner was at one of those Italian places done up with shiny red leather booths and Chianti bottles hanging everywhere. It'd be cheesy if it wasn't for the fact that Agostino, the owner, is a renowned chef and the real thing. You just know that the guy has ties. He could have been an extra in *Casino*. And true to his culinary reputation, the steak looked amazing. I say 'looked' because I have an eating disorder when it comes to food and sex. If I'm going to have sex with a guy later (and I wouldn't be weekending with Nigel if that wasn't a given), I can't eat a lot. And definitely not a steak. All a guy has to do to know if I'm into him or not is watch what I order. If I go for the salad, he knows he's got me. If I order lasagna, forget it. Not going to happen.

As Nigel consumed his New York steak – rare – and I had a few bites of iceberg lettuce with the dressing on the side, we got reacquainted. Our conversation turned into the erotic equivalent of action producer Joel Silver's theory of movie-making. Silver believes that to entertain an audience you've got to have an explosion every ten pages. Nigel and I kept each other entertained by dropping in some sexual reference every ten minutes. Before I knew it, in spite of my intention to resist refills, Agostino was uncorking a second bottle of Domaine Ott. He looked at the oddly shaped bottle of rosé and pretended to be insulted.

'I let you bring your own wine, and you bring this pink shit when I've got the best wine celler in Palm Springs?'

'This is no ordinary pink shit,' I piped up. 'It looks harmless, but trust me, it should come with a warning. "Drink at your own risk."'

'Big risk taker,' he teased Nigel, giving him a friendly slap on the back. Then he smiled broadly at me. 'Forget the wine; it's this guy who should come with a warning.'

'Oh, I've been warned,' I said with a laugh.

Agostino turned to Nigel and winked conspiratorially. 'She's been warned and she's still laughing. What a girl.'

*

I don't care what Nigel says, that stuff gets you in the mood. It's not that you'll end up sleeping with someone you wouldn't sleep with if you were stone cold sober, it's just that if the vibe is there at all, it's the only thing you can think about. And though Domaine Ott may not be a truth serum exactly, our conversation got more and more revealing with every sip. Nigel actually said he missed talking to me. And I confessed that I'd had a few self-induced orgasms with his name on them.

It was two A.M. by the time we got back to La Quinta, and everything seemed to be going great. Except, as Mimi pointed out later, I was a moron not to see the signs. She was referring to the fact that as soon as we were in the room with those two double beds, Nigel took a seat on the edge of his and began talking about what we'd do the next day. He had it all figured out. Where we'd go for breakfast, the bike ride, the spa, the hike, and the Indian restaurant that had the best curry. Mimi's theory is, you don't talk about tomorrow when there's still a lot of today left to be played out.

But I was going with it. Figured we'd talk, then eventually stop talking, and he'd pull me closer or I'd pull him. It wouldn't matter who made the move. But I did *not* expect him to make a move to the bathroom and come back with a bottle of Excedrin PM in his hand.

'Want one?' he asked.

'Do I want a *sleeping pill*?'

'If you take one and drink a lot of water you won't wake up with a hangover.'

'How soon after taking one do you get sleepy?'

'Oh, ten minutes or so.'

Ten minutes? What was going on here? He was in his bed with his night-table light out before I'd even gotten my Prada backpack off my shoulder.

'Good night, lovey,' he said in that lilting English accent that made me want to reenact the Boston Tea Party.

All that Domaine Ott. All that verbal foreplay. All leading up to the big nothing. I sat on the edge of my bed . . . stunned. He seemed oblivious to me and my astonishment.

Finally I spoke up. 'I've got to ask you something.'

'Go ahead,' he said, his voice all forced drowsiness.

'The three glasses of Domaine Ott the other night. Was it with The Draper?'

'Who?'

'You know, the girl from this afternoon. The one who hangs out at your restaurant and hangs all over you.'

'You mean Carolyn? Does she hang all over me?'

'Was it with her?'

'Why?'

'Did you fuck her?'

He sat up. 'Oh, is this the conversation we're going to have now? Is this what you want?'

'No. You're right,' I said. His hedging told me everything I needed to know. 'This is definitely not what I want.'

Sometimes the only move is a quick getaway. So what if it's the middle of the night? I picked up the phone and got connected to the front desk. 'Can you order a taxi for me, please? I need to get back to L.A.'

Nigel turned the light back on.

'Thank you,' I said to the operator. Relieved, I immediately started throwing things into a suitcase. Nigel just watched. Finally he spoke. 'Can't you wait till tomorrow morning?'

'Guess not,' I replied.

Another few silent minutes went by. 'Are you going to be okay?' he asked.

I thought about launching into the principles of avoidable pain versus unavoidable pain. I even considered tossing out my suspicion that Nigel might hate women. Why else does a guy continually encourage a girl to have expectations and then dash them? I wanted to point out that Nigel had escalated the battle of the sexes into a full-blown gender war. But that would involve actually talking to him. I decided to be selfish instead. To give him nothing. Not a lecture. Not a theory. Not anger. Not emotion. Nothing.

'I'm fine,' I said breezily.

'Can I do anything?' He got up and put on his pants.

'No, everything's done. I'm a speed packer,' I said, zipping closed the suitcase. 'Good luck with your new restaurant,' I added as I headed for the door.

He got up and gave me a big hug.

'I'll call you,' he said.

'Great,' I replied. If I got any breezier, I'd sound like a spokesmodel.

He stepped away and gave me one of his long looks. 'Lots of love, darling.'

And as irritating as those words were on the open wound that was my ego, at that moment Nigel seemed so lost. Was this the ending he wanted, or the ending he needed? Did he have any idea what was going on here? Oh sure, by tomorrow he'd have worked out a spin on the whole thing. Probably something along the lines of, I thought she knew what the deal was. But that look on his face said more. It said that men, like women, don't have a fucking clue how things fall into sync or get out of line. Friends. Friends-plus. Lovers. Ex-lovers. Ex-lovers turned friends. Friends-plus turned ex-friends. Which is it? The answer to that can be complicated and dangerous. Domaine Ott or no Domaine Ott.

When I got into the taxi, I had two questions for the driver. 'Have you driven many people to L.A. in the middle of the night?'

'Two since Monday,' he said. 'And that's a slow week.'

'Do you take American Express?'

'American Express, Visa, MasterCard.'

Thank God for plastic, I thought as I settled back for the long ride home.

Five

Jake called a story meeting for Monday at nine P.M. His house.

'Why so early?' I joked as I walked in the door. Jake was notorious for being a late-night guy. It wasn't unusual for him to start a meeting at midnight.

'Because I've got some people coming over later.'

'You've always got people coming over,' I said. 'I've never been in this house when there weren't people around.'

'Yeah, what is it with that?' he asked as if he had nothing to do with encouraging the traffic.

He led the way into his office/den. Office only in the sense that there was a beautiful ebony table that served as his desk. There was also a built-in media center – TV, VCR laser disc, CD player, digital audiotape system. Whatever top-of-the-line electronic toy was on the market, Jake had it – all hidden behind a customized pale wood cabinet. There were two long couches and a coffee table with a huge vase full of flowers and assorted art books, one a famous collection of pornographic photographs. The whole house had been created by what I called Jake's 'A Team,' the best architects and designers in the country. *Architectural Digest* and *W* had tried (and failed) to get the house in their pages. Of course they would love the clean lines, the Japanese aesthetic appropriated for that 'California modern' look – whatever that is. Jake loved being courted by the media but loved turning them down even more. Though he never said so, my hunch is that he was taking cues from the town's elite. Hollywood royalty like Warren Beatty would never consider opening their doors for some four-page spread in a magazine – no matter how glossy the publication. Being so high-profile you could afford to be low-profile was the club Jake aspired to.

'Here's the thing,' Jake said before I even sat down. Then he stopped. 'Alex!' he shouted.

A second later Alex, one of his young assistants, popped into the room. Alex was twenty-five, and whatever energy a typical twenty-five-year-old guy had, his was multiplied by ten just by being around Jake. He was loving every minute of this experience. To him it was the greatest show on earth, and he was lucky enough to have the best seat in the house. He also loved meeting all the actress-models who showed up for parties – or just showed up.

'Alex, where the fuck is the sushi I ordered?'

'It's on its way,' Alex replied calmly.

'On its way is not an answer. On its way where? Is it twenty minutes away? Is it ten? Is it on Mulholland? Is it lost down on Sunset?'

'I'll find out.'

Alex left the room as if he were starting a race. Jake turned to me without missing a beat. 'So here's the thing. I think we need to rewrite three scenes. The studio agreed to the reshoots. This is what I want you to do. I think the Karin character should be a basketball groupie.'

'A *what*?'

'You know, one of those girls who hang out at the Forum hoping to meet a Laker. Or a Bull. Or a Clipper. Or a Knick. Or any guy over six feet tall making over five million a year.'

'Well, I know the type.'

'Not cheerleaders,' he stressed. 'Groupies. *Sophisticated* ones. They know how to play it. It's a perfect setup for Karin. She could be a girl who grew up in one of the tougher sections of Inglewood. Probably could walk to the Forum from her house. As a kid she saw those limos driving up to the Laker games and thought, I want a piece of that. But she's still a neighborhood girl. Knows the cops. Knows the gangs. Get it? She straddles both worlds. She's hanging with Mr. Fat Cat, but she went to high school with the guys who stole the jewels.'

'But the movie's set in Miami,' I pointed out.

'So? They've got a basketball team. Same deal.'

I slumped in a chair and said nothing.

Jake took another sip of his vodka. 'What's the matter?'

'Reshoots? You want reshoots? Does that mean you hate what I've written?'

'Yeah, I hate it,' he said. 'That's why I hired you, 'cause I hate your writing.' He picked up my script and threw it at me. I caught it as if it were a frisbee.

'Writing is rewriting,' he said. 'Look at it this way. We get all this extra money to play with. Don't make me list all the great movies that required reshoots. I might have to slap you.'

I laughed. The slap reference was a quick revisiting of the first time we really talked. Two years earlier. Right here. At his house. A dinner for about twelve. I'd been brought by an actress friend and ended up sitting next to Jake. Just being around his quick wit provoked me to say things I wouldn't ordinarily say to a virtual stranger. After one of my playful jabs, he said, 'What would you do if I slapped you right here?' I looked at him, looked down the table – at the other guests, at the complete lack of privacy – looked back at him, and said, 'Waste of a good slap.' He cracked up, and from that night on we were friends. More and more, this is what I appreciate about Jake. He creates a safe environment in which you can talk as provocatively as you like. My version of free speech.

'Come on,' he said. 'Think about it. A sophisticated basketball groupie. I know you. I know you can run with that.'

He was right. Right about all of it. He was usually right, and what was amazing was that often at the beginning of one of these out-of-left-field ideas, I'd be sitting there thinking, This is crazy. What is he thinking? It'll never work. It'll ruin the whole movie. The tone is off. Way off. And then five minutes into it, I'd realize that what he was suggesting was not only right, it was inspiring.

'It's a big idea,' I said, excited by the possibilities.

He relaxed in his chair. 'Oh yeah? Is it as big as my dick?'

'I don't know, Jake,' I shot back. 'You haven't chosen to share that part of yourself with me yet.'

'That's what I like about you.' he said with a smile. 'You're one of the boys.'

*

The sushi Jake ordered was enough for a cast and crew party, but he and I were the only ones at the table. A half dozen people had arrived over the last hour, but Alex immediately led them down the hallway to the house's party room – a large area in the back overlooking the pool and gardens.

True to my particular eating disorder, having sex on the brain (which I always had around Jake) diminished my appetite. To be polite I put two pieces of sushi on my plate and ate one. Mostly I nibbled on ginger garnish.

We were deep into a creative discussion about the basketball-groupie angle, which of course crossed over into a discussion on women, sex, men, sex, sports, sex, movies about sports, sex, Shaq, sex, Kobe Bryant, sex, season tickets, sex, the playoffs, sex during the playoffs, and sex in the parking lot during the playoffs.

The doorbell rang again. But this time Alex didn't succeed in leading the guests down the hallway. A tall man with longish dark hair, a neatly trimmed beard, and a big grin strolled into the room. It was Teddy, aka King of Bad Values, one of the most powerful entertainment lawyers and a notorious guy about town. Two young girls hung back in the doorway, one blonde, one brunette. Though they were dressed revealingly, their shyness suggested they were new to the scene. They watched, starry-eyed, as Teddy plopped himself on the edge of Jake's desk.

'Hey, enough of this pretending-to-work shit.' He playfully pushed aside a few papers.

Jake eyed the two bimbettes in the doorway, then turning back to Teddy, he smiled. 'What have you been up to tonight?'

'Went to dinner. Dropped by a party.' Teddy paused. Grinned. 'Ran into Claudia.'

'Who?' Jake was clueless.

'Claudia.' Teddy almost shouted. 'Claudia, the girl in the red dress at Orso last week. You know the one.'

'Her name was Claudia?' Jake may not be great with names, but if this girl was at all fuckable, he'd have had it engraved on his brain.

'Wait till I tell you what I found out about her,' Teddy enthused. He loved dangling bits of information as if we were trained seals and it was feeding time at Sea World. The tease in place, Teddy could make his exit. 'Finish this shit up,' he said, pushing a few more of Jake's papers aside. 'The girls want to meet you.' With that he got up, and with the bimbettes by his side, headed to Jake's party room.

Once he was out of earshot, I walked toward Jake, exasperated. 'Can I say something?'

'Go ahead.'

'Teddy has known me for five years now, and he either completely ignores me or, if he does say hi, he gets my name wrong.'

'That's Teddy,' Jake said. 'He's like that with everyone.'

'No, he's not like that with everyone. In fact, the first trait of someone who has earned the nickname King of Bad Values is that he knows your name only if you're a celebrity or have fucked a celebrity.'

'Are you telling me you've never slept with a celebrity?'

I refused to be sidetracked. 'Teddy's a rude asshole,' I concluded.

Jake dropped the pen he'd been fidgeting with. 'Let me get this straight. You're in my house, working on my movie, eating my sushi, *and* you're insulting one of my good friends? Is that what's going on here?'

Oh my God, I thought. He's right. I should have stopped with the celebrity line. I went too far. And then a more horrifying thought. What if I sounded shrewish? Shrewishness is a definite, guaranteed lust-killer.

'You're right. I'm sorry,' I said. 'I don't know what . . .'

Jake put his hand up to my mouth to silence me.

'I'm kidding,' he said.

I must have had a weird look on my face because he repeated it, a little louder.

But all I could think about was that this was the first time his fingers had ever touched my lips. And then this thought. *I am so far from being one of the boys.*

★

By one A.M., Jake's after-hours party was in high gear. That's the way it was with Jake. A story meeting turned into a party and could turn back into a story meeting at any moment. He wanted me to stick around, and I didn't need any extra encouragement.

That night there were twenty or so people, in an atmosphere that was casual yet electric. The electricity came from the presence of a well-known actor and good friend of Jake's. This was a guy who had been in the business for a while. No superstar, but a guy who'd consistently clocked in solid performances and back in the eighties had been nominated for an Oscar for Best Supporting Actor. In person he was unimposing. By choice. His style more no-key than low-key, which might be why he could transform himself into such a wide range of characters on screen. And although he didn't appear to be seeking attention, he was getting it.

You see, Hollywood is ruled by trickle-down cachet, at least for people who crave celebrity heat. And since it's one of the town's most steadfast rules, I guess I should explain.

The town consists of celebrities and non-celebrities. The non-celebrity group consists of cachet cravers and those who couldn't care less. The couldn't-care-less crowd is (no surprise) the minority. Most people in Hollywood, even the most cynical, perk up just a little when a big star walks into the room. Even celebrities perk up when another celebrity makes an entrance, if that celebrity's cachet is equal to or greater than their own. But the hottest heat comes from either the rare megastar with a couple of Oscar wins to his credit or proximity to the latest new star at the point when that star's promise has not yet been diminished by a bad career move or overexposure. In the early eighties, right around the time of his *Controversy* album, the presence of Prince at a club caused ripples of energy throughout the room. Same could be said for Madonna when she did *Desperately Seeking Susan* or Quentin Tarantino right after *Reservoir Dogs*. Jake's actor buddy had never reached that kind of heat, but at this moment, at this party, he was the closest thing to it. And Teddy was playing up to him big time.

I was watching all this from the other side of the room, where I was sitting with a couple of the models who were often at Jake's parties. I've always gotten along with models – who should not be confused with bimbos. Models, even just moderately successful ones, have their own itinerary, their own AmEx cards, and more frequent-flier miles than anyone else in the room. But that's not what I like about them. I like how girly they can be. Hanging out with them can feel like a pajama party. In spite of the sophistication they pick up from hanging out in Paris and Milan, they are capable of indulging in a silly pillow fight. When I'm around them, I feel like I've been zapped right back to my high school years, talking about makeup and giggling about guys. Of course this is generally done while drinking Cristal. And though they're not likely to get into deep discussions about art, politics, or literature, who cares? And even though that night, one of them did spend an hour talking about what she would name her puppy – if she had a puppy – the others were better company than a lot of smug Harvard grads I know.

Jake thinks that's bullshit. He thinks I get along with models because they're superficial pretending to be deep and I'm deep pretending to be superficial. I love the line, but the truth is, all you have to do to be considered 'deep' in L.A. is buy, but not necessarily read, the Sunday *New York Times*.

What Jake doesn't see is that an important part of why I like models so much is that they usually abide by the 'girl code.' They don't need to go after another girl's guy. (Unless he's one of those guys every girl wants, and then all bets are off.) They've got so much male attention, they can afford to be honorable. Bimbos, on the other hand, will go after any guy who can elevate their lifestyle, since they have trouble self-elevating. At the same time they're gushing over how much they love your earrings, they'll be reaching under the table for your boyfriend's dick.

By this point in the party, Jake had moved next to me but was still talking to Teddy's blonde bimbette. Everyone was in a mellow mood. The music was a tape that Alex had made, probably to Jake's specifications – a few seventies classics from Stevie Wonder mixed in with some Wallflowers and Beck – just so the bimbettes and models would get that Jake might be twenty years older than the girls but he spoke their language.

The volume was up, loud enough to feel partyish but not so loud you couldn't have a conversation. Teddy's voice, which is always thunderous, was softened somewhat as he edged in closer to the actor, trying to establish a more intimate, one-on-one rapport. I could see the grin on his face as he cozied up to, no doubt, share some piece of nasty gossip, which is what Teddy always uses as his ante to get into the game. But just at that moment, the tape went silent. Alex had left a ten-second gap between songs, and the only thing filling the void was Teddy's voice.

'. . . I'm telling you, this party tomorrow night will be stocked with pussy . . . including Claudia's!'

He stopped when he realized everyone was looking at him. Did he even for a second wonder if he sounded like a guy pimping for some trickle-down cachet? If he did, he recovered quickly. 'Hey, guys, you're all invited too!' he bellowed. The music kicked in again, and Teddy went back to working the actor.

I leaned over and whispered to Jake, 'Christ, could Teddy suck up any more? Using Claudia to score points. Why doesn't he cut out the middle man and blow the guy himself?'

Jake burst out laughing, which made me feel like I'd scored but made Teddy glare over at us, his suspicion on target. The laughter had been instigated by me at his expense. A tidal wave of guilt hit me. Why was I being so harsh? Teddy may be King of Bad Values but he is just the king. He didn't create the royal tradition.

'You know, Jake,' I said softly, 'if Teddy would just remember my name, I wouldn't be so hard on him.'

'So go fuck a celebrity,' Jake joked.

'Oh, that's lovely advice,' I said as I got up, fully intending to go into geisha mode to purge my guilt. I was about to ask Teddy if he wanted me to refill his drink, but the brunette bimbette beat me to it. As she went to pick up his glass, Teddy grabbed her wrist. 'Wait,' he said. 'Sit down. Tell them about the other night.'

'What other night?' she asked, sitting down next to him as requested.

'At Larry Jones's party.'

'No, no, no.' She hid her face in her hands. I couldn't tell if this was part of the performance or if she was genuinely embarrassed.

'You'll love this story,' Teddy said to no one in particular.

'Don't make me tell it,' the bimbette pleaded. This was no act. Her voice was tense. Her smile frozen.

'Hey, I'll tell it,' Teddy stated as if he was doing her a favor. He looked around the room to make sure he had everyone's attention.

'So the other night, I go to Larry's birthday party. His thirtieth. It's a big deal. You can picture it, right? It's a party for maybe two hundred people, maybe more. At his father's house in Bel Air. No expense spared. And right where you walk in the door, in the front hallway, there's a table and it's filled with presents. And that's where I meet this one.'

He turned and looked at the bimbette, who seemed confused about how to handle the situation. Should she be flattered that Teddy was smiling at her, or upset that he was turning her into a punch line?

'There she is,' he continued, 'standing there adding her little present to the table. A little box from Tiffany. So I say to her, "What'd you get him?" And she says, "One of those little silver picture frames." "Oh yeah?" I say, not thinking too much about it 'cause frankly I don't give a fuck what she got him,

I'm just making conversation. So we're there talking for a while, and people keep coming in and it's getting crowded, so we move into the main room, where the tables are set up. And at first I don't notice it. All I notice is that this one turns white. I'm not kidding. I've never seen anyone turn that white before. So I'm thinking she's just spotted an ex-boyfriend or something, some piece of bad history. But then I see what's she's looking at, and there, in front of every place setting – and we're talking two hundred or something place settings – is a party favor. And guess what the party favor is? A little silver picture frame from Tiffany. Her present to Larry Jones was the same thing Larry was giving out as party favors! Do you believe that? Do you believe that?' Teddy repeated excitedly, as if working the room for more applause.

Now that the story was out, the bimbette looked resigned. She might have been young. She might have been new to this town, but it didn't take a seasoned player to guess that this wasn't the first time Teddy had told this story, nor would it be the last.

*

I sought her out. I didn't expect her to be crying in the bathroom, and she wasn't. She was drinking in the kitchen. Alone. Same thing.

'Can I give you some advice?' I asked.

'Shoot,' she said. She pantomimed a gun in her hand and aimed it at herself. Then she laughed. A laugh fueled by a shot of tequila.

'Two things,' I said.

'Two things? Okay. But two things requires two shots.'

She refilled her glass. She was in self-destruct mode.

'First of all,' I began, 'that story is your story, not Teddy's. If *he* tells it, you'll come off like a dummy. *You* tell it, and you're self-deprecating and charming.'

'Self-what?'

'Never mind. Next time, *you* tell the story. Your way. Make it your joke.'

She thought about it for a while. 'Did you date Teddy or something?'

'Me? Never.'

'I thought this might be a revenge thing. You know, the old girlfriend trying to get the new girl-friend to gang up on the guy.'

'I'm a purist,' I replied. 'I don't believe in group revenge.'

'You're not really Teddy's type anyway,' she concluded.

'Really?' Now I was curious. 'And why is that?'

''Cause . . .' She searched for the right words.

''Cause, you make too much noise. Know what I mean?'

Out of the mouths of bimbettes. I knew exactly what she meant. I *am* too noisy for guys like Teddy. Too opinionated. Too talky. Too in the foreground

'What's the second thing?' she asked, and she chugged her second tequila. 'You said there were two things. What's the second?'

She poured a third shot and offered me her glass.

I took a small swig. 'Learn how to say the emphatic no. Without that, you'll have a tough time in this town. Or anywhere.'

'What do you mean?'

'I mean that there's no and then there's *no*. When a guy like Teddy hears you say no he thinks that what you're saying is yes. It may not be an emphatic *yes*, but Teddy doesn't care. To him, a yes is a *yes*. But if you say *no*, he'll understand that you're not saying no, which is actually a yes. Get it?'

'*No!*' She giggled.

'You got it. Now you've just got to learn how to say *No, Teddy!*'

*

By three A.M. the party was pretty much over. There were still some people around, but Jake and I were the only ones sitting out by the pool. Having his undivided attention gave me hope. As Andrew says, men vote with their feet. If they're there, it's because they want to be there. This was especially true with Jake. He hadn't come this far in his maverick life to forego prime bimbettes to make polite small talk with me – unless that's exactly what he wanted to do.

I've always loved and feared the three A.M. hour. If I'm with the right guy, I'm tempted to pioneer new territory. Cross lines. Seek out the next frontier. I'm not talking about being sexually uninhibited. Getting naked is easy. Or at least it's easy in comparison to getting vulnerable.

So there we were, Jake and I, on an almost-full-moon night, sitting side by side in lounge chairs, talking about sex. No mention of David. No mention of Blaze. I told him about the boyfriend I fucked on a dead-end street in Little Tokyo, and he told me about the woman he picked up in an elevator at the Ritz. Usually when I'm swapping sex stories with a level-one (or -two) crush, I think about how easy it would be to go from talking about blow jobs to giving one. Even the most timid women I know get bold when they're hanging with a crush on an almost-full-moon night. But this wasn't the usual situation. And three A.M. is the truth hour. All that glib stuff I get away with the rest of the time seemed silly. Even if I wanted to avoid the truth, I couldn't. No way I could ignore what was becoming painfully

– and I do mean painfully – obvious. I was madly in love with Jake. This was not a good thing. If I were twenty, twenty-two, twenty-six, okay fine. But I was twenty-eight. It was time to have a relationship. It was not time to be in love with a guy I couldn't have a life with. It was time to leave. Time to go home. Time to move on. Time to grow up.

I didn't leave. I sat there and listened to Jake become more and more personal and confidential, which was his way of wrestling with the three A.M. witching hour. And as I did, a funny thing happened – something that happens from time to time with movie people. We started to do real life as if it were a scene from some movie.

EXT: JAKE'S BACKYARD: MIDDLE OF THE NIGHT

Private. Quiet.

JAKE and ELIZABETH sit on adjoining lounge chairs. A full moon illuminates the beautiful gardens. The air is heavy with jasmine and possibility.

JAKE
Sometimes I hate this house. It's not a good house to
be alone in.

ELIZABETH brushes a strand of hair off her face, hangs on his every word.

91

JAKE (cont'd)
Sometimes, in the middle of the night, I just get out
of bed and check into a hotel.
(a beat)
I love hotels.

ELIZABETH
Why don't you call someone to come over?

He looks at her. No bullshit.

JAKE
At three A.M.?

ELIZABETH
Yeah.

JAKE
I'm not into hookers.

ELIZABETH
I wasn't talking about hookers. Call a girlfriend.

JAKE
That can get complicated.

She reaches over, her hand casually touching his arm.

ELIZABETH
You can call me. I'd come over. And I wouldn't
crowd you.

A moment of highly charged silence. And then . . .

                    JAKE
        And what if I *wanted* to be crowded? Just for
                a few hours.

Her hand moves down his body.

                  ELIZABETH
            Then I'm all over you, boss.

Right at that moment, our real-life movie moment became a real-life *action*-movie moment. Gunshots rang out from somewhere in the canyon. Somewhere close. And a second later, the shattering of glass, followed by a car screeching down the road.

In a flash, Jake was up and running, with me a few beats behind. The second we hit the street, we heard a woman screaming, 'That fucking bastard!' She was standing in front of her black Jaguar, which was parked in the driveway next door. The car's windshield had been shattered. Judging by the bullet holes in the front seat, I'd guess somebody was unloading a .45. I know about stuff like that because of the research I did for my first action script.

'That fucking loser asshole bastard!' The woman hardly acknowledged us. She was about forty and appeared to be wearing nothing but a robe and great suede ankle boots by Stephane Kelian.

'What happened?' Jake asked.

She looked up, focused on Jake. 'Are you my neighbor?'

'The house on the corner,' Jake said as he surveyed the damage. 'What happened?'

'Only one person would do something like this. My psychotic ex-boyfriend. I think it's time I started dating classier men.'

'Proceed cautiously,' I advised. 'There are plenty of classy psychotics out there.'

Now she focused on me. 'Are you my neighbor too?'

'Nope. Just visiting.'

Jake opened the Jaguar's glove compartment.

'Looking for something?' she asked, suddenly sounding playful.

'Looking for this.' Jake pulled out a pen, took her hand, and wrote a name and phone number on her arm.

She checked it out. 'Nice to meet you, Gavin.'

Jake tossed the pen to her. 'No. I'm not Gavin de Becker. That's who you're going to call. He's a security expert. He'll tell you what you should do so this doesn't happen again.'

She looked at him, confused. 'You've memorized the number of a security expert?'

'I believe in security.' Jake shrugged, which was as revealing as he was going to get.

'He's got some psychotic ex-girlfriends,' I added.

The woman reached into her pocket and pulled out lip gloss. As she carefully coated her lips, she seemed deep in thought. So was I, fascinated by this fortyish woman with her wrecked car, standing there in her robe outside her Benedict Canyon house, putting on lip gloss as she contemplated hiring a security expert to protect her from her 'fucking loser asshole bastard' ex-boyfriend.

When Jake and I got back to his driveway, the party was clearly over. The moment we'd had in the lounge chairs by the pool was definitely over. Teddy's car was still there, and through an upstairs window I saw him head toward the guest bedroom with the blonde bimbette in tow.

I stopped at my car. 'I guess I should go home.'

'How soon do you think you can have those scenes written?' Jake asked. Since he was notoriously bad at good-byes, I didn't take this shop talk as any kind of cold dismissal.

'Tomorrow,' I replied. 'Before you wake up, they'll be done.'

'You're that fast?' He smiled.

'When I'm inspired.'

'Fax me,' he said.

I opened the door to my car. It was the critical moment. But as proof of my bad timing, a voice called out from the front door of the house.

'Jake.' It was the brunette bimbette. 'Are you coming back?'

With Teddy and her blonde counterpart off in an upstairs bedroom, she was drunk and available. At that moment I made a point of forgetting her name. Here's a girl who, earlier in the evening, I tried to help. A girl I drank with and laughed with. A girl who knew, even though I didn't tell her, that I had a thing for Jake. How could she not know? It was so obvious even a bimbo would have to pick up on it. Besides, that kind of thing is part of women's radar. And because she knew and would betray me anyway, I relegated her forever to the category of generic bimbette.

'I'm not going anywhere,' he called back.

''Cause I need to talk to you,' she replied, her voice that presex mixture of babyish and slutty.

Jake turned back to me. 'It's easy.'

'Well, if you need easy to get hard,' I said, as I searched for the right comic line to get me out of this situation.

'I need easy to get some sleep,' he said resignedly.

'Okay then, boss, I'm going to let you get your sleep.'

I went to give him a quick good-night kiss. A kiss no different from dozens of other quick hello/good-bye kisses we'd exchanged – but this time it *was* different. This time the kiss lingered longer than the usual friendly Hollywood kiss. Two seconds. Three. Maybe four. Seconds that communicated one message. Regardless of which bimbette he slept with that night, or even if he slept with both, this thing – this undefined clumsy thing he and I had – had a second act.

Before I drove off, I had to have the last word.

'I guess the good news is that I'm not your sleeping pill.'

'And the bad news?'

'The bad news is . . . I'm not your sleeping pill.'

Six

Mimi believes that if you walk out the door with two or more things wrong with your look, there's no way you can have a good day. If it's just a case of bad hair you can get by – finesse it. But if it's bad hair and the wrong shoes, or the wrong shoes and a button missing from your jacket – forget it. I thought about that as I walked out my door and noticed a small ink mark on the sleeve of my shirt. That combined with a skirt that suddenly seemed so last season told me that this was not going to be a fun day. Had I not been running late I might have gone back and changed. Had I been better at the emphatic *no* myself, I wouldn't have gone out at all. I was in one of my hibernation modes. But it's hard to say no to your mother on her birthday and to Mimi when she's on a mission. So there I was with at least two things wrong with my look on my way to doing two things I dreaded.

First stop – my mother's. I guess I should explain the dread. She's my mother, so there's all the usual stuff that goes along with visiting one's mother, made worse by the fact that she's a little crazy and her job makes me a little crazy. I'll give you the short version.

My mother grew up in Portland and came to L.A. when she was twenty-one. It was 1970, and the first guy she dated here, my father, she married. He worked for a record company, and she aspired to be a dancer. She turned auditioning into a full-time job. They rented a house in Laurel Canyon, which was where I was conceived – in a bedroom with tie-dyed everything. At one time the house had been owned by John Sebastian, the lead singer of the sixties group The Lovin' Spoonful. My mother felt that she had arrived. The fact that the house was a simple two-bedroom, one-bathroom fixer-upper didn't discourage her from, especially in retrospect, talking about it like it was a mansion. We moved out of there when I was eleven, when my parents got divorced. By that time my father had left the music business for a job with an accounting firm that occasionally serviced music clients. Happily for me, he still got free records.

My mother moved on to managing an upscale store that sells only the best linens, china, and assorted home-decorating items. This is where the crazy part comes in. The store is a big favorite with brides-to-be who want to register for shower and wedding gifts. And since my mother has a seemingly limitless appetite for fantasy and gossip, she is constantly telling me who is getting married and all the details she can get out of them about their big day. She can go on and on about the six classic shapes of diamonds and why platinum is better than white gold. She loves to fill me in on who'll be saying 'I do' in a Vera Wang and whether the floral theme will be garden roses or some exotic flower I've never heard of.

I wanted to say, Stop. No more. Don't you get it? I'm not interested in being a spectator on the front lines of someone else's big day. Besides, half the weddings I've been to called for an intervention, not a celebration. I wanted to point out that, unlike a lot of girls, I didn't grow up dreaming about my wedding day. I grew up dreaming about my wedding night. And even though that's as true now as it was when I started having honeymoon fantasies, in the seventh grade, this is still not the kind of conversation that a mother should ever have with a daughter who is struggling in the zone. But I said none of this. I took the easy way out. I changed the topic.

'Who are you having dinner with on your birthday?'

We were sitting at the table in my mother's kitchen, a virtual Williams-Sonoma catalog come to life. Every conceivable kitchen aid was on display: blender, mixer, espresso machine, coffee-bean roaster, citrus juicer, all-purpose juicer, and a Calphalon pot in every size hanging from an overhead rack.

She poured herself another cup of coffee. 'I have a date.'

'You do? You do?'

She refilled my cup. 'Why so surprised?'

'You never date.'

'Well, it's not easy being fifty in this town.' She reached for the sugar dispenser and then thought again. Who needs the calories? 'No, it's not this town,' she corrected herself. 'It's anywhere.'

'But you don't look fifty,' I pointed out.

'No one even knows what fifty looks like anymore,' she said, pleased that whatever my image of fifty was, it wasn't her.

'So what's he like?' I asked excitedly.

'He's nice.' She smiled as if she was trying to hold in a secret.

'Okay. And what else?' I probed. 'What does he do?'

'He *owns* a shoe store over on San Vicente.'

This was no mere shoe salesman.

'How long have you been seeing him?' I asked.

'First date.'

'Whoa! First date and on your birthday.'

'He doesn't know it's my birthday,' she stated matter-of-factly.

'You didn't tell him?'

She looked at me as if I were a six-year-old. 'If I tell him, he'll ask me how old I am.'

'How old does he think you are?'

'Younger than fifty.'

'How old is he?'

'Sixty-three.'

'Did you meet him at his store?' I imagined a Cinderella scenario. He fitting her with the perfect black Chanel pump.

'Mine.' She blushed girlishly. 'His daughter is getting married and is registered with us.'

Then without stopping she jumped right in, revving up from zero to a hundred. 'She's got Roger Campbell as her wedding coordinator. Art Luna is doing her hair. And how about this? The centerpiece for each table is going to be . . .'

I tuned out. Sometimes life around my mother can feel like a B-movie thriller. Call it *The Wedding Conspiracy*. Picture me as the protagonist, trapped and panicking. Everywhere I turn, there's another wedding invitation. Another veil. Another peau de soie something or other. It's hell. But the one good thing about being in hell is that it motivates me to get the hell out of hell.

'Is this new?' I asked, picking up off the table some gadget that looked like a small instrument of torture but turned out to be an apple corer. I'd talk gadgetry all day if it kept her off her peau de soie monologue.

'You have got to get one of these,' she said, reaching for an apple to demonstrate. Then she stopped. 'What am I thinking? I'm talking to my daughter who hates to cook, who doesn't even own a can opener.'

'I'm domestaphobic and intend to stay that way.'

'You're going to have to get over that,' she lectured. 'I don't care who you end up marrying, even if he's a rich guy with a cook. Every man likes his woman to serve him occasionally.' She took a bite out of the apple. 'Just don't tell my feminist friends I said that.'

'Don't worry, Mom. In certain sexy situations I have no trouble serving men. I just don't ever want to *have to* serve them dinner.'

She shook her head. 'I can't believe you're my daughter. Where did you come from?'

'Mars, not Venus,' I said. I slid two gift-wrapped boxes across the table. 'Happy birthday, Mom!'

She opened the small box first – 'Crème de la Mer,' supposedly the best moisturizer on the market. Definitely the most expensive. Four hundred dollars? And then the big box – from Mimi's store – the softest, coziest flannel pajamas. What kind of mixed message was I giving my mother? Stay young and stay home?

'Thanks, sweetie.' She gave me a hug. My mother loved birthdays and all holidays. They gave her an excuse to put reality on hold. I envied her. I couldn't put reality on hold even with the help of some fine pharmaceuticals.

Then the phone rang. I could tell Mom hoped it was the shoe man. And when it turned out not to be, the disappointment was swift and obvious. I could tell she was thinking, What if he doesn't call? What if he calls and cancels? I know how my mother thinks. She's got zero confidence in this area. Too much scar tissue. Over the years I've always been surprised by how badly she's dealt with her occasional boyfriends. Okay, maybe her obsession with weddings and gossip is a little wacky, but she's also a very responsible person. In an earthquake she's the one out there in the neighborhood turning off gas valves and handing out flashlights. Experience has made her solid and capable, and yet when it comes to this male-female stuff, she's ageless – which is to say, like the rest of us, she has no idea what's going on or how to change any of it.

Nervously, she added a lump of sugar to her coffee. 'What about you? You seeing that architect guy?'

'Nope.'

'What happened?'

'Nothing.'

'Nothing?'

'Nothing. Guess he just drifted off.'

'Next time,' she began and then paused. She struggled to find the right thing to say. 'Next time when you meet a guy . . .' she shrugged. 'Just know what you're getting into.'

'As if that's ever stopped anyone.'

She laughed. 'Can't argue with that.'

★

'You've got an ink mark on your sleeve,' was the first thing Mimi said when she saw me. The second thing she said was that the informal let's-not-call-it-a-blind-date-but-it-really-is dinner that she had organized on my behalf had turned into a slightly larger party. Only then did she add, 'Oh, and I'm getting married.' She held up her left hand, which now sported a diamond ring.

'Oh my God! When?'

'I don't know.' She shrugged as if the actual date was incidental. 'But the ring is mine,' she said with a giggle. Staring at the diamond as if it were her first-born, she added, 'Probably next year, but we're going to have an engagement party in September.'

'Congratulations.' I was astonished. Just the week before, Mimi had been ready to break up with Evan, now her husband-to-be, because she said they had entirely different metabolisms – whatever that meant to Mimi.

'You don't look happy for me.' She pretended to pout. 'Or are you mad that I invited a few other girls to your blind date?'

'I'm not mad.'

'It might be easier for you this way. No pressure.'

'How many other girls?'

'Just a few, but I told Joe he'd be crazy not to ask you out, that you're the one.' She grinned. 'And he's really cute. And . . . if you two do get together, he would definitely call you the next day, unlike what's his name.'

'David.'

'Yeah, David.'

I knew that was true. Mimi would go ballistic if some guy she fixed up with a girlfriend of hers didn't do the right thing. She was fiercely protective.

'How many?' I repeated, knowing with Mimi that the word 'few' could mean anything from three to thirty.

She snuck another peek at her diamond. 'Well, what happened was, after Evan's ring arrived – Fed-Exed this afternoon – That was my idea. I didn't want to wait till I go up to San Francisco next week to get it. Anyway,' she rattled on, 'I started calling all my girlfriends. I called you first, but you were out.

And everyone said the same thing . . . "Wish I could find a great guy." And I guess 'cause I was feeling so good, I wanted everyone to feel good and I found myself saying, "You should meet Joe. He's the kind of guy I'd be into if I didn't have Evan."' She stopped and caught her breath. 'So now the dinner's turned into . . .'

'Let me guess. Six women and Joe?'

'Seven.'

'Does Joe know?'

'No, but he'll love it.'

'He'll love being the only guy with seven women?'

'Of course.'

I sighed deeply, and I rarely sigh. 'Let me explain something, Mimi. I'm not looking for a guy whose idea of a fun time is having dinner with seven women.'

'Oh, just relax and be happy for me.' She smiled broadly.

'I *am* happy for you.'

'Good. So now all you've got to do is relax.'

Dinner was buffet-style with everyone grabbing a plate and finding a spot in Mimi's cozy, faux-Ralph living room that looked out over Nichols Canyon. Joe sat on the leather couch, a girl on either side, and was having a great time being the center of all that female attention. Now, I happen to be one of those girls who knows in the first five minutes whether or not a guy is for me. I don't need to get to know him. I don't need to figure it out over dinner. And in the case of Joe, I didn't even need five minutes. It was clear he was not for me. How could he be? He walked and talked like a character out of one of Hollywood's not-so-funny comedies I'm sometimes hired to rewrite. The studio usually ends up hating my version because I always put some wise-ass girl in the scene. Usually some version of me.

INT: MIMI'S HOUSE: NIGHT

Seven women and Joe, who is in his mid-thirties. Good-looking. Knows it. He turns to Elizabeth, who is sitting to his right.

> JOE
> So what do you drive?

> ELIZABETH
> Is that some new way of saying 'Hi, nice
> to meet you?'

> JOE
> Come on. I'm curious. What do you drive?

> ELIZABETH
> A Toyota 4Runner. What do you drive?

JOE

A BMW 740i.

ELIZABETH

740i. Hmm. Is that like saying 'I drive the
expensive one?'

JOE

Sixty thousand.

ELIZABETH

Hmmm.

JOE

What?

ELIZABETH

Nothing.

JOE

You got a problem with a guy who drives a 740i?

ELIZABETH

No, not at all. It's just . . .

JOE

Just what?

ELIZABETH

Well, it's been my experience that guys who say
BMW 740i are often the same guys who say things

like 'my twenty-one-year-old girlfriend.' Or
'this thirty-year-old bottle of wine.' In fact, guys
like this generally prefer their wine to be older
than their girlfriends.

JOE
Sounds good to me.

CUT TO:

It didn't matter what I thought of Joe or what Joe
thought of me and my 4Runner. He didn't need my
approval when there were other women around
working hard to get his attention. It was a study in
flirting styles. At the end of the table was the provo-
cateur whose idea of seducing a guy was to shock.
She announced that she'd reached a point in her life
where she would fly only on private jets and only do
coke if she was licking it off a lover's dick. Then
there was the sweet, shy-girl approach. She was
sitting right next to Joe. Barely spoke. But she had
perfected the art of looking at him fleetingly, as if he
were the sun and gazing right at him might blind
her. On the other side of Joe was the shy girl's polar
opposite. A studio executive who approached flirting
as if it was a negotiation. 'I'm in New York for the
next couple of weeks, but will you be available to
catch up the week of the seventeenth?'

Only Julie appeared even less interested in Joe

than I was. That was the tip-off. Even if Julie's not interested in dating a guy, she's usually interested in what's going on with him. She's a journalist – okay, it is entertainment journalism, but still she has a natural curiosity about people. Especially new people.

'You're in some kind of mood today, aren't you?' I teased.

'Just tired.'

But Julie didn't look tired. She looked revitalized.

'Were you out late last night?'

'Pretty late.'

Okay, I was beginning to get it.

'Who?' I whispered excitedly.

'Can't say.'

'Is he married?'

'No,' she replied quickly. 'I don't do that.'

'So why can't you say?'

'Just can't.'

'Was it good?'

'Let me put it this way. He made such a deposit in my sexual energy account, I can make withdrawals from it for the rest of my life and still just be living off the interest.'

A half hour later, Julie and I resumed this conversation in the kitchen. The room was remarkably clean, considering Mimi had just cooked dinner for eight. We sat on the Talavera tile countertop and shared a Marlboro Light. Every time she mentioned her secret lover, she got this adorable goofy smile on her face. 'I don't want to say who it is because I'm not sure *what* it is. It was kind of unexpected.'

'You won't even tell *me*?' I was incredulous. This was a whole new Julie.

'Don't take it personally,' she pleaded. 'Think of it as my private science experiment. I'm trying to see if keeping something secret as long as possible increases the chances of it working out. And it's not that I don't trust you, but if I can't keep something secret how can I expect someone else to keep it secret? See? It's got to start with me.'

'And is he keeping it secret too?'

'That's the plan.'

I passed the cigarette back to her. 'So you guys have a plan. One night and you've got a plan. I'm impressed.'

Just then Joe walked in, and he could tell we were into some serious girl talk. And I could tell he wasn't there looking for me. No, he was searching out the only woman who had paid him no attention. The woman who was still so into her post-sex dreamy state that she'd hardly noticed him.

'Hey,' he said.

'Hi,' we replied in monotone unison.

He offered Julie a cigarette. 'Guess you already found one.'

'I know where Mimi hides them. She's always saying she's quit, but she never quits a hundred percent.'

'Me neither.' He grinned. And he held that grin, waiting for us to figure out that he was talking about more than smoking. He moved a few steps closer to Julie. 'You're on TV, right? That cable entertainment station.'

'Yeah,' she said.

'Cool,' he replied. 'You like working there?'

'No. I'm just doing it till I figure out what I want to do next.'

He nodded as if she'd said something profound. 'I hear you,' he said, and then he winked at her.

The more time I spent around this guy, the more mystified I was by Mimi's instinct to fix us up. We were nothing alike. Not one thing in common. Plus, if this was the kind of guy she'd be with if she wasn't with Evan, what kind of guy was Evan?

'Are you a friend of Evan's too?' I asked.

Joe shook his head. 'Nope, never met the man, but he's got himself a great lady.'

There was something about the way he delivered that line and the way he was leaning on the counter in his jeans and T-shirt. There was something about the way he lit the cigarette he'd brought as an offering to Julie. Suddenly he struck me as having the kind of face you'd see on a billboard.

'You know what? You remind me a little bit of the Marlboro Man. Anyone ever tell you that?'

Looking right at Julie, Joe offered up his best cowboy charm. 'I *am* the Marlboro Man.'

*

I drank too much wine, probably because my two best friends were making zone progress, my mother had a date with a new guy, and I was going nowhere. As I drove home, I made the classic mistake caused by too much merlot. I reached out for someone I knew could make me feel better. I called Jake. I ached to hear his voice. I figured I'd call just to say hi and tell him the Marlboro Man story. He always likes my crazy stories. And it was only eleven P.M.; that was considered early evening for Jake. I justified the call by thinking, Well, he calls me at all hours, and he's not just my boss. He's also my friend. But he wasn't there. Alex answered and being the perfect assistant, he revealed nothing other than that Jake would have to get back to me.

Somewhere around six A.M., my phone rang once. Just once. It woke me up, but by the time I answered it there was a dial tone. Could it have been Jake? David? Possible. It was also possible it was a wrong number. I could hit star 69 and see if Pac Bell could hook me up with the caller. But if I did that, then I might discover that it really was a wrong number.

I decided to forego one of telephone technology's best new features. I decided it was better to hold on to the possibility that it might have been the right guy, who at six A.M. had an aborted urge to call, rather then accept the fact that it was a stranger who misdialed a digit. It might not have been the most courageous thing to do, but it made for some sweet morning daydreams. The proverbial calm before an El Niño–size storm.

Seven

The L.A. Lakers and the Houston Rockets were battling it out on the court. Two rows back, in prime seats that Jake had procured, I was taking in the game with Andrew and Denice, a self-professed basketball groupie. She was my research for the script rewrites, her number given to me by Jake, who'd gotten it from one of his Ashleys. She was happy to get the five hundred bucks Jake was paying her for her time, and even more thrilled by the idea of being a 'creative consultant.' But all you had to do was spend five minutes at the Forum with her to figure out that her prime seat, right behind the Laker bench, was the real payoff. Denice wasn't the kind of girl who could afford good seats, but she was the kind of girl who believed that having a good seat was two-thirds of the way to scoring. As she explained it, scoring came down to three moves: possession, position, and play. 'First you've got to get possession of the ball.' And with her long legs, high cheekbones, and green eyes, she was in possession of the attention of half the

Laker bench. 'Then you've got to get into position.'
Translated, that meant no more than three rows
behind the team. 'And once you're there, you better
fuckin' know how to make a play.'

Andrew had come along for the fun of it and
because there was an extra ticket. (Denice's girlfriend,
who was supposed to be my other research subject,
bailed that afternoon because she had a date with a
Clipper.) It was an odd threesome. The screenwriter
who'd never been to a professional basketball game.
The gallery owner who was on a first-name basis
with a couple of the players because he sold them
art, but couldn't tell you what position they played
or whether their stats were up or down. And the
groupie who knew not only every piece of trivia
about the team but every piece of trivia about anyone
who came anywhere near the team. She knew it all.
Who was hanging with whom, who was angling to
hang with whom. And who was 'jammin' and slam-
min'.' She also knew players' salaries, who might or
might not be traded next season, and such personal
information as whose dick got smaller when he lost a
lot of weight.

Odd or not, this trio worked, mostly because of
Andrew. Two quarters into the game, and Denice
was already laughing and talking to him like they
were old friends. No surprise. Andrew's the kind of
person who is so easy to be around that even on first

meeting, you want to say, Uh, could you just be in my life forever? He's like an antidepressant. Sometimes I wonder if he pays a price for that. I wonder if in the privacy of his home he sinks into some dark moods but, gentleman that he is, would never deign to dump any of that on his friends.

'Yes!' Denice was up on her feet to applaud a three-point play. 'Kobe! My man!' she cheered.

One of the star Lakers, temporarily benched with three fouls, turned around and smiled at her enthusiasm. She smiled back encouragingly, then leaned over to me and whispered. 'See, step number one – got to get your hands on the ball.'

'I think you've got possession and you're in shooting position,' I said. I was getting into this research. Already putting together in my head the lines that would become the new script's dialogue. And just then, at the actual moment when I was thinking things were under control, I saw it. The blonde ponytail. And though this is L.A. and there are millions of blonde ponytails, I knew, I just knew this wasn't one of the millions. This blonde ponytail was an out-of-towner. There she was, Blaze, Jake's Miami Ashley, the art student, a long way from her classroom. And just like in Miami, she was holding on to Jake's arm in a way that made him visibly puff up with pride. The sight of them almost made me sick. Instinctively I knew Blaze was out here at Jake's invitation. I knew it the way the streetwise girls in my action scripts always know when they've stumbled into danger. Blaze was no longer just an on-location bimbo. She was an on-location bimbo imported to Jake's hometown. I suddenly felt weak and dizzy – a concussion to the heart.

'Yes! Yes!' Denice was on her feet screaming again at a blocked shot and rebound that gave the Lakers the ball and the last shot of the first half. Only then did I notice that Jake and Blaze were not alone. There, dateless but clearly enjoying his very expensive floor seat (no doubt paid for by Jake), was David, my one-night stand whose parting words, 'We'll talk,' apparently came with no expiration date. I had no interest in talking to David – now or ever. But if that was the price I had to pay to hang with Jake, no problem. Price paid. Deal done. When the halftime buzzer rang, I was up and out of my seat even faster than Denice, and she was not a girl to waste one minute of halftime sitting still.

*

'You didn't mention you'd be here tonight too.' I directed the comment to Jake.

'Lakers/Rockets,' he replied as if it were a match-up he couldn't miss.

But I suspected he loved having a big public arena so he could show off Blaze. Sometimes it wasn't enough for Jake to be an alpha male. He had to be publicly alpha.

'Hi, you,' David interjected, giving me the briefest of kisses.

Hi you? Was that meant to be more or less intimate than saying my name? And then it hit me. *Oh my God. He doesn't remember my name.*

'Hi, David,' I replied coolly. 'Having fun?'

Having fun? Where did that come from? What was I saying? What I was really saying was, Where the fuck have you been and how come you haven't called? Could he read between the lines? Of course he could.

'That pass from Kobe to Shaq.' He nervously glanced at the court as if at that very moment some kind of instant replay was taking place. 'Amazing.'

'I want to meet Kobe Bryant,' Blaze announced.

Of course you do, I thought. He's the player of the moment. The star of the second quarter. Third quarter you'll want to meet whoever outdazzles him.

Jake looked at her suspiciously. 'Why do you want to meet Kobe?'

Uh-oh, I thought. A flash of jealousy. Usually Jake was happy to pass his current bimbo around as if she were a dessert and he was offering everyone a bite. But jealousy over this kind of girl was a new thing.

'Why do you think?' Blaze laughed. 'Wrong person to say that to. You think everyone has sex on the brain all the time.'

He dug his grip into her waist. 'I know *you* do.'

They were moving into that little new-lovers circle-of-two thing that really makes me want to puke. Far too cute and far too much information.

I scanned the crowd. 'I've got to get back to work,' I announced and cut out of there as if I had some better place to go.

Halftime at a Laker game made me feel the way I feel at certain Hollywood parties and premieres — like I'm operating at an extremely high level of free-floating anxiety. There is no sanctuary. Not for someone who works in the business. There's always a studio excutive or two who either jerked you around on some project or who hasn't yet returned your call. Then there are the people you've worked with, who at the time treated you like you were one of the family, but now that the movie has come and gone barely have the energy — or motivation — to nod in your direction. All of this makes me feel incredibly edgy, and not in the good way.

Also in the mix, a number of big celebrities whom you don't want to be caught staring at, lest they take you for another intruding sycophant. But it's hard not to look at the star of the season's hottest comedy who is hanging with the pop diva who's topping the charts. And how do you not look at *Oscar de la Hoya*? And if Michael Jordan's in the house, forget it. And hovering around these stars are the basketball groupies who don't know what 'sycophant' means and wouldn't care. They didn't get all dressed up in short skirts and high-heeled boots to have their game slowed down by good taste. Around them I feel like a different gender. The subfemale gender.

The closest thing to an oasis was Andrew, who waved me over to where he stood between two women in groupie gear. 'I'm here doing your research for you,' he said. 'This is Alana and Robin. They're friends with the Lakers.'

'More than friends with some of them,' Robin said with a laugh. 'But I don't kiss and tell.'

'Where's Denice?' I asked, needing her expert guidance.

'Oh, she's working it,' Alana said, glancing a few yards away to where Denice was talking to an ex-NBA star. I couldn't tell you his name, but I did recognize him from some fast-food commercial. They didn't look like they wanted to be interrupted, so I took my tape recorder out of my pocket and hit record.

'So, Robin, what's it like to date a Laker?'

She perked up as if I were Diane Sawyer.

'To be honest, we didn't actually date. See, he's kind of married.'

'Kind of?' Alana interjected sarcastically.

'Yeah, kind of,' Robin repeated adamantly. 'I don't go out with married men who are in love with their wives. Just the ones who are having problems.'

Andrew shot me a look that said *Watch this*. 'What if he's in love with his wife *and* having problems?' he asked.

Robin looked slightly annoyed, but it's hard to be annoyed at Andrew. He's so boyishly disarming, especially with that lock of hair that falls over one eye. And even though he's not what basketball groupies are shopping for, he's got his own appealing style. That night he was wearing orange pants that looked like you could snowboard in them, and a black T-shirt. More artist than art dealer.

'If I'm in bed with a guy,' Robin explained, 'I can tell if he's in love with his wife or not.'

'You can?' Andrew was amused. 'But you've got to be in bed with him to find that out. And you've got to "kind of" date him to get into bed with him, right?'

'Whatever,' she concluded, with what is quickly becoming the number one entry on my most over-used words in L.A. list.

About two seconds later, she and Alana had moved on. My tape recorder went back in my pocket. Andrew grinned mischievously and put his arm around my shoulder. 'Aren't we having fun?' That's the thing about Andrew and me. We always have fun. We've had fun at a car wash. We've had fun being stranded in the Denver airport with all flights canceled because of a two-day blizzard. We certainly should have been having fun at a Laker game surrounded by a group of colorful basketball groupies. But I so clearly wasn't.

He turned serious. 'Are you okay?'

'Andrew!'

'Sorry,' he said. 'I forgot.' Early in our friendship, I'd confided that when I am feeling fragile the worst thing to say to me is, *Are you okay?* I wasn't trying to be difficult, but I didn't think it was a good idea to burst into tears in an aisle next to one of the VIP areas at the Great Western Forum.

Just then I saw Denice 'drop the ball' with her ex-NBA star. Her focus shifted to Jack Nicholson, who was heading her way with a couple of his pals. She stared boldly at him, confident that she'd be acknowledged. It was as if her youth and beauty entitled her to attention from a man who is known for appreciating youth and beauty. But Jack sailed past, his focus on the court, where the Lakers were warming up for the second half. By the time Denice turned back to her ex-NBA star, he too had moved on. It was turning out to be one of those nights.

'You should take a cue from Jack Nicholson,'

Andrew said once Jack and his buddies had passed us by as well.

'Do you know him?'

'No, but I know a great story about him.'

★

L.A. abounds with Jack stories. People love dropping his name. Even implied proximity to Nicholson is guaranteed cachet. Whether these stories are true or not, who knows? They range from 'I got into an elevator with Jack . . .' to 'I was up at Jack's house and . . .' But Andrew wasn't a name dropper, so anything he said came with high credibility.

'Legend has it that an acting teacher named Jeff Corey told his workshop this story the night before Jack won his first Academy Award. It seems that back in Jack's early days, before things got easy after *Easy Rider*, he was doing an improv in class. When he finished, Corey said, "There's nothing there, Jack. It's not working. There's no poetry there." And Jack looked up at him, eyebrows raised – you know the look – and said, "Did you ever consider that maybe it's there and you just can't see it?"'

I needed some help on this one. 'And that's my cue to . . .?'

Andrew playfully squeezed my arm. 'Numbskull, your situation with Jake. With David. Maybe it's there and *they* just can't see it.'

'What's there?'

'*You*. The poetry of you.'

Not to go melodramatic, but now tears did fill my eyes. That was the nicest thing any guy had said to me since I'd entered the zone. But I had to pull it together. Denice had suddenly rejoined us – solo.

'Where'd the guy go?' I asked.

She carefully pulled her fingers through a clump of her hair as if untangling it were more important than any guy. 'He drifted off. Guys are weird sometimes.'

I envied her. Why couldn't I just wrap up a guy thing by saying 'He drifted off, guys are weird sometimes,' and move on to obsessing over a clump of hair?

'Is he an old boyfriend?' I wondered how blasé this girl could get.

'We have an on-again, off-again thing,' she replied.

'How long has it been off?'

'Four, five months?'

At the same moment, as the remainder of the crowd in the hallway started to head back to their seats, we both saw him. Her 'on-again, off-again thing' was off in a cozy huddle talking to Robin and Alana. I watched Denice carefully, curious as to how groupies handled such moments. She handled it perfectly. She simply looked at them and then back at me and said, 'As Michael Jordan once said after his team lost the first game in the playoffs, "There's still a lot of basketball left to be played."'

*

The third quarter of the game was mostly a blur for me. All I could think about was my double rejection. Jake and David. I imagined that anyone who looked at me could see that I was a girl who had been doubly dumped. No way to hide it. I imagined that if the TV camera lingered on my face for a moment, Laker announcer Chick Hearn would say, 'And taking in all the exciting Laker action tonight – the saddest girl in the world!'

And of course, I hated myself for feeling this way. Why couldn't I be more like those other girls . . . Denice, Alana, Robin, and Blaze, girls who felt entitled to everything and felt that any guy who didn't get it was an idiot? I'd grown up around girls like that. L.A. is full of them. Often the girls weren't even that great, but their attitude said, Buddy, you are lucky to even be in my time zone. And it worked for them. For a while, anyway. I'd seen those same girls at forty, and it wasn't a pretty picture. Attitude hardened into anger. Being a haughty bitch without a résumé works only when you're young. In Hollywood that means under twenty-six. And I've always been too ambitious to develop a game plan that gives

127

you only a short run on a crowded field. But it was tempting. A girl like that could call a guy in the middle of the night because she found a spider in her apartment, and he'd break speed records to get over there and rescue her. I (even in my Hollywood youth) could come upon a psychokiller in my bedroom, and the guy I'd call might be inspired to dial 911 before going back to sleep. An exaggeration, but that's what halftime at this Laker game was doing to me.

By the time the fourth quarter was under way, the Lakers were never more than two points ahead or behind. The crowd was going wild, and I became even more fixated on Kobe's performance. His three-point baskets were nothing but net. It wasn't his skill alone that had me mesmerized. To take high-risk shots at that stage of the game took guts. He was playing smart but not safe, leading me to wonder if the really smart ones never play anything too safe. And if that was the case, I wasn't as smart as I thought I was. When you got right down to it, just how courageous was I? A few flirtatious moments with Jake. Taking a chance on David. That doesn't take guts. That just takes an active libido.

The last thirty-five seconds of the game were tense. Tied score. The Rockets had possession and were dribbling down the court. The Laker defense was tight. Thirty-four seconds left. Thirty-three, thirty-two, thirty-one . . . and to the horror of the Laker fans, Houston scored. Time-out called.

'Fuck,' Denice said. 'But thirty seconds is enough time,' she added knowledgeably.

I watched Kobe as he huddled with his coach and team-mates. He showed no signs of tension. Everyone else in the Forum was practically jumping out of their skins, and he looked like he had ice water in his veins. The buzzer sounded. End of the time-out. This is my research, I realized. This has to go into the script.

INT: FORUM: NIGHT

A packed house. Last seconds of the game. Enough energy and tension to blow the roof off. All eyes on the court, including those of the camera-ready photographers, reporters, and legendary announcer CHICK HEARN.

CAMERA PANS: past the Houston bench, past the VIP floor seats, past the Laker bench, where coach KURT RAMBIS nervously paces.

The players take up their positions. The next few moments are a fast-paced series of images: Bodies in motion. Jumping. Running. Dribbling. Blocking. Falling. Sweating.

And through it all, the familiar voice of an excited CHICK HEARN narrating the action.

CHICK HEARN (o.c.)
Kobe Bryant takes the ball out to the sidelines. He
throws to Harper, who dribbles toward the basket
before passing to Shaq. Shaq looks for an opening.
Not there. Pippen doing a good job on defense. Shaq
passes the ball back out to Kobe. Four seconds left
on the shot clock. Kobe spins, goes for the three-
pointer . . . IT'S GOOD!

The crowd explodes.

CHICK HEARN (cont'd)
Lakers ahead by one, and Houston has no time-outs
left. Pippen receives the inbound pass, goes for the
twenty-foot jumper. No good. Off the rim, Rice has
the rebound and the Lakers win it ninety-eight to
ninety-seven!

CAMERA PANS – REACTIONS from the crowd, including
one girl who seems transported by the victory.

CUT TO:

'You're hooked now aren't you?' Denice asked
devilishly, as if she had just introduced me to a
controlled substance. Then as if she were dangling
the promise of an even better drug, she added, 'Wait
till you watch a Laker/Utah game.'

★

'Hey, Elizabeth.'

Andrew and I were walking briskly through the parking lot when those two words slowed me down. I turned to see David, standing next to his car. Jake and Blaze were nowhere in sight.

'What a game!' I said breezily. I might have slowed down, but I wasn't about to stop.

'Come here for a minute.' he beckoned sweetly. 'I want to show you something.'

'Go ahead,' Andrew said. 'I'll meet you by the car.'

When I got over to David, he'd already pulled a blueprint out of the backseat. 'Check it out. I'm finally building my house.'

'You are?' I studied the blueprint like the novice that I am. I had no idea what any of it meant, and at that moment, I didn't care. All I was thinking was it would have been easy for him *not* to call me over. We both could have used this evening's awkward run-in as a way of punctuating our one-night flirtation. Period. End of fantasy. And for me, end of any lingering expectation.

'Yeah,' he said, 'I'm finally doing it.'

'What next?' I teased. 'A dog?'

'No pets. No kids. No wife. Not yet.'

'Oh, that's right. You're the guy who doesn't even want to be responsible for a houseplant.' A Self-Contained Unit in action.

'I travel a lot.'

'Get a cactus.'

He smiled. 'When am I going to see you again?'

'Oh, is your New York-trained actress girlfriend out of town? Is she the kind who prefers to be called an *actor*. I never understood that. What – are waitresses waiters now?'

'You don't waste any time making your point, do you?' he said.

'Is there a speed limit I've exceeded?'

He laughed. 'Not yet.'

'You know, you can also get ticketed for driving too slow.'

'Well, you know where I live,' he quickly replied. 'Stop by sometime.'

A few clever lines came to mind. I could have kept this banter going forever. David's last words assured me that I was within reach of a sure thing. An easy two-point basket – a bank shot off the glass. But having just witnessed the Lakers' triumph, I decided there was nothing smart about this approach. Nothing courageous. I decided to move out into three-point territory and go for the riskier shot.

'You know, David, it's not that I haven't done this kind of thing before. Meet someone. Spend the night. Don't hear from them. Eventually run into them somewhere. Hook up again. Have a few laughs.

Sex. I'm not saying it's not fun, but I'm not into that setup anymore.'

'I never thought you were.'

I looked at him with disbelief but said nothing. Fact is, I hate talking to a guy about relationship issues, especially when there isn't even a relationship to talk about.

'I had to take care of some things before I called you again,' he explained.

'I get it,' I said, letting him off whatever hook he thought he was on.

He picked up an *LA Weekly* lying on the front seat and pulled a pen out of his pocket.

'Is that guy you're with your boyfriend?'

'Andrew's a friend.'

David jotted down a number and tore off that piece of the page. 'My beeper number. Maybe sometime next week we can get together. I'll call you too.'

'Sure,' I replied, coolly, pretending I, like Kobe, had ice water in my veins. 'Maybe sometime next week.' I walked off before that fake ice could melt.

★

Andrew was listening to the radio when I got in the car. He lowered the volume. 'So?'

'His pager. He gave me his pager number.'

'Is that bad?'

'It's not his cell-phone number. God only knows what I'd have to do to work up to getting his cell-phone number.'

As Andrew eased the car out of the parking lot, I saw Jake and Blaze, looking very much like a couple, heading toward Jake's Porsche. She was holding his car keys and tossed them to him when he got to the driver's side.

Let it go, I told myself. *Let him go. Get on with it. Look elsewhere. Keep moving. Don't look back.*

Andrew cruised onto the boulevard and turned up the music to teenage-level high. It may not have been the velocity and optimism I craved, but it was the next best thing – velocity and distraction.

Eight

It used to be that getting ready for a date meant a good solid hour at the gym, a half hour in a Kiehl's mango bubble bath, and a fifteen-minute phone pep talk with Mimi or Julie. But being in the zone called for additional preparation. And being in the zone *and* having a date with David called for serious additional preparation. It meant bringing out the big gun. It meant a trip to Davenport.

Davenport is my therapist. He's not one of those Southern California volleyball-playing therapists. The man is an athlete of the mind. In my first session with him I was bemoaning my fate as a person with no safety net. He sat there stone-faced and said, 'You're right, you don't have one.'

'Well,' I complained, 'that's a very difficult thing. You know, I'm up there on the high wire. I could fall. I could die.'

'Yes, you could,' he agreed. 'That's life.'

'But other people have safety nets.'

'Some do,' he agreed.

'So . . .' I said, waiting for him to explain the unfairness of the world.

He looked at me earnestly. 'You know that safety net you think you want? It's barbed wire.'

Talk about tough love. Davenport just dropped it on you. *Here are the facts. No whining. Deal with it. If you can't, then stay stuck. Your choice.* Since Davenport's forte was clarity, and the side effects of being in the zone included confusion, bad judgment, and frequent self-deception, I thought a session with him would be the best antidote to the fantasizing that had started with the call.

It had taken David a week, but he did finally call and ask me out. And he was funny and sweet, and since Jake was preoccupied with Blaze and I was preoccupied with trying not to think about Jake, giving David another chance seemed like a reasonably good idea. The second I hung up, I started thinking about all the things that were right about David. From there it was a short step to remembering what a good fuck he was (the guy knows how to hold a note, you know what I mean?), and from there an even smaller step to remembering how nice it was simply to lie next to him in bed. Great skin. Left unchecked, I could easily upgrade his status to Mr. Got to Have Him and forget about the fact that he didn't call after our first night together. No matter how impressive his note-holding and smooth skin, that fact alone would always make him a jerk.

*

'I don't understand dating,' I concluded, forty-five minutes into my session. 'I don't understand it, and I don't think I'm very good at it.'

This is not an easy thing to confess when you're feeling so exposed. I was sitting directly across from Davenport on a black leather couch beneath a large skylight. The overhead lighting illuminated every flaw. And though hiding flaws may be counter-productive to therapy, I saw no reason I couldn't compartmentalize: expose my soul, hide my blemishes.

This is also not an easy thing to confess to a therapist who looks like he could be one of the faces on Mount Rushmore. Talking dating to Davenport is like talking makeup with a Founding Father. For a second I thought I might have pushed the envelope of inanity, but he replied as he often did with a statement that was both true and irksome.

'The most important thing to remember about dating is never to take it personally.'

I laughed. Sometimes the truth is so fucking annoying there's nothing else you can do.

'But how do you do that?'

I understood the *concept*. That was easy. Davenport

had given me this lecture before. When two people meet, there is an initial sizing-up. Does he/she meet my standards? Is he hot enough? Smart enough? Cute enough? Is he wearing the right shoes? But the real deciding factor is not whether or not two people would look good together in a DKNY ad but whether or not their psychological cases tap into each other. If they don't, you could look like Cindy Crawford and still end up getting dumped.

Knowing this has only made me feel better way after the fact. The first blast of rejection has never been lessened by such rational concepts, no matter how accurate or brilliant. Damn! Why is it that an epiphany in a shrink session has yet to keep me from hours spent daydreaming or, more precisely, dick-dreaming about some ungettable guy. But then again, maybe an ungettable guy is what my particular case is all about.

'Not taking dating personally requires more Zen than I'll ever have in this lifetime,' I said.

I sounded whiny but consoled myself with the thought that I was whining about a bigger issue than dating. I was whining about the whole setup. The whole rigged game.

Davenport shifted in his seat. And though he never looked at his watch in the middle of a session, I was sure he was counting the minutes, and who could blame him? How many times was he going to have to go through this stuff with me?

'It's a direction,' he said. 'That's all. A way to approach it. Look,' he was winding up the hour, 'you know the deal. Nature's running the show. It's about perpetuating the species. Men and women are brought together for the purposes of replicating DNA. If you don't have a kid within two years, chances are you'll break up and find someone else who taps into your case and replicate with him. Or not. And move on again.'

'But,' I protested, 'if I completely accepted that biologically driven theory of coupling, I'd never be able to enjoy another love song on the radio or see a romantic comedy at the movies.' I paused. 'Actually, I despise romantic comedies. A cute couple – destined to live happily ever after – endure a series of cute misadventures before falling into each other's arms in a loving but never lustful embrace. Music crescendos. Fade out. The last time I experienced anything close to that sweet, sappy scenario, I was in the fifth grade.'

As I babbled on, I became aware that my whining had lost all pretence of being about any bigger issues. I was now simply another L.A. woman complaining to her therapist about her dysfunctional love life. Could I be any more clichéd?

Davenport jumped in. 'There is another playing field, you know. One where you're not set up to fail.'

He was going to get spiritual on me. I knew it. He did that from time to time. And it was one of the things that was fascinating about him. I loved that all his scientific data had logically brought him to a position that included thoughts on God and the higher self. But I wasn't ready to hear anything spiritual. You have to be in the right frame of mind to really hear that stuff. It's like sex. If you're not in a receptive mode, it can feel like a Monty Python skit.

'You got an address for that playing field?' A bad line, I know, one I wouldn't even put in a romantic comedy. But our time was up, and all my brain cells were focused on trying to find some bit of wisdom that would help me make it through the night.

Davenport took out a piece of paper and wrote down a few books. *The Fantasy Bond*. *Love and Sexuality*. The Bhagavad Gita.

'Is this my homework?'

'Your date is your homework.'

He checked his watch. I took out my checkbook.

There was one more thing I had to say, though I really didn't want to. I wanted to let the issue slide. I wished I could ignore it. Or, better, overcome it. But it wasn't going away. I had to face it.

'Uh . . . I know you're going to think I'm nuts, but I've got to tell you, this skylight is not patient-friendly.'

For a moment he said nothing, and then he took my check and laughed. With me or at me? I have no idea.

*

The Friday before Oscar night is always a good party night in L.A. In fact, the best parties are the weekend of the big night, which is not as big a night as you might think. Sure, local news can't stop hyping the show. Yes, as Oscar day goes on, there is a kind of frenzy in the air until six o'clock, when an eerie quiet and synchronicity descend over Hollywood. But it feels more like a state of siege than a celebration. Okay, I'm a little jaded. Years ago I lost the ability to watch the show with the requisite amount of antici-pation and suspension of disbelief.

I blame part of that on a girl I once knew who won an Oscar for Best Supporting Actress. In her acceptance speech, her eyes teared up as she delivered a heartfelt thank-you to her loving husband, who was her mentor and her inspiration. The audience was touched. The applause was grand. But how much of an inspiration could her husband have been? For six months she'd been having an affair with my next-door neighbor and, we later learned, with her trainer as well. Another moving Oscar moment.

Davenport is much harsher about the whole event. He believes that Oscar night in L.A. is one giant invitation to depression. He should know. He's a therapist to half of Hollywood. As he sees it, people relegated to spectatorship feel like losers. Those who are nominated but don't win, are not – in spite of what they claim – happy just to have been acknowledged. And if you do win, then you've got to figure out why winning hasn't made you as happy as you expected.

I don't know about that. I think I'd be pretty happy to win. And even not as happy as I thought I'd be would be good enough. On the other hand, if I had to chose between a date with Oscar and a date with Jake – no contest. Not that it seemed likely to be an issue. I hadn't heard much from Jake since Blaze's arrival, and action writers never get nominated for Oscars – or for anything else. Anyway, Academy Awards night is no big deal for me, but it was for David, which was the shocker.

'Can't get together with you that night,' he said. 'I have to watch the Oscars.'

Have to? He's an architect. Why does an architect *have to* watch the Oscars? Was he going to stay home and watch them alone? Was he off to some Oscar-viewing party? Or was it bullshit and he was just busy that night with his New York-trained actress girlfriend? I didn't pry. Instead we settled on a Friday-night date.

'What do you want to do?' he asked when he called that afternoon.

'I don't care.'

This is the part of dating I truly don't understand. What's the point of going to dinner or a movie or an art exhibit or anything else when the point of the date is to end up in bed? Is it to see if you want to fuck the guy you're out with? I already knew I did. Why couldn't we just skip the preliminaries? I'd have no problem with a plan to meet at his place or mine at let's say ten P.M. A little conversation, maybe some champagne or whatever, and then *bam* – you're onto it, into it, all over it. I always have better conversations postsex anyway. Pre-sex talks sound like a lengthy personal ad – fake version of me seeking fake version of you. But I didn't have the guts to come right out and suggest we cut to the good stuff. Some guys love this approach. It saves them time and money (you can forego the expensive dinner at Matsuhisa). But other guys take it as an insult, as if you're turning them into nothing more than your live-action dildo.

'Well, whatever you want to do is fine with me,' he said.

'Yeah, right.' I laughed. 'Guys always say that, but

then you say something like, "Great, let's go bowling," and they say, "Bowling? You want to go bowling?"'

'If you want to go bowling, we'll go bowling,' he replied, with zero enthusiasm. 'But I've got a sore knee from a skiing accident, so I might not be able to actually bowl.'

'Well, that sounds like fun. I can actually bowl, and you can actually keep score. Forget it. I wasn't serious anyway.'

'Well, figure it out and let me know what you want to do; I've got to go into a meeting with a client.'

Now this is the part of dating I really, really hate. The figure-it-out-and-let-me-know part. I don't want to figure it out. I feel like I'm doing the guy's homework.

'My agent is having a pre-Oscar party,' I said before he could hang up. 'And since you're an Oscar fan . . .'

'Sounds great.' He perked up. 'I'll pick you up at eight.'

*

Parties thrown Oscar weekend tend to be big-dick events. Agencies who have Oscar-nominated clients like to flaunt their success by throwing the kind of bash that'll be talked about the next day and the day after that. Caviar, champagne, and security guards are the common denominator. The deciding factor in the big-dick contest is the celebrity head count. Who scored the most VIPs? CAA? ICM? UTA? William Morris? But equally important in creating a buzz about the party are the noncelebrity guests (like me) who have been invited as a necessary contrast to the rich and famous. You can't have a successful celebrity party without an audience.

I usually pass up these invitations, but it's not wise to pass up too many. Being a recluse is not how the Hollywood game is played. And when I do go, I like to take a girlfriend, usually Mimi or Julie because they'd totally understand if within five minutes of arriving I suddenly announced that I had to get out of there. They'd also understand if I wanted to stay till two A.M. An unconditional support system is what you need at such evenings. Besides, these girls know how to work a room and, if need be, find their own ride home.

Taking a date to one of these things is much trickier. And taking a date who's not in the industry can be disastrous. Who will he talk to? Will he be bored? Will he watch me working the room and decide I've got neither style nor substance? Will he be so enamored of the stars present that I'll be less enamored of him? That aside, I expect a guy to check out beautiful girls. And I don't mind a guy checking out beautiful well-known actresses, because my theory is they're less alluring in person than they are as screen icons. As I once said to a guy in a bar who was trying to dis me by saying I was no Julia Roberts, 'You don't get it. Julia Roberts is no Julia Roberts.'

The actress competition didn't bother me. What worried me and what I saw as potentially disastrous was bringing a new date onto my turf and seeing him completely differently from the way I did when he was operating from his own mission-control center. The fish-out-of-water scenario often works in romantic comedies, but rarely works in dating scenarios. I call it my fireman theory. See a guy in fireman duds with a big hose in his hands. Watch him act like a hero, and suddenly you're getting as hot as the fire he's putting out. Take off the hero uniform and stick him at a Hollywood party, and you won't even notice him. Do I think that's smart or right or mature or any of those good things? No. But Hollywood parties, especially pre-Oscar ones, have a powerful effect on all who attend. Upon entering, be prepared to be plunged right back into junior high. Imagine every adolescent anxiety and insecurity times ten. Who's hot. Who's not. Who's in. Who's soon to be out. Who's talking to whom. Who's flirting with whom. Who came with whom. Who's leaving with whom. Bring a non-industry date into that environment, and it's trial by fire. For the record, I think it's always better to hang out with a guy on his turf, unless he's one of those guys who fits in anywhere. One of those guys who's so charming he becomes fresh meat in Hollywood's feeding frenzy. If David turned out to be one of those guys, even Julia Roberts might take notice.

★

'Hey, David.' A tall young man with a high cool quotient approached, smiling.

Three seconds into the party and David, not me, was the one being called to. 'Hey, Rodney, how you doing?' The tall man waved back and kept moving.

'Is he a friend of yours?' I asked, knowing Rodney to be one of the up-and-happening managers in the business.

'I designed the addition to his house.'

'Who else do you know here?'

'You mean other than Sly, Bruce, and Whoopi? No one.' He grinned to let me in on the joke.

'For a second you had me.'

'You know what I like about you?' he said. 'You're so gullible.'

'Me? Gullible?'

'Yeah, you. Tough-chick action-writer you.' He took my hand and led me toward the bar. 'It's a good thing. Balances out your natural arrogance.'

'My what?'

He was laughing. 'I'm just trying to loosen you up a little.'

'Why, do I look tense?'

'White-knuckled terror. You're not shooting the rapids, you know.'

'Oh yes, I am,' I replied as I spotted a producer I'd once worked for unsuccessfully, a producer I swore I'd never work for again, and my agent – the host of the party – who nodded in my direction and then embraced a more important client.

'Then my advice is enjoy the thrill,' David replied.

Five minutes into the party, and this is what I was thinking: I really do like this guy, and I hope Julia Roberts is a no-show.

★

Every good pre-Oscar party should generate at least one story that travels through Hollywood with the force of a Santa Ana wind. This one looked like it was barely going to inspire a few breezy anecdotes. A sexaholic director was hitting on the seventeen-year-old daughter of a European actor, and a female studio executive who had one martini too many had fallen into the pool. The word was, she'd done it on purpose to show off her new tits. And with her soaked shirt clinging to her body like a second skin, she was definitely an advertisement for the surgical skills of her doctor. Aside from that, though, there was nothing going on. No headlines. Nothing for the next day's e-mail.

But around midnight, the host got lucky. Or unlucky, depending on whether throwing a memorable party is worth a memorable migraine. I was stepping out of the bathroom when I spotted an actress who twenty years earlier had had a five-year stint on the A list but since then had done little but marry twice and divorce fast. That night she was solo and whacked out of her mind.

'Rodney Swift just broke a guy's jaw over some girl,' she announced as she checked her hair in a hallway mirror. Was she talking to me? She didn't even know me. She was talking to anyone within earshot. 'And the girl's blonde. They'll think it's me. They'll think it's me,' she said as she continued to play with her streaked locks. 'The tabloids love to trash me. I fucking hate the First Amendment.'

With that she darted into the bathroom and, with the door ajar, tapped into a vial of coke with a fingernail and snorted the powder as daintily as if she was dabbing on perfume.

I walked down the hallway, more curious than alarmed. This was not the kind of house, or the kind of party, where bad or wild things happened. And at first nothing seemed even slightly out of order. Guests milled around. Music on. Laughs. But then I saw that out in the backyard there did seem to be some kind of commotion. As I got closer I noticed a security guard was talking to Rodney, who looked like he was about to implode. A dozen or so people surrounded a man lying on the ground. I turned to another guest standing nearby.

'Do you know what happened?'

'Ask her.' He pointed to a distraught girl, a one-time video vixen who was being consoled by a small group of women. She was one of those girls whose best assets are blonde hair and a great body, and even though she was upset she did her best to flaunt them.

By then someone was helping the guy on the ground to get up, and the crowd parted to give him breathing room. I recognized him as a waning rock star who at one time had been managed by Rodney. I'd last seen him at a party at Jake's, where he spent the whole night drinking martinis and talking to Harry Dean Stanton about Buddhism. Tonight he had a cut lip, and blood all over his four-hundred-dollar Gucci shirt. Only then did I realize that David was the one helping him to his feet and keeping a tight grip on his arm. Suddenly I felt as if I was watching a scene I'd written. What followed could have been a page out of one of my early unproduced action scripts.

EXT: BACKYARD: NIGHT

> ROCKER
> (to Rodney)
> Come on, asshole. You want to try that again?

> RODNEY
> (not looking for round two)
> Just leave her . . .
> (glancing at video vixen)
> . . . the fuck alone.

The PARTY'S HOST steps between them. If ever there was a time for this AGENT to show off his negotiating skills . . .

> AGENT
> Guys. Come on. If I wanted a fight, I would've invited Tyson.

> ROCKER
> Who the fuck are you?

> AGENT
> I'm the person throwing the party.

> ROCKER
> That's nice. Next time, serve better vodka.

Suddenly, with a fake that would earn him cheers in the NFL the ROCKER spins around, executing a 180 that puts

RODNEY in range. Talk about a hidden weapon. Who'd expect a glob of SPIT to shoot out of his mouth and hit the mark?

BULLSEYE on RODNEY'S forehead. We're at war.

RODNEY goes ballistic. Like a madman trigger-happy with an Uzi, he fires a stream of unintelligible words. He'd prefer to throw fists, but now everyone's in the mix. Stopping a fight or starting one? Hard to tell.

The two SECURITY GUARDS get a piece of the action while the AGENT nervously makes a call on his cell phone.

DAVID's the one who takes control. Grabbing the ROCKER by his Gucci lapels, he pushes him away from the crowd.

DAVID
You don't do that kind of thing HERE. You get that?

It's attitude not muscle that keeps the ROCKER in check.

ROCKER
Had to spit. He's too much of a pussy to deserve a punch.

DAVID
(conspiratorially)
Let me explain something . . .

As DAVID maneuvers the ROCKER toward the exit.

CAMERA PANS:

to VIDEO VIXEN, hands on her slim hips, tits thrust forward, cover-girl pout. She's already been forgotten by both guys and everyone else. A Helen of Troy wannabe.

CUT TO:

A half hour later, as David and I were leaving, my agent stopped us at the door. He shook David's hand. 'Nice work back there,' he said.

David accepted the compliment graciously. 'He's not a bad guy, he just has a knack for finding trouble.'

'Music people,' my agent said as if that summed up the situation. He was smiling at David the way I'd seen him smile at potential clients he was trying to woo.

'It was a great party,' David said, making a move to leave.

'Come back again.'

'Invite us,' I said.

Only then did my agent turn in my direction. 'Always nice to see you here.' He swung back to David.

'Thanks again, David.' Obviously he'd found out David's name, though not from me, since he hadn't said one word to me all night until now. Then he did something uncharacteristic. He hugged me good-bye. I took it for what it was. Trickle-down attention.

★

Much later, as David and I were on the freeway, speeding back to his place, it occurred to me that not only had he passed the Hollywood party test, he even got to play hero. He became a fireman. He took out the big hose and extinguished the flames. Question was, how'd he do it? How'd he get the rocker to cool down in six seconds?

'What'd you say to him?' I asked.

'I told him he was about two seconds away from being laughed at.'

'And that worked?'

'Men hate being laughed at.'

'Are you betraying your gender by telling me that?'

'It's no secret. It's not the information as much as the delivery. Got to say it with the right inflection. Got to make him feel like he's letting down the team by acting like an asshole.'

David illustrated his point by giving three different readings of the same line.

'You don't harbor any secret desire to be an actor, do you?' I asked.

'The only secret desire I've been harboring is to fuck you again.'

I put my hand between his legs. 'Secret's out.'

★

It was good. Even better than the first time. But what is really good sex? I've thought about this a lot. So have all my girlfriends. There has been lots and lots of girl talk about the definition of really good sex. I don't have a definition as much as I have a story.

Picture a girl who is, as most are, insecure about her body. Picture this girl putting on a bikini at the beginning of the summer. She looks in the mirror and thinks . . . *There's no way I can walk around wearing this.* But she packs it in her suitcase anyway. Now imagine that girl on a Greek island. The first day there, she timidly puts on the suit. By the end of the first week, she hardly ever takes it off. By the end of the third week, she wishes she'd bought a skimpier one, and by the end of the month, she wishes she didn't have to wear anything at all. Fucking David was like a month on Santorini. He took me from feeling insecure to feeling like a sex goddess, and if that isn't good sex I don't know what is.

So there I was, in the throes of being an uninhibited goddess, when the phone rang. Five times. Then it stopped, and almost immediately rang again. *This is interesting*, I thought. It's two-thirty in the morning, he's fucking me, and his phone is ringing.

'I've got to answer it,' he said. 'If I don't, she'll come over.'

I assumed 'she' was the New York-trained actress girlfriend. 'Go ahead,' I replied calmly.

He managed to reach over and pick up the receiver without putting me on hold. His dick wasn't going anywhere.

'Hello,' he said, trying to sound as sleepy as possible. 'Yeah? Is that right? I'm glad it went well. Two curtain calls! That's great.'

I moved my hands down his back. He didn't seem to mind. I took that to mean that even while he was on the phone with his New York-trained actress girlfriend, I had an all-access pass to his body.

'Did you go out afterward?' he asked her. 'Did you have fun?' He sounded sincere. And as his voice continued to grow full of warmth and maybe even love, his dick retained its redwood-tree-trunk proportions inside of me.

Should I feel bad about this? I wondered. Should I feel slighted? Should I feel diminished in some way? Should I be concerned at the ease with which he juggles two women? Whatever I should or shouldn't have felt, the fact is, I didn't feel bad. I was more curious than anything else. Is this the ultimate example of embracing ambiguity? Was I pioneering new territory here? Did this constitute a threesome?

Suddenly I remembered the Best Supporting Actress whose acceptance speech years earlier seemed the height of hypocrisy. Now I thought, Life is messy – and maybe that's okay. Then I thought. No wonder I can't write romantic comedies.

When David got off the phone, he offered no excuses or explanations nor did I want any. We continued making love, even more intensely than before. He looked right at me in a way that was more intimate than a thousand I love you's. Whatever this is, it's authentic, I decided. If not, then come Sunday night, he should be up there picking up an Oscar.

Nine

I woke up in my bed at noon, feeling a little bad. Not because I was back in my bed. I loved that. I have no trouble spending all night with a guy and then getting in my car and driving home at six A.M. In fact, I prefer it. The reason I was feeling a little bad was because I'd reached too high the night before. It's like when you overexert yourself at the gym but don't feel it till the next day. I'd overworked my sexual outlaw muscle.

But at least it was a Saturday. A perfect Dad day. A perfect time to seek out the illusion of a safety net, which for me meant going to the only place that always makes me feel safe. A golf course. I've always felt that nothing bad will ever happen to me on immaculately kept greens. Well, nothing except the public humiliation that comes with swinging and completely missing the ball. My rep on the course is I have two shots – surprising and embarrassing. I'll never shoot under a hundred, but so what? After nine holes (who has time for eighteen?), I'm pretty mellow. Mellow and ready for an all-American treat: a cheeseburger and a diet Coke. It's as close to a Norman Rockwell painting as I get.

When I got to the course, my father was already at the driving range. He was on his second bucket of balls and had found his rhythm. For a few minutes I watched him from the deck of the clubhouse. I could have watched him for hours. It's the way I imagine I'll feel about watching a child of mine – a boy – work hard at something that matters to him. Father or son. Sixty or six. It doesn't matter. Both trigger the same protective instinct.

Besides, I think of my dad more as a traveling companion than a parent. He loves the description. It appeals to the side of him that came of age in a tie-dyed, hippie-esque world. A world where sharing a journey and sharing a joint were what it was all about. And even now, in spite of the conventional trappings of his life – second wife, two kids, a dog, and a house in the Valley – there's an aging hipster in there somewhere.

★

'I saw your boss the other day,' he announced.

'What?' I had just blown three shots on the fourth hole trying to hit out of a sand trap.

My dad nudged the ball into an easier spot. It was either cheat or we were going to be there forever.

'You saw my boss? You saw Jake?' I swung and this time connected. It wasn't pretty, but the ball landed on the green.

'Bill Coleman has his account,' he explained as we got back into the golf cart.

That didn't surprise me. Live around Hollywood long enough and you begin to see how things are connected in unexpected ways. Your mechanic has a sister who is the nanny of the children of an actor you just had a meeting with. Your acupuncturist turns out to be best friends with the best friend of the man you just spent the night with. Or, my favorite, discovering mid-exam that my gynecologist went to Hebrew school with the producer I was currently working for. It wasn't that Jake was a client of the accounting firm my father worked for that threw me, it was the fact that he showed up at their office. Jake never showed up at an office, not even his own expensively appointed one on the studio lot.

'He's looking good for a guy who lives the life he lives.'

I detected a twinge of jealousy in my father's voice. Had my dad taken the road most traveled (in Hollywood), he might have happily lived a bad-boy life.

'Did you talk to him?' Suddenly I imagined a nightmarish conversation that began with my dad saying, My daughter talks about you all the time.

'I told him to keep his hands off you.'

'You did not!'

My dad was out of the golf cart and studying the ball's placement, about twenty yards from the green. I was right behind him.

He reached for his lob wedge. 'What's wrong with that?'

'What's wrong is, he might do it.'

Silence. I couldn't tell if it was because my dad didn't want to think about his daughter with one of Hollywood's notorious bad boys or because he was so into concentrating on his next shot that, for the moment, he didn't care. His setup and follow-through were almost perfect. The ball landed six inches from the hole.

He smiled. 'Your name never came up.'

In some ways, that was even worse. As I walked over to my ball, I considered the slight of not even being mentioned. I considered Andrew's theory that we never know how much or how little space we take up in someone's life. I considered the possibility that I took up an infinitesimal space in Jake's. I considered giving up on Jake *and* my golf game. In fact, I thought I *had* given up on him. I thought I'd talked myself into a state of calm resignation, but all my dad had to do was mention his name and I was rattled.

I stared at the ball in front of me, trying hard to

concentrate, but it was useless. My swing barely connected. The ball did a bunny hop and landed three feet away.

'I have no middle game,' I whimpered.

My dad handed me a different club. 'It's the hardest part of the game to get.'

Made worse, I thought, by the fact that in every area of my life I felt like I was struggling with the middle game.

That's what the zone is all about. Not the exhilaration of a shot off the tee. Or the comparatively easy task of putting. No, it's the area in between, an area occupied by sand traps and other man-made obstacles. Lovely, I thought, just fucking lovely.

*

Lunch at the clubhouse was a ritual with us. It was like a scene out of the life we were supposed to be living. Father and daughter spending a fun-filled afternoon on an upscale public course, followed by lunch in the cozy dining area. It was like something right out of a brochure for the joys of middle-class living. And though I found the dining room to be a bizarre hybrid of sports bar and ski chalet, and would bet anything that the person who designed it believed lots of dark wood paneling equals class, I couldn't deny that it worked. It was comfortable. It was family. It was *safe*. I even liked the quiet drone that came from the TV set that was always tuned to some professional golf game. Nothing soothed me more than listening to golf commentators speak in that specialized whisper they use when covering tournaments.

We always sat at one of the tables near the windows, and we never talked about anything too serious. The light touch I didn't have playing golf, I excelled at in conversation with my dad. That afternoon it was almost three by the time we sat down. There were only about fifteen or so people in the room, most of them men. My dad seemed tired, but who isn't tired? Career. Maintenance (whatever it takes to look and feel good). Relationships. I'm beginning to think we can choose only two, but we're all exhausted trying to have three.

'Everything good with you?' It was my standard question to my dad. I always asked hoping he'd say yes, and always feared the day he'd say no.

He nodded. 'You know . . . work is work. The kids are great.'

The kids were my half brother and sister, ages eight and six. I adored them, but around them I felt ancient.

'And Janine?' Janine is my stepmom, thirty-eight years old. Restless and impressionable. She's been married to my dad for ten years. Married him when she was my age.

'She's learning how to make wigs. She thinks it's an industry that's about to take off.'

An industry? I was tempted to push it. What does she mean, an industry? Does she think there'll be a General Motors of wigs someday? But I knew better. My dad always defended Janine through all her crazy phases.

'Where do you go to learn something like that?'

'Minnesota,' Dad replied wearily.

'She's in Minnesota?'

'Just for a week.'

I tried to read him on this one. Was he upset she was gone? A little relieved? My stepmother wasn't easy to deal with. Based on my stories, Davenport described her as a predator posing as a house pet. I wanted to like her, though. She was beautiful. She could be fun. In fact, she could be delightful. We had things in common. But every time I thought, *Okay*, this can work, she'd throw some nightmarish fit that inspired me to dub her a delightmare.

'And after she studies for a week, what happens? She gets her diploma in wig-making?' I tried to sound interested, not judgmental.

'Something like that,' he said.

I must have appeared slightly skeptical because he quickly added, 'She's good. We're good. We're going to take a vacation next month. Just the two of us. Mexico? Hawaii? Someplace like that. Janine's mother will watch the kids.'

He sounded upbeat, but he's my dad. I can read between the beats. It wasn't that hard to do since he hates vacations, hates flying, hates hotels, and hates the beach. This wasn't a vacation, it was a concession. It was couples therapy with a resort backdrop. I could just picture him sitting at one of those hotel bars by the pool, bored out of his mind but trying to look like this vacation was the greatest idea in the world. But then again, maybe Janine would put on some sassy little wig she had made and saunter over in her Victoria's Secret miracle-bra bikini, and a tired marriage could get a big shot of juice. Not that it was an image I wanted to dwell on.

'So you dating anyone?' my dad asked, jacked up on three refills of iced tea.

'If dating implies some agreed–upon pattern, an assumption of consistency . . . then no. I'm not dating.'

'But you're seeing someone?'

'Well, let's put it this way. I saw someone last night.'

'One of your bad boys?'

'They're never mine, which is what makes them bad.'

'Bad meaning good?'

'Bad meaning impossible to have, which isn't always good but usually is interesting.'

'Can't have interesting forever.'

'Why not?' I really wanted to know. It was one of those moments when I welcomed some enlightened fatherly advice.

'Because even bad boys get old.'

That did it. I had to defend my guys, especially Jake. Jake now and Jake's future as an aging Hollywod bad boy.

'Old's got nothing to do with it,' I argued. 'Not with the kind of bad boys I'm talking about. I'm not talking about wild guys who know how to party. A real bad boy has to be accomplished. He's got to be a guy who has done things. He's got to have made at least one trip to the top of the mountain. If not more. He's a bad boy because his gigantic spirit demands diversity. That's always going to be interesting to me. I don't care about the spiritless lazy boys getting drunk on champagne at base camp.'

My dad looked at me with the strangest expression, as if he were temporarily disoriented by having stepped into the wrong party. And then, as if backing out of the room apologetically, he said wistfully, 'It was a lot easier being a bad boy in the sixties. All you had to do was smoke pot.'

*

It took about twenty minutes for us to reenter our faux Norman Rockwell scenario. But we did. We managed to get back to small talk and move on to dessert (all-American pie à la mode). Then the television set above the bar caught our attention. Gone was the golf commentator's soothing drone, replaced by a news anchor's snappy patter.

This newsbreak reported a 'tragic event in Fresno.' Apparently a middle-aged couple had gone to see a marriage counselor. Halfway through the session, the wife took out a gun and shot her husband in the arm. At which point he whipped out his gun and shot her in the chest. A full report was due on the five o'clock news. The therapist, as yet, had no comment for reporters.

The clubhouse got very quiet. The men all looked a little depressed. No kidding. Isn't that a classic male nightmare? The hysterical woman who pushes your buttons until the unhappy marriage erupts in a barrage of gunfire? My father pushed away his apple pie and finished off his iced tea.

'What a world this is,' he said. And I knew, even without having been there, that there was a time in the sixties when 'What a world this is' meant fun, not fear.

As he walked me to my car I thought about whether he had ever cheated on Janine or if Janine had cheated or was cheating on him. Suddenly, all I wanted was to believe he was happy.

'Hawaii,' I said. 'I think you and Janine should go to Hawaii. Everyone says it's a special place.'

'Have you been to Hawaii?' He looked confused, as if he'd missed a piece of my life and couldn't figure out how it happened.

'No, but if I ever get over my bad-boy thing and can find a great guy like you, I'll make sure we go there.'

That sentence tells you everything about how much I wanted him to feel good. I don't talk like that. I don't think like that. I don't write like that. If I did, I'd be making two hundred thousand dollars a script writing romantic comedies. And even though I am in the zone and crave a legitimate boyfriend, that doesn't mean I'm fantasizing a week in Kauai with a guy who's lost his edge.

My dad mulled it over. 'Could be good. They've got some good golf courses there. And it's important to do something different every now and then.'

I put my arm around him. 'You'll love it.'

'We'll see,' he said as we reached my car. 'Call me if you need anything.'

'I'm fine,' I replied. That was our deal. He always offered to be there for me if I needed him, and I always let him off the hook.

He gave me a kiss on the cheek. 'Be careful around men like Jake.'

'What's the worst he can do? Break my heart? It's been broken before.'

'Men like Jake . . .' He left it at that. He'd done his parental duty.

'Don't worry,' I said. 'Nobody can annihilate me without my permission.'

He looked relieved. 'That's my girl.' He smiled and walked away.

Ten

The worst part of being a screenwriter is pitch meetings. It's bad enough when you're there to pitch a story that you've come up with and are passionate about; at least then you can console yourself with the thought that if they don't like it, maybe they just aren't smart enough to get it. Your passion protects you from self-doubt. It makes it easier for you to exit the room calmly after they've said, 'We'll think about it and get back to you,' which, translated, means 'It's a definite pass.' It also makes it easier to shake their hands politely and say, 'Thanks for your time,' which, translated, means 'Fuck you, blind man.'

But when you're going in on a pitch that is a take on someone else's idea, an article the studio bought, a remake of another movie, or an executive's idea of high concept (my favorite being 'bicoastal' – that was it, the whole concept), it's harder to tap into the self-righteous 'Fuck you, blind man' attitude. But it's very easy to feel wobbly and insecure as you try to sell your take on their idea when they don't even know what it is but claim they'll know it when they hear it. And often the only thing they really want to hear is Tom Cruise's agent calling to say he's interested.

That morning I seriously contemplated never doing another pitch meeting . . . ever. But it was an unlikely reality, since even A-list writers are subjected to them. However, in their case they're meeting with the guy who can say yes. I only meet with mid-level executives or producers who at most can say maybe. And even when a maybe turns into a yes – usually after several grueling story sessions – I don't get the big bucks. I do okay. I have a nice lifestyle but nothing fancy. No BMW 740i – not that I want one.

My meeting was with Renée Larkin, a producer with solid connections at all the big studios and a project in need of a rewrite. My agent had set it up and considered it a feat. 'Renée will meet with you,' he said excitedly, as if she were the pope. 'I called in a favor,' he added, letting me know that this had everything to do with him and nothing to do with my résumé.

This is not the way I like to make an entrance, but I needed to line up my next job. And though the odds were against me, and Renée's rep as a bitch had provoked more than one writer to say, 'I'd rather work at McDonald's,' I was doing my best not to sink to such a low level of self-esteem that even I wouldn't hire me.

What made this particular pitch meeting even worse was that it was at Universal, a studio that always makes me feel like a factory worker. It's the most corporate-looking lot in town, especially if you enter through the gate next to the building known as the 'black tower.' But even the other side of the lot – the public side, which boasts Universal City-Walk – is a scary place. I may be jeopardizing future deals at this studio, but I've got to ask, *What were they thinking?* We'll put together this fake city street, fill it with souvenir shops, restaurants, and movie theaters, and it'll improve the quality of leisure time? Maybe for people who like a fake life. It feels like Disneyland without the rides. I'm more comfortable with real life on real streets. I'd rather go see a movie on Hollywood Boulevard even though it means navigating around hustlers and teenage runaways.

When I finally exited the five-story parking garage, convinced I'd never find my car again, I was facing five production trailers, none of which had a sign out front. I walked up the few steps to the first in line and knocked on the door. It was opened by a girl who appeared to be in her early twenties.

'I'm looking for Renée Larkin's trailer,' I said.

'This is it. Are you Elizabeth?'

'Yeah.'

'I'm Jordan, Renée's assistant.' She nervously looked inside the trailer, where I glimpsed Renée on a mobile phone, talking and pacing the confined area like a caged tigress.

Jordan waited to catch Renée's eye and then indicated me standing there. Renée nodded as if she was acknowledging a room-service delivery.

'Come on in,' Jordan said. 'Can I get you something to drink?'

I took a seat. 'Nothing. I'm fine.'

It was a small trailer. I couldn't help but study Renée. She was tall. Big-boned. Fortyish. Not unattractive, but painfully single (common knowledge in town). She was wearing a tight suit and high heels. She glanced at me once, but there was nothing welcoming about that glance. She wasn't exactly saying *Make yourself comfortable, I'll be with you in a minute.* She was saying *I'm smart and successful, and I'll get around to you when I get around to you.*

As she continued to talk on the phone, she sat down and intermittently took bites of a salad. When her lemonade glass was empty, she tapped a fork on it, and Jordan rushed to refill it. And I mean rushed. She looked like she was on the fast track to a nervous breakdown. God forbid she should spill a drop.

I'll admit it, that little scenario inspired a rush to judgment. I decided Renée was a Leverage Abuser. Have power, will torture. And her favorite object of torture was any girl who worked for her, especially if that girl was considerably younger and prettier.

Renée took notes on the back of a script and scowled at Jordan as if she was the reason for whatever wasn't going right at that moment. What is it with women like Renée? I thought. These are the very women who talk a feminist line in public but in the semiprivacy of their own production trailer, treat their female assistants like, well, faceless factory workers. Where's the sisterhood in that? I felt a theory coming on.

Maybe it comes down to this. There are women who feel pretty and women who don't, which has everything to do with how they felt about themselves growing up. Renée struck me as one of those women who grew up not feeling pretty, and even on days when she's looking good, she doesn't really feel it. Jordan, on the other hand, probably grew up knowing she was cute, and even on days when she's looking bad, she still feels like a pretty girl, just one having a bad day. Maybe what we had here was a woman who never felt pretty now in a situation where she could get back at the kind of girl who almost always feels pretty.

Renée finally got off the phone and turned her attention to me. 'Did your agent explain the idea?'

No greeting. Okay, fine. Not a problem for me. I appreciate getting down to business.

'Yep.'

She picked up a piece of paper, her phone sheet. 'Jordan, didn't we return Tom's call?'

'He's not back till tomorrow.'

Renée tossed the sheet. 'I don't care when he's getting back; I want him to know I returned on Tuesday, not Wednesday.'

Jordan immediately picked up a phone and placed the call. It was then that I noticed a twelve-inch Buddha statue and a small vase of flowers on a shelf. A makeshift altar. *Ah*, I thought, Renée's one of those . . . spiritual on the outside.

'So, let's hear it,' she said, her attention swinging back to me and our meeting.

I did my best to contain my performance anxiety and launched into the pitch I'd worked up for Renée's project about female detectives in L.A. I prefaced it by saying, 'Obviously this territory has been done before, so we have to have a fresh angle.' I suggested that these girls should be good at what they do, but not so good when it comes to managing their personal life.

'They should be struggling like everyone struggles. They should make mistakes. One of them could even be involved with one of the bad guys, a counterfeiter – *not knowing* he is a bad guy.'

I added the 'not knowing' part because my agent had stressed that Renée wanted a big commercial movie. Having the female lead *knowingly* fall for one of the bad guys was too dark for the sunny summer blockbuster Renée was shooting for.

Renée had no reaction to this. None. No sign of any kind that I had said anything that made sense or that she found even mildly interesting. Pitching to someone who doesn't react is like making love to someone who operates only on receiver mode. Eventually you either get bored or you turn it into an exercise in masturbation. I turned the pitch into an exercise in mental masturbation. If she wasn't going to react, I'd try to tell it in a way that at the very least was entertaining to me.

'I see the lead as one of those girls who could have been a teenage runaway hanging out on Hollywood Boulevard. She's been on her own since fifteen. Now, at twenty-five, she's smart, streetwise, and resourceful. But even she gets seduced by this slick-talking skankster counterfeiter because, let's face it, even the smartest woman is vulnerable to the right line from the wrong guy.'

It was one of my favorite concepts, but Renée still had no response. In fact, she looked like she was barely breathing. I was tempted to check her pulse. Talk about hostile. I'd never before pitched to some-one who didn't give me the courtesy of some kind of reaction. Even a phony one.

I continued on, weaving my favorite lines and

scenes into the story. At least one of us was enjoying this dead-in-the-water meeting.

'Ultimately, of course, our star detective turns in the bad guy even though she loves him. It's kind of like what Bogart has to do at the end of *The Maltese Falcon* when he finds out Mary Astor is the killer.'

Still no sign of life from Renée. Her deadpan expression was insulting. Okay, enough. What to do? I couldn't come right out and say, *If Tom Cruise was pitching this same idea you'd be smiling and laughing your ass off.*

But I did have some ammunition. With a woman like Renée, you can always play the sex card.

'We also need a second key male in the story. A good guy, but not someone who is so good he's predictable. He's the one who helps our girl solve the case, but he's also capable of throwing her up against the wall and kissing her in a way that makes discussion irrelevant. You know, one of those guys who is so sexy, sleeping with him is like getting a blood transfusion. You wake up in the morning and say, Okay, maybe he's not the most sensitive guy in the world, but he can do THAT! Wow!'

My 'wow' said everything. It said, I know about the wow experience. I've had the wow experience and look forward to more wows in my future. How about you?

Renée tilted her head to the side and looked at

me condescendingly. 'You've obviously been working for Jake,' she said.

I looked at her without saying a word, and she
held her stare. What we had at that moment was an
undeclared battle. She viewed me as the enemy. To
her, I was one of those girls who hung out with the
very guys she despised. She felt rejected by them and
in return felt compelled to reject anyone they
accepted. Even if I had two Academy Awards on my
bookshelf, Renée would not want to work with me.
Of course, she would because I had two Academy
Awards. She'd work with me and pretend to adore
me if that got one of her projects a green light. But
it'd be a sham. The sides were drawn. From the
second I'd arrived she'd been a cold bitch, and with
the last part of my pitch I'd justified her coldness. I
was in their camp. The camp that chose sex over
sensitivity. So there we were. I looked at her as a
leverage abuser with a bad sex life, and she looked at
me as a slut with no leverage. You could say that I
was reading a lot into this, but I have to tell you, this
has happened before. When Jake's your boss and
mentor, you become the target of a lot of female
hostility. These women act as if I've betrayed my
tribe by signing on with the kind of guy who will
never ask them out. I wanted to say, Look Renée,
he hasn't asked me out either, but so what? Yes, he
dates bimbos. Yes, he chases youth and beauty. But

he's about a lot more than who he fucks, and if you don't see that then maybe you should stick to mindless summer blockbusters.

The rest of the meeting was an exercise in doubletalk. Like that scene in *Annie Hall*, when Woody Allen and Diane Keaton are making small talk over a glass of wine. Their small talk is the dialogue, but their thoughts are in subtitles.

INT: RENÉE LARKIN'S PRODUCTION TRAILER: DAY

Renée and a young screenwriter, Elizabeth West, are finishing up a pitch meeting that has gone badly. A certain amount of tension between the two can be sensed.

Renée crosses her arms and legs. 'Tightly wound' doesn't begin to describe her.

                    RENÉE
          There's another way of going.

SUBTITLE: You're wasting your time and more important . . . mine.

               Elizabeth puts away her notes, snaps her
                    Filofax closed.

                    ELIZABETH
          What direction are you thinking of?

SUBTITLE: I doubt that you have any idea what you want, but let's pretend you do.

> RENÉE
> I'm thinking something lighter. Something closer to
> a spoof of *Charlie's Angels*.

SUBTITLE: Your ideas are too dark and boring. Go get a job in the indie film market.

> ELIZABETH
> I don't do spoofs.

SUBTITLE: That's the worst fucking idea I've ever heard.

Renée laughs. A sarcastic laugh.

> ELIZABETH (cont'd)
> I'm not good at them. I'm also not good at puns.
> Spoofs and puns. I'm not your girl.

SUBTITLE: True. I'm not good at them. And if you'd bothered to read any of the scripts my agent sent over, you'd get that.

Renée picks up a pen.

> RENÉE
> Wait. Let me jot that one down. Not good at spoofs
> and puns.

SUBTITLE: You're stupid *and* arrogant.

At that point subtext became text. Renée jotted a line or two on a notepad, then suddenly stopped and held the pen up to Jordan.

'What's this?'

'It's your pen.'

Renée held up the scribbled notes. 'Is this a fine-point black refill? Looks like medium blue to me.'

'They were out of the black,' Jordan explained.

'And there's only one store in L.A. that sells Waterman refills?'

She threw the pen across the room, narrowly missing Jordan's head. Jordan's eyes filled with tears, which she quickly blinked back.

'Looks like that Buddha's really working for you. Renée,' I said.

She looked confused. Did I dare to insult her, or was this just one of those jokey things writers say? I broke into a goofy smile, which only confused her more.

Truth was, all I wanted to do was get out of there. It didn't matter that suddenly she got sweet with Jordan. 'If you want to go to lunch now and run those errands of yours, that's fine.'

But wait – there was one more screenplay moment to be played out.

INT: RENÉE LARKIN'S TRAILER: DAY – CONTINUOUS

Elizabeth gathers her stuff and stands up. Renée stays seated.

                    RENÉE
          We'll get back to you.

SUBTITLE: Fuck you.

                  ELIZABETH
          Thanks for your time.

SUBTITLE: Fuck you, blind man.

As Elizabeth heads for the door, something makes her stop. She walks to the spot where Renée's pen landed. She picks it up and hands it to Jordan.

                                      CUT TO:

The second I got outside, I wanted to run. The high-stakes game that comes with being a freelance writer means that rejection, even by someone you don't want to be in the same room with, triggers panic. I'll never work again. I'll have to move into a cheap studio apartment. I'll have to beg my agent to set up pitch meetings with lowly assistants. I conjured up a half dozen bleak scenarios. I wanted to get in my car and get as far away from the Renée Larkins of this world as I could. If I could only *find* my car in the maze of the five-story parking garage. Nothing like panic and no sense of direction to make me crave signs of life elsewhere.

I flipped open my cell phone and checked my voice mail. No message from David, but to my great surprise, there was one from Jake. I called right back, not expecting to get him. It wasn't even noon yet. He might just be getting up. But Alex put me straight through.

'What's going on?' Jake asked.

'Just had a meeting with Renée Larkin.'

'Big job title, no pussy power,' he said.

I laughed. That was my kind of haiku.

'Why are you meeting with her?' Jake asked

'It's called making a living. Though I'm not very good at it. I'm never going to be able to work for people like Renée.'

'We should talk about that,' he said.

I wasn't sure what he meant. He could be hinting at another assignment, or maybe he was just being nice. Sometimes it was so hard to figure which Jake I was dealing with – boss or friend.

'What are you doing next Monday night?' he asked.

Now I was really confused. For a second I thought he might be asking me out on a date, but Jake wouldn't be thinking date at 11:30 A.M. This had to be business.

Without waiting for an answer, he went on.

'There's a test screening of the movie in Glendale. Eight o'clock. Alex will give you the details.' And then, without a good-bye, he was off the line, and Alex jumped on.

One minute on the phone with Jake had wiped out the negative effects of my meeting with Renée. Even fleeting contact with him was a mood changer. 'Consider yourself a necessary voice and don't ever be talked out of it,' Jake had once said to me. And he'd said it in the middle of an afternoon story meeting – not in the middle of some late-night, drugged-out party rap. No one else in Hollywood talked like that. Especially not an action director to a writer reworking a blow-it-up/shoot-'em-up finale. Jake believes in me. I have to remember that. Remembering that might not get me my next job, but at least it will keep me from feeling like a faceless factory worker.

Eleven

It had been a while since Julie, Mimi, and I had done a girls' night dinner at Orso. Tonight it was just the three of us and our cell phones, all carefully in view on the tabletop. Power on. Ready to receive. In my case, there was only one possible caller – David. Shortly after the Nigel disaster I'd gotten a new number. Shortly after David and I had our Oscar date, I decided he was the only one I'd give it to. I liked knowing that when the phone rang, it could only be him. Problem is, it never rang. When David did call – and lately he was checking in regularly – it was always on my home number. But still I carried around my cell phone, placing it on table after table at dinner after dinner. It had become a modern-day version of *Waiting for Godot*.

We were sitting out on the patio. Prime spot at a prime time. Mimi loved it. She thrived on the whole social thing. It was her version of watching TV – an ongoing soap opera with plot lines that would never pass the network censors.

'There's Whitney Bennett,' she said.

Julie turned. 'Where?'

'The table in the corner. She's the one facing us in the black leather jacket.'

Julie swung back around. 'That's Whitney Bennett? I thought she'd be prettier.'

Whitney was mildly infamous around town because she could party as long and hard as any guy. It helped that she had a small trust fund, so she didn't need a real job and never had to get up early.

'She's one of those girls who can look really good or really bad,' I explained. 'I've seen her looking better, but what doesn't change is that perfect body of hers.'

'And her willingness to share it,' Mimi added.

'It goes beyond willingness. Whitney's a Puller,' I said.

'She is?' Julie took another look. 'She's never tried to pull me.'

'Or me,' Mimi piped up. 'What about you, Elizabeth?'

The answer to that was no. I'm not a likely target for Pullers because when it comes to that kind of sex, I'm not a natural team player. Let me explain. Generally speaking, a Puller is a girl who can occasionally attract a high-profile guy but knows she doesn't have what it takes to keep him. So rather than just be one of the many girls he dabbles with for a few months, she extends her stay on his playing field by pulling in other girls for threesomes. That way she stays in the loop, hoping if she stays long enough some kind of relationship might take hold. This isn't as far-fetched as it sounds, since a few Pullers have done quite well in Hollywood. And elsewhere. You don't have to be that well traveled to get that Pullers are an international phenomenon.

The thing about Whitney was, she was good at pulling but bad at parlaying her pulling into anything more than a reputation as a fun girl. And as I'd concluded long ago, when guys designate you a fun girl it usually means you'll do blow, blow them, and not get hysterical when they eventually blow you off.

'How do you know Whitney?' Julie asked.

'I met her at one of Jake's parties.'

'Was he . . . ?'

'I don't think so. But who knows who a guy like Jake calls up on a rainy Monday night in November.'

'Vile,' Mimi declared.

'Who's vile?' I asked, ready, as always, to defend Jake.

'Not who. What. Threesomes.'

Julie and I remained silent.

Mimi's mouth literally dropped open. 'You're kidding? And you didn't tell me?'

'They're not easy to pull off,' Julie said. 'It takes a special man to host that party.'

Mimi couldn't figure out if Julie was kidding or not. She looked to me for a clue.

'Sex is not about democracy,' I said. 'Chances are, someone's going to feel slighted.'

'Yeah.' Julie nodded. 'But there's still about a five percent chance that threesomes can be fantastic.'

'Five? Hmmm. Maybe ten.'

'You're both crazy,' Mimi concluded, still not sure whether or not we were serious.

I laughed. 'As Davenport says, triangles are tough unless everyone has the same-size candy bar.'

★

A half hour later we were still talking about sex, and I was still thinking about triangles. The friendship triangle. I was thinking about Mimi, Julie, and me, and how I was the one with the smallest-sized candy bar. Mimi was engaged and had her store. Julie was having a secret romance, and though she was slumming with her job at a cable network, she had a standing offer to return to local news. I had a cell phone that never rang and no definite job prospects. Not that Mimi and Julie were keeping score.

Mimi poured herself another glass of wine from the carafe on the table. 'Oh my God, Elizabeth, that waxer you told me about practically got gynecological on me. I mean she's great. I've never looked sexier. I went for the runway strip. It's very *Penthouse*. But then I decided to really go for it. So yesterday when I was getting my hair colored, I made them mix up some extra formula so I can, you know, dye the carpet to match the drapes.'

'I prefer the hardwood-floor look myself,' Julie admitted.

Two guys at the next table overheard this exchange – we weren't exactly whispering – and started laughing.

'They're cute,' Mimi said looking at Julie. Now that Mimi was engaged she wanted the whole world to be matched up.

'Not interested,' Julie said.

Mimi turned to me. 'Elizabeth?'

I looked over at the cuter of the two. He was young. Maybe twenty-two. He was wearing a sleeveless T-shirt and jeans. Though his exact ethnic origin was indeterminate (some combination of white, black, and Cuban?) the mix produced an extraordinary face. He'd lucked out in the genetic lottery. His eyes really got me. Soulful eyes – reminiscent of Tupac Shakur's – and amazing triceps. It was a combination I would have gone for in a second before I hit the zone. And even being in the zone wouldn't necessarily have stopped me from engaging in table-to-table flirting. What stopped me was my cell phone – a reminder of David. To my surprise, Mr. Maybe was becoming present even in his absence.

'I don't think so, Mimi.'

'Okay, okay. But there are going to be lots of cute guys at the wedding, so don't bring David.'

'If we're still seeing each other, I'm bringing him. When you meet him, you'll really like him.'

'I haven't forgiven him yet for not calling you right away after the first fuck.' Then, typical Mimi, she laughed and added, 'Evan could probably cheat on me and I'd deal with it, but if he didn't call when he was supposed to, engagement off.'

'We all have our own personal deal-breakers,' Julie said, 'It's amazing any two people can stay together.'

Right then, my cell phone rang. Thunderstruck doesn't begin to describe how I felt. An answered prayer can really throw you. But it didn't throw me so much I didn't answer the call with the most alluring hello I could muster.

'Janet?' the unfamiliar voice on the other end of the line shouted.

'Janet? No, this isn't Janet. What number are you calling?'

'Sorry,' the voice said without further explanation and hung up.

I couldn't believe it. Thunderstruck by a wrong number.

I had to walk off the disappointment. I pretended to go to the ladies' room, but instead I stepped outside and had a cigarette. It was a beautiful L.A. night. A lot of my friends think the perfect city would be L.A. during the day and New York at night, but I don't agree. A certain kind of L.A. night can simply overpower me. Those are the nights that inspired me to get a convertible when I was sixteen. To drive aimlessly, top down, tunes cranking. On this kind of night, you're just so happy to be alive. And even if there's no guy in your passenger seat, you feel sexy anyway. This was one of those nights, but it required getting on the open road. Pacific Coast Highway up to Trancas and back would be a good ride. Or Mulholland from Coldwater Canyon west to the beach.

'You know, you *can* smoke on the patio.' The information was given by Whitney Bennett, who had walked out of the restaurant with her dinner date, a middle-aged, well-dressed man who marched over to the valet to hand in his parking ticket.

'I know,' I said, putting my cigarette out.

'So what's going on?' she asked.

'The usual. Work. Working out.'

'All work and no play . . .' she said as she struck a seductive pose, thumbs inside her low-waisted Earl jeans.

'Oh, I get out now and then.' My response was intentionally flat.

She looked over at her male companion to see if he was okay. He seemed to be, standing there waiting for his car, checking his watch.

'Have you ever met Robert?'

'No. Never have.'

'I'd love for you to meet him. He's fabulous. An investment banker. Based in New York, but he just bought a house in Brentwood. He's going to start having fabulous dinner parties. You'll have to come.'

'Just let me know when.' I made a move to go back inside, hoping she didn't have my number and wouldn't ask for it.

'He wants to get into the movie business. He has tons of money to invest. Maybe he can buy one of your screenplays.'

'Is that right?' I said. I was suddenly stalled in my getaway, but not by the lure of a possible deal. Yeah, right, like I hadn't heard those promises before. When you grow up in Hollywood, you learn early on not to accept candy from strangers. No, I was frozen in place because I was mesmerized by the upper half of Whitney's face. It didn't move. No lines. No movement. Nothing. She was thirty-seven or thirty-eight, and her forehead was as wrinkle-free as a fifteen-year-old's. She'd Botoxed out. Those injections that paralyzed your facial muscles were the latest rage. In moderation it worked, made you look younger, more relaxed. In excess, it turned you into a freak.

'Whitney!' It was her rich date beckoning.

She kissed me – get this – on the lips. 'I'll call you,' she said, as if we were old friends.

I watched the two of them get into his Mercedes. And I thought, I don't ever want to be her. Maybe ten years ago she was a lot like me. It was a terrifying thought. At that moment I felt an uncharacteristic desire to settle down with a normal guy, have a couple of kids, and get the fuck out of Hollywood. But there was another voice in my head that weighed in with a powerful argument against that. It was Davenport's. Years of therapy taught me that if I followed through on this uncharacteristic urge, there'd be a good chance that someday I would wake up in my state of so-called domestic bliss in equal terror. There I'd be, in the middle of a conversation with a next-door neighbor, a woman who, like Whitney, was ten years older. Except this woman would be inching her way toward a matronly sub-urban look and a sexless future. Mid-conversation I'd be overcome by a different urge, an irresistible urge to pack my bags and come running back to Hollywood.

★

When I got back to the patio, the two guys from the next table had joined our group, the cuter one sitting in the chair next to mine. They'd ordered another round of drinks, and everyone was loose. So loose that they were talking about what goes into the perfect blow job. The consensus was saliva, enthusiasm, and technique.

'Technique is a big category. Got to be more specific,' Julie said.

'Breathing,' I said as I sat down. 'The importance of breathing correctly cannot be underestimated.'

'You know how to tell if a girl's going to be good at blow jobs?' This was from the other guy. He might not have had soulful Tupac eyes, but he too was immediately likeable. 'If you've just started seeing a girl and you say, "Baby, what do you think of blow jobs?" and she says, "Only with someone I'm really in love with," then you know her performance is probably not going to be in the top one percent.'

Mimi laughed the loudest. 'But you know,' she said, 'the best sex *is* the sex you have with someone you love.'

Julie jumped in. 'I think that's more a girl thing than a guy thing.' She looked at the cute guy next to me. 'Right?'

'We all want to be cruising on the love drug,' he replied, imitating the voice of the king of love Barry White.

'Are you?' I asked. 'In love?'

'Not yet.'

'It's hard, isn't it? It shouldn't be.' I was a little drunk. 'Why should it be so hard to fall in love and stay in love? The whole system's fucked.'

He put his hand on my arm. 'We're all seeking new gods.'

I didn't expect that to come out of his mouth. I didn't expect him to say something that rang so completely true. I didn't expect his touch to inspire blow-job fantasies. I wasn't so buzzed I didn't understand that I was being tested. It wasn't that I didn't have the right to go off with this guy. Who knows what David was up to? But when you're in the zone, nothing is simple and easy anymore. All roads lead back to the big question . . . *What am I doing with my life?*

I picked up my cell phone and held on to it as if it were a lifesaver.

'Waiting for a call?' he asked.

'Ah, no, just draining my battery and setting myself up for disappointment. It's kind of a *Waiting for Godot* thing.'

'*Waiting for Godot?* I just read that play.'

Oh great, I thought. Now I'm really being tested. He's got Tupac's eyes, he sounds like Barry White, and he reads Beckett.

It wasn't easy, but I passed the test. The two guys

moved on to a dance club on Wilshire after I turned down the invitation to join them. It was not my favorite way to end a Friday night, but it was how so many of them do end.

EXT: ORSO PARKING LOT: NIGHT

Elizabeth, Mimi, and Julie wait for their respective cars to be brought around by the valets.
All three are talked out. They've covered it all. Men. Sex. Love. Marriage. The zone. Four hours of it. Nothing left to say – except . . .

> MIMI
> (remembering)
> Oh. How's work?

> JULIE
> Okay. And you?

> MIMI
> Same. Elizabeth?

> ELIZABETH
> It's work. It's fine.

Typical end to a typical girls' night out. Four hours spent talking relationships, four seconds spent talking career.

CUT TO:

I got in my car, cranked up the radio, did a quick U-turn, and headed toward the beach. It was a night made for driving and music. Until my cell phone rang. I was fully prepared for another wrong number.

'Hello?'

'Hi, sweetheart, it's me.'

David had never called and used the familiar 'it's me' before, nor had he ever called me sweetheart.

'Hi!'

'What are you doing?'

'Just leaving Orso.'

'Where are you going?'

'That depends.'

'Want to come over?'

I did another, faster one-eighty. 'I'm on my way.'

Twelve

Test screenings are often held in places like Burbank or Glendale, communities that are a half-hour's drive from Hollywood but might as well be Des Moines. I always feel like I'm traveling to the Midwest when I head over the hill and get on freeways that I've only heard of in local news metro traffic reports. You know, a two-car collision on the L.A. Interchange or a fender-bender on the 140 East, something like that.

This is a world of shopping malls and more shopping malls. It's a world of families with lots of kids. These are people who don't care about 'the trades' but take *Hard Copy* as gospel. These are people who gladly waited in line to see *Titanic* over and over again. These are people who are at ease in malls, while I fear I'll never get out alive. A mall is worse than the Universal lot. The entire structure feels like an eerie maze created by Stephen King. Is my car parked on E7 red or was it E7 orange? Or was it F7 red? Or was it F7 red east? Or F7 orange west? And why do I have to park in a place that requires me to walk for what feels like a mile through endless displays of unwanted merchandise before I spot the sign for the cineplex?

That's my usual mall experience, but because this was a test screening put together by Jake's machine, the directions were impeccable. Jake made them fax over not only a map but also a detailed description of which entrance to take into the parking garage, the best level to park on, the best section of that level, the actual distance between the elevator door and the front of the movie theater, where you get your parking ticket validated, and whom to call in the case of an emergency or a question.

The big issue was, whom do I bring? David was my first thought. He's Jake's friend, has an interest in his work and presumably in mine, but Julie talked me out of it. Her advice was, Never bring a guy to an event that could bring out your needy, insecure side when you're just beginning a relationship.

Mimi was busy with wedding stuff, and Julie was just busy. Ever since Mystery Man came into her life, I assumed 'busy' meant busy with him. That left Andrew. He's not a big fan of these kinds of things. He's more the type to rent a video and call it a night. I hesitated even to ask. But I did, and he said yes, and there we were, walking through this hideous mall together. Andrew was more cynical than usual, which fit right in with my mood.

He looked at a display in a video store window – huge ads for a just-released teen flick.

'I know the guy who produced that,' he said. 'Last week he bought a painting from Pace Wildenstein for two hundred twenty-five thousand. I ran into him in Beverly Hills the day of the sale, and you know what he said? He said, "There's a lot of money to be made selling teenagers a bogus version of their culture."'

'If only I were better at bogus,' I said, 'maybe I wouldn't have an anxiety attack every time I open my American Express bill.'

He didn't laugh, not that it was that funny, but it actually seemed to put him in a worse mood. Hmm, I thought, something is going on here. 'Are you going through that money thing that guys get into?'

'Which money thing?'

'You know, guys have all this pressure to be financially secure by forty. It's the male equivalent of the pressure women feel to be married by thirty-five.'

'Is it?' he replied listlessly.

'Davenport says for men it's all about cash; for women it's all about men.'

'Well, then I should be in a great mood today, because I sold a major Ed Ruscha work today.'

'You did? That's great! So why are you so glum?'

'Glum? Am I glum?'

He was bullshitting, but so what? Sometimes bullshit is an effective moat around one's castle, and I figured if he ever wanted to put down the draw-bridge I'd be right there. The castle metaphor came to me 'cause there were posters up for a Warner's animation film – something to do with a kidnapped princess. It's not as if I go around saying things like 'Such-and-such is the moat around your castle.'

★

When we walked into the theater it was filled nearly to capacity, mostly with grown-ups – which isn't to say that some of them weren't in their twenties. What I mean is, regardless of age, they all seemed like people who had the kind of nine-to-five job that rules out the kind of adolescent, indulgent lifestyle people in Hollywood can perpetuate, at least until their first heart attack. It was an audience more suited to a warmhearted Disney family film than to a hard-edged action flick.

The last two rows of seats were reserved for the studio execs, agents, producers, director, and assorted key players. Jake was standing in the aisle next to his seat. Lately, I'd become pretty good at concentrating on David and trying to get on with my life. Mind control had been working beautifully – until I actu-ally saw the person I was trying to forget. Suddenly he was all I could focus on.

Blaze was standing next to him in a short skirt and sweater, looking like Gucci Spice. She had more bravado about her than she'd had in Miami and at the Laker game. It was as if she'd recently climbed a couple of notches and wasn't about to keep that climb a secret. She saw Andrew and me walk in and chose not to acknowledge us. Well, she didn't acknowledge me. She checked out Andrew. I could read her expression: Who is he? Should I know him? Is he in the business? But then she quickly turned back to Jake, who was busy talking to a young studio executive who had worked on the project. This was a guy who couldn't figure out if his role model should be Jake or Steven Spielberg. Wild man or family man? Steven was richer, but it looked like Jake had more fun. The exec's solution was to talk about his kid around Steven and talk pussy around Jake. That is, when he wasn't talking percentages, projections, and merchandising, which he must have been doing at that moment because Blaze looked totally bored. Not nearly as bored as Jake. He hated this stuff. Used to love it back in his early days – on the first movie, the second, even the third. He loved the business as much as the show. But now it was, as he liked to say, 'all dollars and no sense.'

Andrew nudged me to get my attention. He may not know many of the players in the film business, but he knows types as well as anyone. He looked at the guy playing up to Jake and whispered, 'Are you now or have you ever been a studio executive?' I laughed so loud, people stared. I didn't care. I was at a test screening of the first big movie I'd worked on. Inside, I was a wreck, but thanks to Andrew, I looked like I was having a grand time.

When Jake and Blaze took their seats in front of ours, I couldn't resist tapping Jake on the shoulder and joking, 'I'm surprised you showed up.'

'I like to surprise them every once in a while.'

By 'them' I knew he meant the suits who were always on the verge of writing him off as a talented but crazy guy whose lifestyle was catching up with him. A guy who would have to pay for his sin of breaking the rules and letting you know he was getting away with it. Jake knew that a lot of people secretly – and some not so secretly – were waiting for him to fall. Waiting for the day they could shake their heads and say, 'Too bad. He was a smart guy, but his demons took over.' 'Pity is really a coward's way of saying *hooray!*' was one of Jake's gems, and he knew that many in Hollywood couldn't wait to throw him a great big pity party.

'What's with the crowd?' I asked. 'Is this what you wanted?'

'This is marketing's idea of a cross section. I feel like I'm in fucking Utah.'

I'd seen Jake go nuts over this kind of incompetency before, but not this time. He simply smiled at Blaze and dug into their shared bag of popcorn.

★

It was fifteen minutes into the movie before I could breathe normally. It's hard sitting there listening to your words being judged by an audience. Any line that worked, I credited to brilliant acting; any that didn't, I blamed on myself. Midway through the film, I braced myself for one particular scene. I was afraid I'd made it too corny. Too sentimental. The studio wanted it out because they said it slowed the pace. Jake wanted it in because he said it revealed something about a complicated character. How it tested would go a long way toward determining the final cut. As the scene began, I studied the audience. They were attentive as the screen filled with . . .

INT: MOTEL 6: EVENING

ED, 40s, tough, smart, an ex-cop turned thief and would-be counterfeiter. With him is his shifty, sweaty partner, WES, 35. They are regrouping after a botched robbery. ED puts on a clean white shirt before reaching for the phone.

WES
What'd you do that for?

ED
Do what?

WES
You change your shirt to make a phone call?

ED
I'm calling my mother.

WES
Yeah, so?

ED
She's 80 years old, in a nursing home in Providence.
She's got this picture of me as a guy who wears a
clean shirt, has a good life.

WES
It's a *phone*.

ED
Yeah it's a phone. But I do it for her anyway.

He buttons the shirt up to the top, straightens out the cuffs.

ED (cont'd)
Besides it's easier to act the part, when I dress the part.

Thankfully, no one walked out. I could relax.
From this point on, the movie was mostly flashy

hardware, flashy stunts, and a driving rock sound track. You didn't have to be an action fan to enjoy that ride.

*

After the screening, the lights got turned up and the marketing team passed out questionnaires to the audience. Everyone else congregated in the lobby to talk about how the movie played. Comments were bandied back and forth, though not in my direction. Andrew and I stood in the middle of the lobby like two kids on their first day in a new school.

'Do we have to stick around?' he asked impatiently.

'I don't know.'

He checked his watch. 'I've got to make a call.' He took a step toward the exit.

I grabbed the sleeve of his jacket. 'What did you think?'

'Didn't I tell you?'

'No!'

'I didn't? Sorry. I can't believe I didn't tell you it's the first action movie I've ever liked.'

With that he headed outside. I watched him on his cell phone, wondering who was on the receiving end.

The audience was filing out of the theater. Marketing executives were scurrying about with stacks of completed questionnaires.

'Here's one of the writers.'

I turned around to see the same young studio executive who had been playing up to Jake earlier. Now he was playing up to Blaze. He held one of the questionnaires. A woman wrote that she enjoyed the film but couldn't recommend it to her friends 'because,' he read directly off the page, 'there are things in it that go against my religious beliefs.' He smiled. 'Did you write something sacrilegious?' He was trying to be playful and charming for Blaze's benefit. I'd seen this guy work the wives and girl-friends of bigshots before.

'You tell me. You just saw the movie,' I said.

Always politic, he replied, 'Yes, I did, and I really enjoyed it.'

Blaze was just standing there, so I tried to bring her into the conversation. 'Personally,' I said, 'I love the idea of someone enjoying something in spite of the fact that it goes against her religious beliefs.'

'I don't think you should make fun of a person's religious beliefs.' She turned pleadingly to the studio executive. 'You know what I mean, don't you?'

Okay, now, I know what a fetching look is. That look she gave him fetched her an ally. Or silenced a foe. The executive went for, if not the high road, certainly the safe road. 'Everything's allowed,' he concluded, as if he were offering some wisdom worthy of Solomon.

I don't know why I felt the need to explain myself, but I did. 'What I'm trying to say is, here's a woman who is open-minded enough to enjoy a movie even though it may express certain ideas that go against her religious beliefs. It was a compliment.'

I looked around for Jake. Why wasn't he here to put an end to an argument that was bordering on the absurd? But he was involved in one of those head-to-head discussions that come with a do-not-disturb sign.

'Compliments like that . . .' Blaze said sarcastically, as she dug into her bag for something.

My first thought was that she was searching for her thick-framed 'intellectual' glasses. But no. Instead she pulled out a pack of cigarettes and lit up.

I turned to the junior executive. 'You know what I'm saying, don't you?'

'I hear both of you,' he hedged and then excused himself to chase down one of the marketing execs and find out whether those questionnaires made it more or less likely he'd be getting a big bonus this year.

Blaze and I were left standing together without any buffer. I fully expected her to continue her attack, but instead she turned instantly sweet.

'Do you smoke?' she asked, offering me her pack.

'No, thanks,' I replied cooly.

'Does this bother you?' she asked, waving her cigarette. ''Cause I can put it out.'

Suddenly she was beyond sweet, she was meek.

'I actually like secondhand smoke,' I said, a little disarmed by the abrupt transition. For a second I considered the possibility that I was dealing with a genuine split personality.

'Don't you hate people who make a big deal about smoking? So worried about getting a little smoke in their lungs.' She chuckled.

'And yet,' I added, 'they'll sit there eating a bucket of buttered popcorn. Like that's not going to jam their arteries.'

'Exactly.' She laughed, bumping shoulders with me as if we were high school chums and this was our traditional 'go girl' ritual.

I got it. The second the exec left, Blaze had no need to be serious. She had been trying to sound smart, and opinionated, to get his attention. She was sending this message to him: *I'm more than just a pretty face*. And, of course, she was. She was a pretty face with enough ambition to launch the next NASA shuttle. I was inconsequential to her master plan. She could use me to showcase her serious side, but other than that I was just someone to hang with until Jake or somebody else who could further her career moved into striking distance.

'Are you liking L.A.?' I asked. Now that I was onto the game, I was curious to see just how fake-friendly this girl could be.

'It's perfect for me,' she replied.

'How long are you visiting?'

'Visiting? I moved here.'

Whoa. Jake often imported girls from out of state but just as quickly sent them home with a Rolex and a couple of designer dresses.

'You did? Where are you living?' I asked, trying to sound only mildly curious.

'With Jake, of course,' she declared, once again bumping my shoulder. Only this time it hurt.

*

I was ready to leave, but Andrew was still on the phone. He looked all wound up. It occurred to me that maybe he was back to doing drugs. I sat down on the bottom step that led to the upstairs balcony seating. I watched as Jake dealt with the business-people. He was good at it because they were a little afraid of him – more so when it looked like he wasn't about to fail. That pity party would have to be put on hold. Judging by the smiles and handshakes, I'd guess the suits felt confident of a moderate-sized hit. I should have felt good about that too. Even though

I wouldn't get screen credit on the project – that honor went to the first three writers hired – it would be a nice unofficial credit. It could get me another job. A big job. And another one after that. I could feel the adrenaline building. Then again, what if, in spite of expectations, the movie didn't do all that well? What if it came out, made some money, and quickly and quietly went away? What if my best shot at success generated a few pitch meetings but nothing more? The adrenaline was still building, but now it was fear-driven. That's what Hollywood does to you. One minute you're on the verge of getting sucked into the big golden fantasy, and the next you feel like a huge has-been.

Thinking about all this made me crave drugs, and I wondered if Andrew was carrying. Sometimes staying in touch with the stuff that really matters in life, not the stuff Hollywood can offer and just as easily take away, requires a little help. That said, I'm no druggie, and I hate loser drug addicts who can't control themselves. If I ran the world, recreational drugs would be sold only to healthy, balanced people. People who know how to use them to enhance their life and keep their values clean. But then again, I'll never rule the world or be confused with anyone who wants to.

Andrew was bobbing his head, StarTAC to his ear, pacing nervously. I hoped he wasn't back on drugs, because he couldn't handle them. If he could, he wouldn't have crashed and burned the first time around.

'Don't look so worried. As test screenings go, this one wasn't bad.' It was Jake. Solo. For a change. Blaze was nowhere in sight. He handed me one of the audience cards. 'This guy liked the scene with Ed on the phone with his mother.'

'So is it in or out?'

'It's always a battle.'

'But the screening went well, right?'

'This one went well. Next week's audience could hate it, and the same guys who are talking sequel will be trying to cut the budget for prints and ads.'

He didn't seem worried. And he looked really good. Why does that always happen? When you finally see the guy you're trying to forget about, he looks so fucking good.

'The audience loved Karin's last line to Lester,' he said

' "So now that you're no longer my boss, can we finally fuck?" that line?'

'That's the one. Even this old lady sitting across the aisle laughed.'

'Yeah, well, most women can relate to that situation. Working for a guy and trying to be professional, but really, deep down . . . you know.'

Did he know? Did he know that now that the

film was about to lock, I was technically no longer working for him? The terms of my contract had been fulfilled. This was it. He must have known, and if he knew then was he bringing up that line because he was saying *Let's fuck?* No, no, no. A guy like Jake doesn't need to use a line. He doesn't have to seduce in a roundabout way. He could just look at me and say, 'Midnight. In my bed. Be there.' And I would.

'Hey, ba-by.' Blaze had reappeared. 'Ready to go?'

Her arms encircled Jake's waist. She smiled at me over his shoulder. 'I'm making Jake drive me to this spot I found up off Mulholland. It's the highest spot of the canyon, and you can see both the Valley and Hollywood, but it's really, really quiet 'cause it's off the main road. And it's so beautiful on a night like this. There's a blue moon out there. Second full moon this month. That means it's really, really powerful.' She gave him an extra squeeze.

More and more, with every 'Hey, ba-by,' I was really growing to dislike this girl. Why don't I like Jake less for liking her? I wondered.

★

'She's like a Victoria's Secret ad, provocative and little-girly. She's like a killer who arrives on your doorstep in pigtails holding a bunch of daisies.'

I was obsessing over Blaze while Andrew and I

hung out in my kitchen and raided my refrigerator. Leftover takeout. Andrew had his cell phone on the table turned on – waiting for some important call. I could relate.

'Okay, what's going on? Who's supposed to call you?'

'Can't go into it. I'll tell you someday. Just not now.'

'Does that mean soon?'

'How's David?'

Not the smoothest segue, but if Andrew needed to change the subject that was all right with me. I believe in giving my friends a lot of room. Didn't mean I wasn't worried about him. Didn't mean I didn't want to make him feel better. But at the moment I had no idea how.

'David's fine. Actually, we've been getting along great. I spent the whole night at his place last week. And I have to say, not only is he great to sleep with, he's great to sleep with. One of those guys who gives you a lot of room, but who also knows how to cuddle, and . . .'

I stopped when I realized that not only was Andrew totally bored by this, so was I. Cuddling is not exactly a scintillating subject. I challenge anyone to come up with a good cuddling anecdote.

Andrew picked up his cell phone and held it in his hand as if he was willing it to ring.

'But you'd be out that door in a second if Jake called,' he pointed out.

'Separate issues,' I replied.

He picked up his jacket and put the phone in his pocket. This was not a happy guy. I resorted to a cliché. I hugged him, hoping that would help. It didn't. We weren't good at hugging. We were both too awkward and self-conscious.

'It's Jake you love, but you'll settle for David.'

'Andrew,' I said calmly. 'I was born without the gene for settling. And in case you haven't figured it out yet, so were you.'

'Well,' he sighed, 'if that's true. we're both in more trouble than I thought.'

Thirteen

Bachelorette parties are rarely fun. How can they be?
Unlike men, most women don't feel the need for a
Dionysian group experience. What are we going to
do? Stand around and watch some hunky stripper do
his dance for the bride-to-be? Boring. Get drunk and
go to some raucous club? I don't think so. What
usually happens at one of these things is that a bunch
of women get together at some restaurant, have a
couple of drinks, share a few personally revealing sex
stories, and maybe give the bride-to-be some sex
toys. And when Mimi's the bride in the spotlight,
even that's pushing it. Mimi always struck me as
someone more interested in what she would wear to
bed than what she would do in bed. In fact, I think
one of the reasons she wanted a bachelorette party
was that it gave her an excuse to buy a Versace dress.
Putting on one of those skintight numbers was
Mimi's version of a fling. It was wild and, even on
sale, definitely reckless.

The restaurant she chose for the party was Les

Deux Café, a trendy hangout made trendier by the fact that it was located on an untrendy street off Hollywood Boulevard. In warm weather the patio/garden was the place to sit, and Mimi had requested a table for twelve near the entrance. So there we were, twelve women in a prime spot at Les Deux, one wearing Versace and the others not exactly dressed down. We were getting a lot of attention. More than the up-and-coming actor and his gorgeous girlfriend but not as much as . . . Hef. There he was with another elderly man and twins, young and blonde. Was that a twinkle in Hef's eye? I'd like to think that in this Viagra era, Hef is ready, willing, and oh-so-able to lead us and *Playboy* into the new millennium.

'Hef is a god,' one of the girls at our table said. Another girl, one of those brainy types who never lets you forget that she graduated from Yale Law School, let out a short, sarcastic laugh. 'A god? Why? Because he encourages women to flaunt their fake tits?'

It was too early in the evening for me to get argumentative. I needed another drink before I could take on the Establishment, I had to pace myself, so I simply said, 'Everybody flaunts. Flaunt your IQ. Flaunt your tits. What's the difference? We all use whatever we have to get where we want to go.'

The Yalie looked as if she wanted to blow the

smoke from her Dunhill in my face. And I think she might have, but Mimi interceded. 'Oh shut up, everybody. This is my party, and we'll laugh if I want to.' Then she left out a raucous laugh and ordered another vodka.

There were several women present who had also been at Mimi's dinner for the Marlboro Man, plus a few girls I'd known for years. But Julie and I always stuck together. That afternoon we'd already put in an hour on the phone, but we still made sure we sat next to each other. Who better to do running commentary with than Julie, someone I could totally trust and who did commentary for a living?

'Look around,' she said. 'Guys keep checking out this table, but not one of them would ever approach. I don't blame them. Twelve women – too scary.'

'But how great it would be if a guy did come over. Davenport says if you want to see what women are really about, watch their group dynamic change the second a guy enters the picture.'

'Some single women go into a feeding frenzy,' Julie laughed.

I looked around the table. 'Two married, one engaged, at least three with serious boyfriends – four if I count you.'

'I guess you could call it serious.'

'You *guess*? Didn't you tell me the sex is great?'

'It's not just the sex; it's the whole thing that

comes with it. We're great together in the middle of the night. It's our day life that doesn't fit together.'

'What does that mean? He likes Italian food and you like Chinese?'

'No,' she replied. as if what I'd said was ridiculous. Okay, it was.

'Well actually . . .' She paused. 'Maybe that's one way of explaining it.'

*

A dinner scene like this is one of the hardest things to get right in a screenplay. If you concentrate on one or two characters, you lose all sense of the group energy. And if you split the focus among too many characters, you lose the momentum that comes with following the main story. My solution is always to split the focus but never, ever drop the plot line.

EXT: LES DEUX CAFÉ; PATIO: NIGHT

Twelve women at a table. Spirits high. The woman at the center of attention, MIMI, suddenly stands up, tugging on her Versace dress.

MIMI
Where's Jennifer?

Julie, seated across from her, glances toward the entrance.

JULIE
An hour late. That's not okay.

MIMI
(loudly)
What's Jennifer's cell-phone number?

Elizabeth, seated next to Julie, interrupts her conversation with the waiter.

ELIZABETH
I don't know. I don't even know MY cell-phone number.

MIMI
It's my party. I'm the only one allowed to be late.

Mimi shrugs, not that upset. She sits back down, catches the waiter's eye.

MIMI (cont'd)
Another Ketel One martini, straight up, three olives.

CUT TO:

THE OTHER END OF THE TABLE:

Two dinner guests compare notes. They're a study in opposites. One is very sophisticated, Ivy League-educated and proud of it. The other is pretty. Looks like she grew up on a surfboard. She did.

YALIE

Mimi's the only person I know who's ever bought
a Versace.

SURFER

I have an actress friend who got one for free
'cause she had a hit series and was going to the
Fire and Ice Ball.

YALIE

Maybe Mimi bought it because Evan likes that kind
of thing. I know guys like him. Investment bankers
who buy their girlfriends pearls. Want them to look
classy in public, trashy in private.

SURFER

The best affair I ever had was with a guy like that. I
had a whole wardrobe I wore only over to his house.

YALIE

Mimi would probably go along with any excuse to
add to her wardrobe.

A trace of bitterness can be detected, but the YALIE covers
quickly.

YALIE (cont'd)
She looks good in red.

DISSOLVE TO:

LATER: MIMI AND ELIZABETH: mid-conversation

> MIMI
> She was so great. So helpful. I was going to go for
> the bone-white china, but she pointed out that the
> off-white with burgundy trim was much more
> versatile. And linens. I'm in awe of what she knows.
> The cotton thread count. And the history.

She pauses dramatically.

> MIMI (cont'd)
> She knows which celebrities sleep on Pratesi and
> which sleep on Ralph Lauren.

> ELIZABETH
> You are the daughter my mother always wished
> she had.

CUT TO:

MID-TABLE: YALIE and a perky BRUNETTE talk conspiratorially.

> YALIE
> I've met Evan only once.

> BRUNETTE
> I've met him three times. He's nice.

                    YALIE
              What's the deal?

                   BRUNETTE
              What do you mean?

                    YALIE
I can see why she's into him. He's attractive, comes
        from a good family. Has a good job.
                   (a beat)
Mimi's a great girl, but guys like that usually go for
         girls who are more . . . educated.

                   BRUNETTE
She's just like his mother. That's what she told me.
She may not have a Yale education, but she's smart
          enough to know how it works.

                  DISSOLVE TO:

MUCH LATER: JULIE and ELIZABETH watching MIMI
table-hop.

                    JULIE
Hard to be excited about a friend's marriage when
           her fiancé hates you.

                  ELIZABETH
            He doesn't hate you.

JULIE
He doesn't like me. Or you. We don't fit into his
snobby San Francisco world. Of course, if I became
Katie Couric or you became Robert Towne . . .

ELIZABETH
That's depressing.

JULIE
Fuck him.

ELIZABETH
No. I mean it's depressing that the best-known
screenwriters are men.

SUDDENLY MIMI is back:

MIMI
Does anyone have Jennifer's cell-phone number?

Not a question anymore but a punchline that sends MIMI
and some of the girls into peals of laughter.

CUT TO:

Two hours into the dinner, the storytelling began.
The idea was that we'd go around the table and
each girl would share some risqué episode from
her life. It wasn't a new idea. I'd been to four
bachelorette parties in the past two years, and three

of them required story swapping. The key to making this work is to tell a story that has at least a little shock value without spilling any secrets that you'll regret having aired the next morning. It's not a difficult line to walk. All you have to do is pick either an incident in your distant past or one involving someone who no longer rates space in your Filofax.

Most of the stories were short. Something as simple as 'When I was eighteen, my boyfriend had a pickup truck and one time I sat on his lap and fucked him while he was driving down the four-oh-five.' The girl who shared this golden moment looked like the type who was wild at eighteen. At twenty-eight she still seemed to be speeding down a road without seeing where she was headed. These days she wasn't getting fucked by guys as often as she was getting fucked over by them.

Another woman, an older woman – in her forties – a local designer whose stretch jeans were a big seller at Mimi's store, offered up a story about an orgy in Paris back in the early seventies. The key part of the story was a man at the party whose dick was so long he could tie it into a knot. 'Which fascinated all the women, but none of them would go near that thing,' she explained.

'One question,' Mimi asked, slurring her way through another drink. 'What drug were y'all on?'

Mimi appropriated a slight Southern accent when she was drunk.

'Who knows?' the designer replied with a kind of world-weary sophistication that's unusual in L.A. Not that there aren't sophisticated people here, but to be world-weary implies experience, experience implies age, and, well, you get the idea. In L.A., twenty-five can be too world-weary for a lot of guys.

'I have a story.' The statement was delivered with the crispness of a starched uniform. It came from the Yalie, the control freak, who had been nursing the same glass of white wine all night. Julie and I perked up. This ought to be good.

'After my junior year at Yale, I was summering in Italy,' she began. Julie rolled her eyes. As if anybody in Hollywood cares about an Ivy League education. 'I fell asleep on the beach. When I finally woke up, it was because this gorgeous young Italian had kissed me awake.'

The whole table went into stunned silence. *That's it?* Mimi had just told a story about a wild night on 'ludes. Julie had confessed to a one-night stand with a professional wrestler. And I'd shared one of my hideous Nigel episodes. Here we were, telling stories about being drunk, being with the wrong guy, doing the wrong thing, being messy, and the Yalie tells a story about being Sleeping Fucking Beauty? Is that the point? I thought. She's a princess and we're all stupid sluts? Is that what's going on here?

'I have to pee,' Mimi said, getting up and climbing over a chair.

'Me too,' I said, because really, what comeback is there to someone who basically says, 'I have a perfect fairytale life'? How great for you, how boring for the rest of us. But I didn't come up with that line till the moment had passed and I was in the ladies' room.

Two lip pencils, two lip glosses, and two lipsticks were spread out on the counter. As drunk as Mimi was, her hand was steady when it came to doing her makeup.

'Bet you're surprised,' she said as she studied her lips in the mirror.

'By what?' I asked, trying to make my lips look as model-perfect as hers.

'Surprised Evan and I moved up the date.'

'I know you're not pregnant.' Not Mimi. A girl who believed in doubling condoms.

'No. Definitely not pregnant.' She continued to study herself in the mirror. 'Evan wasn't good with a long engagement,' she said. 'We've had more fights over this thing, and we never fight. Planning this wedding could be grounds for a divorce.'

'You ever have second thoughts?'

'Why would I? Evan's great. A good provider.'

'A good *provider*?'

At the same moment we both started to laugh. Something about the word 'provider.' A word that's supposed to connote something desirable and positive but which at that moment seemed silly, something closer to a waiter than a love object. But even with all the laughing I wasn't convinced Mimi was a happy girl.

'As long as you're sure it's what you want to do,' I said.

'Hell, darlin',' she replied, slipping into her Southern cadence again, 'no one's ever sure.'

When we got back to the table, Julie grabbed my arm. 'Look,' she said, pointing to the other end of the table. Jennifer had finally shown up, and she'd brought with her a *man*. And not just any man. A director. An A-list director whose last film had been nominated for a Golden Globe.

Jennifer waved to Mimi. 'Sorry I'm late, but I've been working with Pierre.' You knew she loved saying 'working with Pierre,' as if just saying it put her on the A-list too.

'Working on what?' Julie whispered to me. 'Isn't Jennifer a pastry chef?'

'She found out she's allergic to sugar, so now she wants to produce.' Only in Hollywood would that not seem like a stretch.

Jennifer pulled up a chair for Pierre, oblivious to

the fact that she had broken a cardinal rule by introducing heavy-duty testosterone into an all-girl gathering. It was Davenport's theory in action. Mimi seemed momentarily disoriented by the intrusion. Was she losing control of her own party? Clearly, she was no longer the center of attention. Instead, everyone was focused on the guy – even if focusing on him meant consciously *not* focusing on him – ignoring him as a way of possibly attracting his attention. I say this not because I can read everyone's mind or know exactly how they're feeling but because I know how I was feeling, and when it comes to these issues, I'm one of the herd.

Mimi glared down the table at Pierre until finally he held up a glass of wine, a toast to her. Then he said something in French that only the Yalie understood. But Mimi didn't need a translation to go from gloom to glee. Being toasted by an A-list celebrity at your bachelorette party wasn't such a bad thing. In fact it was a very, very good thing. One for the memory book. And then because she was drunk and we had just had a bonding moment in the ladies' room, she leaned over and explained. 'He did direct one of my favorite movies.' And then because Mimi is better at knowing who's famous than knowing what made them famous, she added, 'Didn't he?'

★

Bachelorette parties often have a stage two. Once dinner is over, it's time to move on to a place where guys are invited. That tells you everything about the difference between men and women. Men don't plan bachelor parties so that around midnight they can hook up with their girlfriends. By midnight, they're too wasted and too into watching or playing with the invited hookers to even think about checking back into their real life.

But by the time we relocated to Bar Marmont, our group had increased by a dozen guys. Evan was not among them. His bachelor party was under way up in San Francisco, and he wasn't due in L.A. till the day before the wedding. Even if he had been in L.A. there was a good chance he wouldn't have shown up here. In the year that he and Mimi had dated, we rarely all hung out together. In many ways he and Mimi had separate lives and separate circles of friends, and neither one seemed particularly interested in bringing the two together. As Mimi once put in, 'We're merging companies, not staff.'

Another no-show was Andrew. He'd called the bar and conveyed his apologies with a bottle of champagne but without an explanation for his last-minute cancellation. I really missed him. He and I always had such fun at these things. Getting a little buzzed with girlfriends is fine, but sometimes that second or third glass of champagne makes you crave male attention, even if it's from someone who's practically your brother.

With the exception of Pierre and an older man who seemed out of sync with the drunken frivolity, all the guys present I'd known for years. None had date or brother potential. Not one was my type, but they all were perfect friends for Mimi. Beyond friends. They were her hobby. She loved trying to fix them up or dress them up. How often had I listened to her hang on the phone with one of them? 'She's a super girl, super,' she'd say. 'She's on the best terms with all her exes.' Or, 'The gray lightweight cashmere sweater with the khaki pants. That's a perfect look for you.'

'You're hot,' someone said. It was the older man, the only person there I didn't know at all. Not even his name.

I jumped because his hand was on my shoulder. His hand might as well have been on my forehead, because he was talking about my temperature.

'I know,' I said. 'Sometimes when I'm feeling claustrophobic I go up a couple of degrees. It'll pass.' I took an ice cube out of a water glass on the table and held it against my neck.

'I had a girlfriend once who always ran a couple of degrees hotter than normal.'

'Is that right?' I was trying to figure out who this guy was. Had Mimi told me about him? Whoever he was, I guessed he was one of her newer recruits. Mimi was a pro at appropriating people. One minute they're in her store, browsing, the next she's in their life, facilitating.

'You're the writer, right?' he said, zeroing in on me.

'Uh, yes. And you're . . . ?'

'I'm Max.'

'Max?!' It was more of an exclamation than a question because the second he said his name I knew who he was. Not only had Mimi told me about him, I'd heard about him for years. 'Being Max is more than enough.'

'Enough for what? For whom?' He smiled mischievously.

'Enough to keep this party going till closing time.'

*

Okay, I have to stop here. Stop the way I always like to do toward the end of the second act of one of my action scripts. I love putting the action on hold for a moment and taking a couple of pages to introduce a character who has nothing to do with the plot but comes into a character's life and says some interesting and helpful stuff and then goes on his way. Always, without exception, the studio cuts this scene from the script. 'It doesn't advance the story,' is the usual reason given. My argument is, it advances the story if part of the story has to do with how these characters think and feel, but I always, without exception, lose this argument.

But this kind of thing happens in real life all the time. And from the second Max introduced himself, I knew this was an act-two moment. I knew it because that ice cube against my neck did nothing to cool me down and because, although I didn't I know Max, I knew *any* interaction with him rated, at the very least, the equivalent of a three-page scene.

You see, you don't grow up in L.A. – in the film business, with parents who were part of the counter-culture – and not know who Max is. In the seventies, he was it. The producer of some of the coolest movies. Movies that changed the culture and changed Hollywood. And he did it with small budgets, using nonstars. And when one of his films hit it big, he'd send five-figure bonus checks to the actors – even those who had just a few scenes in the movie, because Max believed in redistributing the wealth. He was a symbol of Hollywood moviemaking when ideas were sexy. Before the high concept and Wall Street ruled. Before Universal CityWalk existed. Before people like Renée Larkin became as ubiquitous as bottles of Evian. Before a movie lived or died based on opening-weekend box office, Max was the man.

Jake worshipped him but had never met him. Not that he hadn't tried. But Max hadn't been part of the

Hollywood scene since the early eighties. He never showed up for premieres or parties. He did his hanging out in his house up in the hills with a small circle of friends. The fact that Mimi could get him to come down off the mountain to a bar on Sunset Boulevard on Saturday night was a testament to her considerable energy.

'Mimi didn't tell me you were coming.'

'Mimi didn't know.' He reached behind the Yalie to get a bottle of champagne out of the ice bucket and filled both our glasses.

'That's right, you're probably not the RSVP type. You're more the don't-count-on-me-but-don't-necessarily-rule-it-out type.'

'Or count on me but maybe rule it out.'

'I don't get it,' I said as I studied his face. Not hard to see what a cutie he must have been in his twenties and thirties. Still was, in that sixty-year-old hipster way. 'What's the difference?'

'Always start from hope,' he replied.

'Why?' I pressed, not willing to let him off the hook with some clever turn of phrase.

'Live dangerously,' he said.

We talked for hours. But it wasn't the usual verbal volleying. That would have been fun but ultimately unsatisfying. I've volleyed with some of the best, and usually it just gives me a headache and few usable lines for my next screenplay. What Max and I got into was the kind of conversation you might have with a friend you've known for twenty years. We covered the big issues. Life. Love. Abandonment. Betrayal. Power. Soul. And of course sex. I couldn't resist crossing that line. I told him that meeting him was a unique experience because usually when someone's been in Hollywood for a long time, you've heard a lot about them. From their ex-girlfriends, their friends, or their friends' friends. And because tantalizing items of gossip are currency in Hollywood, it's not unusual to meet someone and know everything about the way they fuck and nothing about the way they think.

'But I'm different?' he asked wryly.

'Yes, you are. Because I've heard so many stories about what it was like working on your movies, I know not only everything about the way you fuck, I also know a lot about the way you think.'

He laughed and to his credit didn't ask how he rated as a lover on the ex-girlfriends' rap sheet. He didn't seem to need to boost his ego with some thirdhand compliment. And even though he seemed tired, less by the late hour than by having put in six decades on planet Hollywood, he had a vitality and confidence about him which I assumed came from knowing he had delivered big-time to all those ex-girlfriends and still could.

From time to time people looked at us, no doubt

wondering what was going on between us. At one point, Mimi came over and sat on Max's lap like an irrepressible, playful puppy. 'I love him. Isn't he great?' she said. Max just smiled. This was one guy Mimi would never dare tell whom to date or what to wear.

'Do you know how we met?' Mimi laughed.

'Can't imagine.'

'Beverly Hills Courthouse. We were both there for overdue driving violations. Neither of us can stand to wear seat belts.'

'Living dangerously?' I asked him.

'Oh,' he said with a smile, 'there are stories I could tell you.' He didn't need to. It was part of the legend.

When Pierre came over to shake Max's hand, it was as if he were kissing the Godfather's ring. He was showing respect for a guy who had made some of the great ones. Max was gracious but wasn't about to dump me for some high-profile adulation. He got points for that. Of course the Yalie tried to get in on the action, saying she'd read a piece in *The New Yorker* about the twentieth anniversary of his finest film.

'That's not what *The New Yorker* was saying twenty years ago.' He chuckled.

I don't remember exactly when I realized that the group had shrunk to six and the bar's doors had closed. I hadn't even seen Julie leave, but I figured there was a good chance she'd cut out to hook up with her mystery guy.

Max and I were the last to leave. The valets were gone. We stood in the parking lot, each of us with our car keys in hand. I was counting on this conversation continuing somewhere, sometime, but I ruled out its happening in this lifetime. Who knew when he'd come down off the mountain again? In any case, we'd covered enough ground to keep me inspired for months. I even had the satisfaction of having Max acknowledge that he'd never vetoed a second-act character moment . . . unless it was badly written.

'What are you working on now?' he asked.

'Just finished a rewrite.'

'What are you working on for you?'

'For me? I don't write for me. I get hired to . . .'

'Yeah, yeah, I know. That's paying the bills. I'm talking about working on something that comes from inside you.'

'You mean a spec script?'

He rubbed his forehead and tried again. 'Whatever you're doing . . . go deeper.'

I probably should have left after he imparted that weighty advice, but he had been so enlightening and smart about so many things, I couldn't let him leave without getting his take on the issue that was controlling my life these days – the zone.

'I hate giving advice,' he said. 'Besides, I have none. No advice is my advice.'

'C'mon, Max.' I had had enough to drink and the conversation had been intense enough that I thought I could get away with pestering him – at least a little. 'I know you've already figured me out. I know you understand this relationship business better than I do.'

'My track record is no proof of that.'

'Fuck résumés.'

'Okay. I'll tell you this. It's not advice, it's a thought . . . one that came to me recently, although I think it also came to me thirty years ago, but I ignored it then.' He paused as if second-guessing his impulse to say anything at all. 'Falling in love with someone's potential is usually a bad idea.' With that, he kissed me on the cheek and headed for his car.

'Wait, wait,' I said. 'That's it?'

'That's it,' he said. 'What do you expect? You're smart, you're pretty, you're funny, but I'm not getting any pussy out of it.'

'Now that's a good exit line.'

*

I was floating on inspiration long after he'd pulled out of the parking lot and headed west, while I took off going east. *Live dangerously; start from hope.* It sounded like a good motto. Would I still love it tomorrow?

Suddenly I wanted to go home and work. I wanted to write. A novel. An essay. Five essays. I wanted to write a new screenplay. A screenplay that had nothing to do with high concepts or studio formulas. The kind of screenplay Max might have produced back in the seventies, when he and Hal and Warren and Jack and Roman and Evans were calling the shots.

I also had an urge to call Mimi. I wanted to tell her that I had a whole new definition of a good provider. But it was three A.M., and Mimi wouldn't get it. She wouldn't understand why I was so excited by an experience that didn't have a third act.

Fourteen

Is admiring the foundation of a house a little like falling in love with someone's potential? That was the question I asked myself as David gave me a tour of what was to be his dream house. Aside from the foundation and the basic frame there wasn't much to look at. It was beautiful though, and made more beautiful by the fact that it was very private.

'I figured it was time,' he said, in the tone guys often use when they're announcing their engagement. It's a tone that makes me nuts. If I were their 'intended' it would *really* make me nuts. I don't want someone to marry me because it's time to settle down. I want someone to marry me because they're crazy about me. Though I'm not so dense I don't know that being in the zone is another way of saying that I'm looking for a more serious guy because I figure it's time. At the very moment that I was silently criticizing David, I was guilty of doing exactly the same thing.

Sometimes it feels as if time is the biggest demon

around. My Buddhist friends tell me that time is not linear. Davenport says the subconscious has no sense of past or present. Fine. Right. Except there David and I were, walking around his property, doing things and saying things to the thunderous ticking of a clock. But it wasn't ticking so fast for him that he was ready to launch into a phase of conventional domesticity. Yes, he was putting down roots, but he was an SCU, and I wasn't kidding myself. They were the roots of a fabulous bachelor pad. So what was I doing there? I was giving it a little more time. We were getting along too well and having too much fun to make an exit.

Still, I couldn't resist probing. 'Aren't you going to get lonely living up here all by yourself?'

'If I do,' he said, 'I'll sell it.' And then he added, 'I don't get lonely.'

Okay, guys who don't get lonely are not good candidates for Mr. Maybe. Compatibility and fun were not going to be enough to launch this into a real relationship. But there are five things that can happen in an evening that can make a girl forget that fact. And though they don't have to happen in that particular order, this is the way they happened that night. These five things had me thinking that maybe Jake knew what he was doing when he made that call back in Miami. Maybe David was the perfect guy for me.

The first of the five things that sucked me into a state of maybeness was that David and I discovered we were in total agreement on Wilhelm Reich. I know, but bear with me.

'I love Wilhelm Reich,' I said in response to a comment David made about a biography he'd recently read of the Austrian psychologist. I know I sounded like a bimbo trying to sound smart. I could have made a more intelligent comment. Something along the lines of, 'It's impossible to disagree with his theory that sexual fulfillment is essential to personal well-being, and yet we all know people who would opt for a house in Bel Air over a lively libido.' Or I could have quoted extensively from some choice Reichian passages. But it seemed anti-Reichian to be leading with my brain at that moment.

'He got it right,' David remarked.

'I can't believe you believe that too,' I exclaimed. 'He's one of my guides. Know what I mean? One of the ones I go back to and reread.'

'One of the ones? Who else is guiding you?' he asked with a twinkle in his eye. In fact, David had been twinkling all afternoon. But seasoned Hollywood girl that I am, I had to consider that maybe the only thing the twinkling meant was that he was having problems with the twenty-one-year-old sophisticated New York-trained actress and wanted to make sure his backup option was secure.

Still, a twinkle can be encouraging. 'Well,' I said, 'Cameron Crowe's a guide. He's one of my favorite filmmakers.'

'*Say Anything* . . . was great,' David agreed. 'I don't know one girl between twenty-five and thirty-five who didn't love that scene where Cusack . . .'

'Shows up outside of Ione Skye's house with the boom box blasting?'

'That's the one. And *Singles* was smart. Smarter about relationships than most movies. But *Jerry Maguire* . . .'

He didn't have to finish. 'It wasn't my favorite either.'

'Too happy an ending for you?' he joked.

'I don't rule out happy endings. Do you?'

'No, just that one. I never believed Tom Cruise would go back to Renée Zellweger at the end. He would have to have undergone a complete transformation before I'd buy that.'

'Ah . . . you said the word.'

'What word?'

'"Transformation." I decided it's *the* word for the twenty-first century.'

'Is that so?' He seemed more amused than interested.

'It's actually a very sexy idea.'

'I'm sure it is.' He smiled.

'I think of it as third-stage sex. First-stage sex is

procreation. Second-stage sex is recreation, and third is transformation. In other words, I believe the perfect fuck can change your life.'

'Can you reach stage three without going through stage one?' he teased.

'Of course.' And then, more seriously, I added, 'You got a problem with procreation?'

'Not ready for that,' he said. 'Not yet. Not for a long time.'

Okay, if a girlfriend of mine were telling me this story, I'd say, *Stop*. This is not going to work out. This guy is not going to change anytime soon. He might wake up one morning five years from now and think, I really *do* want a wife and kids, but that'll be in *five years*. Could be more. We all know men in L.A. who don't even start thinking about kids until they're fifty. David could easily be one of those. But it's hard to hold on to that argument when the guy is right there in front of you and all you can think about is how much you want him. This is when reasonable doubt becomes your ticket to fantasy. Though the preponderance of evidence suggested David was not the kind of guy a girl in the zone should continue to see, he wouldn't be convicted by a jury of his SCU peers. The fact that he and I were in sync on Reich and Crowe made me feel as if we were part of the same tribe. It's like being fourteen and finding out that another kid in your class is obsessed with the same obscure band you've been listening to for months. It immediately ups the chances for an ongoing relationship.

Wait. There's more. As the sun was sinking over the edge of the canyon and I was basking in the golden light (the most flattering of the day) and our synchronicity, David did the second of five things that pushed me closer to believing that it, whatever it is, might all work out. He wanted to show me where he was going to put in a cactus garden – 'not as big as the one at the Getty, but better.' As he led me though an obstacle course of construction junk, he took my hand. That simple gesture, holding my hand, sent a jolt through me. The truth is, up until that moment he hadn't held my hand. We had been all over each other's bodies but hand-holding was not part of our repertoire. And just as certain kisses can feel more intimate than sex, David's holding my hand while guiding me to the site of his future cactus garden made me feel more connected to him than even those kinds of kisses.

I've polled guys on this issue, and they all say that hand-holding doesn't necessarily mean anything, particularly if you're helping a girl step over a stack of two-by-fours. It's the male ego taking a leadership position or, in a minority of cases, a small act of chivalry. Yet that simple gesture got me thinking the thing I pride myself on never thinking: *This could be going somewhere.* I generally hate that phrase because too often that thing that is going someplace ends up going, going, gone. To even think something is going someplace is to jinx it. And yet there I was, jinxing myself, but not for long, because David caught my attention with the third thing on the list of five.

'Are you hungry?' he asked.

'A little.'

He pulled out his cell phone. 'I'm not in the mood to go to a restaurant. What if we ate here?'

'Here?'

'Yeah.'

I hesitated. Not because I need the comfort of an actual table and chairs but because I didn't think of David as the *alfresco* type of diner . . . unless it was on the patio of The Ivy.

'Okay,' I agreed, not asking how or where or what. I was just a passenger on this part of the trip, and happy to let him be my guide.

What followed next could have been a scene out of a Hollywood-style romantic comedy. Picture Greg Kinnear and Jennifer Aniston in a script written and directed by Nora Ephron. David had a banquet of food and wine delivered from The Grill. It was a testament to his power of persuasion that he pulled this off, because The Grill doesn't deliver, and if they did, they probably wouldn't deliver this far up Coldwater Canyon, and they definitely would not be talked into making a side trip to pick up candles.

Music was provided by the car's radio. I liked the fact that David didn't try to dazzle me with his favorite CD or cassette. It was take-what-you-get on L.A.'s Mega-100 FM. When a song with a Latin/rock beat came on, I got up and danced for him. Let me say right here that the biggest benefit (and I do believe it's big) of having gone to a public high school in Los Angeles was the exposure to ethnic diversity. I grew up in a Benetton ad. Among the mix were a lot of great dancers, and just by hanging out with them at parties and, later, at clubs, I picked up their rhythm. I knew how to work it. When I'm inspired, I feel like I'm in touch with my inner Tina Turner.

Dancing was my way of thanking David for surprising me and continuing to surprise me. I loved his 'guide potential.' I loved that he was smart and knew about a lot of things I knew nothing about. I felt we could talk for hours and still feel as if we were just getting started. And, of course, I loved making love to him. Right there. On the ground with a starry sky overhead.

That's when he did the fourth of the five things that brought me closer to imagining he could be the one. After the usual great sex (and, this time, simultaneous orgasms) he didn't move. I'm not talking about the time a guy spends lying on top of you after fucking to catch his breath. Or the courtesy time he'll spend there so it doesn't seem like he can't wait to get off and move on. David stayed there as if there were nowhere else he wanted to go. He stayed there until he got hard again and we got into it all over again.

The fifth thing happened as we were pulling on our clothes.

'We have to come back when the house has a floor,' he said.

This may not seem like a big deal, but the use of the pronoun 'we' and the future tense, along with the previous four happenings, made me feel as if we were on the verge of coupledom.

'I like the way you give a tour,' I said, envisioning sex in each room, as well as on the upstairs terrace and the downstairs patio. Sex everywhere but the cactus garden was my plan.

By the time we drove down the canyon it was almost midnight. Traffic crawled in front of the clubs between Doheny and Crescent Heights. At first, everywhere I looked I saw couples. It was that time of night. Time to pair off. Time to throw caution to the wind and hope it was aerodynamic. I imagined all along the boulevard, couples making plans for tomorrow or the next day or the day after that in first person plural.

But then I picked up on those who were out of the love loop. A pissed-off girl in thigh-high boots jerked away from her boyfriend's arm and stormed off without him. Three guys outside the Rainbow looked like no amount of tequila was going to make up for the fact that they weren't going home with girls in thigh-high boots. I also spotted two people walking to their car – together but miles apart. The guy looked like he was into no one but himself and the woman like she'd be into anyone but him.

Where did David and I fit on this continuum, I wondered? Were we going somewhere, or had we already arrived? Was this as far as we were going to get?

I looked over at him, his hair still tousled, a cigarette in his hand. Who smokes while driving these days? No one. Not even him. But it had been an unusual night. So unusual that I decided to see if we really were in new-pronoun territory.

It was not a decision to be made lightly. Andrew once told me he had lost interest in a woman midsentence because she jumped into 'we' mode on their first date. David might be one of those guys who jammed on the brakes if a girl got too 'we' crazy. But I decided to start from hope and live dangerously. Not only would I go for the pronoun, I'd hit the accelerator.

'We should think about getting out of L.A. one of these weekends.'

If he had come back with some vague reply or no answer at all I wouldn't have been surprised. Getting out of town together can take a relationship to a whole new level. It was possible, even probable, that David wasn't interested in taking me to that level. Or in taking anyone to that level. Not now. Not for a long time. But he didn't say maybe, or one of these days, or could be good. He said, 'Why not?' And he said it as if signing on for a great adventure.

Those two words summed it up for me. *Why not? Why not* think about it? *Why not* do it? *Why not* believe it? *Why not* believe in us? In it, whatever it is? In him? In me? In luck? *Live dangerously, always start from hope . . .*

In the back of my mind I did have an answer to *Why not?* More than an answer – I had a list of reasons that argued against *Why not?* But I wasn't about to go there. Not after a five-point evening.

Fifteen

I loved Mimi's wedding. No bridesmaids. Her intention was to spare her best friends the ordeal of buying and wearing a dress they hated. But her dress was perfect. From the front, very snobby San Francisco. Proper, and delicate lace. But the back spoke to her Hollywood roots. Completely bare all the way down to two inches *below* the waist. I also appreciated the relatively brief ceremony. No poems. No declarations. Most of all, I enjoyed how beautifully Mimi handled her family – always the trickiest part of any wedding. Throughout the reception, anytime one of her crazy relatives – and that included two stepfathers and her real father, whom she refers to as Bio-dad – did something particularly kooky, she'd turn to one of her friends and state a four-word refrain that effectively punctuated the craziness. When a bitchy cousin told her she looked tired (imagine it, telling a bride on her wedding day she looks tired), Mimi simply stared at the bitchy cousin, turned to Julie and me, shrugged, and said, 'See how that is?'

Whatever arguments Mimi and Evan might have had planning this day, it looked like she got the wedding she wanted, and he was loving every minute of it, too. It was at the Santa Barbara Biltmore, in a room with a terrace overlooking the ocean. Every detail could have come with the Martha Stewart stamp of approval. How much does an event like this cost? I thought. Am I a freak because I can't imagine spending thousands and thousands of dollars to get married? I'm all for a good party, but is any wedding really ever a good party? Mixing family and friends sounds festive in theory, but it's rarely a recipe for a truly fun time.

I'm not complaining. I was with my foolproof date – Julie. Taking a guy you're seeing to a wedding is risky. People often relate to an unmarried couple at a wedding as if the twosome were auditioning for the part of bride and groom. This can make a guy feel crowded, and as we all know, a guy's response to that is fight or flight. On the other hand, bringing David up to Santa Barbara for a wedding would be a good excuse for us to get out of town for a weekend. It was a tough call. Eventually I did ask him, he couldn't make it ('work'), and I was relieved.

For a second I thought of showing up with Andrew, but he kept changing his mind about what time he wanted to leave L.A. and what time he had to be back, so I finally just told him to forget it. I'd meet him there. It wasn't like him to be so indecisive. It also wasn't like him seemingly to be enjoying a drink at the reception with Joe, the Marlboro Man. Talk about a study in opposites.

'Do you think Andrew is drinking again?' I asked Julie.

'No,' she said without even glancing in his direction.

'Hmm. So that's a club soda, not a vodka tonic?'

'What do you think? Andrew's going to blow years of sobriety to have a cocktail with Joe?'

'What do you think the two of them are talking about?'

'I don't know. It's a wedding,' she said. 'Weddings do strange things to people. I had a ten-minute conversation about fly-fishing with Mimi's uncle. A subject I know nothing about and care nothing about. But if you're stuck in an elevator with someone long enough, you can find almost anything interesting.'

There was a sharpness to her tone that I knew had nothing to do with being at the wedding. Julie loves weddings. I suspected it had something to do with her mystery romance, which remained a mystery in spite of my and Mimi's best efforts to crack her vow of silence.

'Glad you two are here.' It was Evan, being the perfect host. 'It means a lot to Mimi and me.'

I'm sure he'd said the exact same thing at every table he'd stopped at, but he did sound sincere. Evan had one of those boyish, appealing faces that made you want to believe him, even when your instincts told you there was more to the story. Giving him the benefit of the doubt came easily. Plus, he had the winsome confidence of a young man who had found his niche. Finance was his forte, and he swaggered through the room like a budding Wall Street king.

'You're going to have to come up to San Francisco and visit us,' he added.

'When's Mimi moving up there? Not for a while, right?' She hadn't mentioned it.

'By the end of the month,' he replied.

'What about the store? Will she re-open up there?'

'You know Mimi,' Evan smiled as he moved off to be the perfect host at the next table.

I turned to Julie. 'I guess I don't know Mimi. Don't know her well enough to have guessed she'd close shop move up north without even mentioning it.'

Julie took it in stride. 'You know, the thing about Mimi is, she seems to be the one who's most likely to end up on *Oprah* spilling her guts, but the truth is, she's more private than anyone I know.'

'Not more private than you. You and your mystery guy.'

'That's different.'

'It is?'

'I'm private about just this one matter. Mimi is private about her whole life. She just got married to a guy we hardly know or know anything about, and we're her best friends.'

'You've got a point there. Maybe she doesn't trust us.'

'Nah. I think it's just the way she is. It's her version of good manners. As if sharing her private thoughts would be an imposition on her friends.'

'But she always wants to hear *our* private stuff.'

'She loves it. Loves the challenge of making it all better.'

I knew Julie was right. 'Mimi's going to make a great mom.' A second later, this thought hit me: *I'm not so sure I will.* Couldn't dwell on that.

'I still don't get why you have to be sooo secretive about your guy.'

Julie accepted champagne refill from a waiter. 'Because we live in Hollywood. People root for relationships to fail here. The second they hear you're seeing someone, the gossip begins. And it can't be ignored. It has an effect. It's like having a third person in bed with you. If I'm going to have a third person in bed with me, it isn't going to be Hollywood.'

'Can't argue with that,' I laughed.

'Besides, when it starts to fall apart, you don't have to explain what went wrong to everyone you run into.' She paused, distracted by a woman barreling toward us. 'Like this gossip queen,' she said, as a woman in her mid-thirties, blonde, and trying way too hard parked herself at our table.

'You know who's here?' she said excitedly. 'Pierre Lanier, the director of *Three Nights at the Ritz*.' This gossip queen, or 'gossip reporter' as she called herself, did weekday-morning reports for a local news station. I assumed she and Julie knew each other, maybe had even worked together at some point.

'I think he's here alone,' she continued. 'I didn't see a date. Is that a bad thing to say? That I'm already checking it out? Hell, I'm single, why shouldn't I?'

As the gossip queen launched into melodrama, I realized I was entering the haze. That's the particular condition that, at least for me, is synonymous with wedding receptions. Since weddings tap into all kinds of conflicting emotions, I end up drinking more and more champagne to keep the circuits from overloading. Too much stimulation accompanied by lots of suppression results in the haze. Everything starts to look and feel a little fuzzy. Conversations take on a surreal quality – and the gossip queen's was surreal to begin with.

'I mean, we were more than engaged,' she complained, as she continued to divulge her latest guy crisis. 'He had me looking at houses. Million-dollar houses. The day before I found out, I was with a real estate agent, looking at a place that would have been perfect for us. The very next morning, I'm picking up bagels at a deli in Beverly Hills, and as I walk past a newsstand I see his name on the front page of *The New York Times*. Turns out he'd been arrested in Manhattan for fraud and embezzlement.'

'How long were you dating?' Julie asked.

'Four months.' The gossip queen sighed. 'And I didn't even like him that much at first. He wasn't at all my physical type. I talked myself into the relationship. I told myself I should be with a stable man for a change. Even though he was sexually dysfunctional. What I had to do to get him off was not fun.'

'So much for stable men. Now what? Back to the wackos?' I joked. I was uncomfortable hearing this much personal information from someone I didn't know. Even Julie looked uncomfortable.

'Fuck that,' she laughed. 'I'm going to go introduce myself to Pierre.' She stood up and extended her hand. 'Nice to meet you two,' she said as she glided off to find the A-list director.

I looked at Julie. ' "Nice to meet you two"? I thought you knew her.'

'Seen her around. Never actually met.'

'Does she tell that story to everybody? To total strangers?

'It's a wedding,' Julie reminded me.

Remembering Julie's earlier comment, I added, 'It's an elevator.'

★

The haze persisted, made even hazier by the late-afternoon sun. Julie had wandered off to find the Marlboro Man for some reason, while Mimi and I shared a Marlboro Light on the terrace. My nemesis from the bachelorette party – the Yalie – strolled over.

'I can't find my date,' she said, which was her way of letting me know she had one.

'Mix and mingle,' Mimi giggled. 'The key to a successful party. My stepmother's motto.'

'It was really a lovely ceremony,' the Yalie said. She was one intonation away from a fake British accent, which meant I was one intonation away from an attack of Britaphobia. 'Except,' she continued, 'I had a bit of a problem with the minister.'

'Did you?' Mimi asked, handing me the cigarette and aping the Yalie's accent.

'That's like saying you've got a bit of a problem with vanilla ice cream,' I interjected, 'or the color beige. The man didn't exactly inspire controversy.'

She ignored me. 'That speech he gave about how just last Saturday he was called to the home of two elderly people who wanted to be married. But, when he arrived – '

Mimi jumped in to get to the point. 'The woman pulled him aside and told him they'd already gotten married fifty years ago. I thought it was cute that they wanted to renew their vows. It was my favorite part of the ceremony.'

'It was lovely, I agree,' the Yalie nodded. 'However, I was at a wedding up here three months ago. Same minister. Same story.'

At that moment I wanted to find Mimi's bitchy cousin and introduce her to the Yalie. Those two had inner lives that could have been separated at birth. But Mimi had a better solution. She looked at me, shrugged, and said, 'See how that is?'

★

I can't remember a wedding I've been to in the last few years that didn't have at least a couple of celebrities present. That's just the way it is when you're in this business, or one of the businesses that services this business.

Mimi knew a lot of celebrities because of her store, but there were only two present at the reception. One was Pierre, who almost overnight had become Mimi's best pal. He was in between projects and in party mode. The other was an old friend of Mimi's, a twenty-six-year-old TV actress who was on a hit sitcom. Of course the two celebrities were sitting at the same table because that's what celebrities do. They hang together. I ended up hanging with them because Pierre waved me over. He recognized me as the girl Max had spent hours talking to at Bar Marmont. Trickle-down acceptance. Ordinarily I would have waved back and moved on, but in the haze, it's easy to float from table to table and move in and out of conversations. One second everything feels intense, the next you couldn't be more blasé. Or, as was the case when I was sitting there with Pierre and the ingenue – sometimes you feel intensely blasé. Which was a particularly unusual reaction for me because they were talking about my favorite topic – sex.

'He's a bad fuck,' the actress stated, referring to some actor she'd had a fling with. Rumor was, she had dated him for the publicity. The two did make the cover of *The Star.* 'He acts like he's the new James Dean, but let me tell you, there's not a drop of rebel in that boy.'

'What does that mean?' Pierre asked, as if he were having trouble translating.

'It means he gets drunk, fucks for five minutes, and falls asleep.'

Pierre smiled, but he's French, so I couldn't really read the smile. He could have been thinking What a charming, brash American girl, or he could have been thinking *What a stupid cunt*.

'I almost cast him in a movie last year,' he said, 'but the financing fell apart.'

'I loved your first film,' the ingenue flirted.

'*City Girls* was great,' I agreed. 'It's the dark side of *How to Marry a Millionaire*.'

The ingenue scowled at me as if I'd stepped on her lines.

'I got lucky,' Pierre replied. 'I had a producer who knew how to talk people into writing the big check for a small art movie.'

The actress frowned.

'What?' Pierre asked.

'That producer!' She practically hissed.

'Is he a bad fuck too?'

'Well, that's not where I was going, but I've heard he is.'

Just then the Marlboro Man walked by with a generic bimbo on his arm. He glanced at the actress, waved.

'What about him?' Pierre teased. 'What's he like in bed?'

'From what I hear, he doesn't get a lot of requests for a repeat performance.' The ingenue laughed as if her response was worthy of Dorothy Parker.

Pierre leaned in closer. Being French, he brings a lot with it when he leans. It's seductive. It's mysterious. It's also a little annoying, but the actress was definitely going with that. Loved the attention.

'Let me ask you something,' he said, his voice growing deeper, more intimate. 'You know those women who go around saying this guy's a bad fuck, that guy's a bad fuck? Does it ever occur to them that maybe *they're* a bad fuck?'

For a second the haze lifted, and with total clarity I realized I'd just witnessed a brilliant knockout. The A-list director who'd hung on the ropes came back with the decisive punch. The actress would need more than ten seconds to get back on her feet.

★

By six P.M., the haze had become dangerous. It was affecting my judgment. I couldn't distinguish between a good idea and one that would cause me heavy regrets the next morning. Having a cell phone made the situation worse, because cell phones allow you immediate gratification. If I had actually had to walk out into the hotel lobby, ask the desk clerk where I could find a phone, find it, and place the call, I might not have gone through with it. The initial impulse might have been overtaken by a flash of restraint. But that little StarTAC cell phone was right there in my bag, which was in front of me on the table. His number was programmed into the system. There was no time for a flash of restraint. Before I knew it, I was sitting there saying, 'Hi, David.'

'Hi,' he said, sounding a little groggy.

Was he taking a nap? Was it a bad connection? 'Did I call in the middle of something?'

'Uh . . . no. I'm just here,' he replied.

Could he have come up with a more vague response? I don't think so.

'Getting a lot of work done?'

'Yeah, yeah,' he said quickly. 'How was the wedding?'

'It was beautiful. But you would have hated it.'

'But you're having a good time, right?'

Something about this conversation made me anxious. But because I was aware of the state I was in, I couldn't tell if my anxiety was justified.

'Hmm, I don't know. I guess I am.'

At the moment, I really didn't know. Didn't know anything. Didn't know why I had called him or what I was looking for. He seemed so different. Not that he wasn't being nice. He was being *very* nice. Too nice?

'These things are good for you. It'll turn up in your work. As you always say, everything's research when you're a writer.' He sounded sincere, encouraging, even loving.

'Not everything. I do keep some things private.'

He laughed. 'I'll talk to you when you get back to L.A.'

'Okay,' I agreed and hung up.

I tossed my cell phone back into my bag. I wish this thought hadn't occurred to me but it did. It did more than occur to me, it went right to where I breathe. It struck me that on the phone David sounded exactly the way he'd sounded when he'd answered his phone that night at 2:30. This time was he fucking the 2:30 A.M. girl while talking to me? Or was I being excessively paranoid? Without my judgment in top operating form, I was flying without radar. And if that doesn't give you motion sickness . . .

I needed to get outside. I moved quickly, as if I had a particular destination. Once out the door and on the terrace, I looked for a neutral area. Someplace where I could stand and not look conspicuous but also not be near anyone I knew. I walked to a corner and struck a pose, gazing toward the Pacific as if I were just another tourist having a pensive ocean moment. A few yards away, a youthful-looking man, probably in his early thirties, was puffing on a cigar. He was impeccably dressed, but his tie was loosened and his blond hair mussed. It was the studied rumpled look you often find on bratty rich boys when they put in an appearance at one of their parents' fancy events.

Don't strike up a conversation, I silently begged. *Ignore me. Ignore me. Ignore me.* And he did. At first. I thought I was safe, so I let my gaze wander across the terrace. At the other end, I noticed Evan talking to a girl. Could be a relative for all I knew. But even from where I was standing, I could see he was working his charm. That's when the rich boy spoke up.

'That's Evan for you,' he said, cryptically.

'What does that mean?' I asked suspiciously.

'Do you know him?'

'I know Mimi.'

'Ah . . . *Mimi*.'

He picked up a brandy glass from the ledge and took a sip.

'Who's the girl he's talking to?' I asked.

'Oh, some girl. Evan has lots of friends.'

'Then he and Mimi are going to have quite a Christmas card list.'

'I think that girl,' he glanced in Evan's direction, 'will be on a separate list.'

Okay, I had to ask him. 'Are you from San Francisco too?'

'Yes, I am.'

The way he said yes made me peg him as an insufferable snob.

'Is that a San Francisco thing then?'

'Is what a San Francisco thing?'

'Implying that the groom will cheat on his wife to someone who, for all you know, could be the bride's sister?'

He took a leisurely puff on his Monte Cristo before saying, 'Mimi doesn't have a sister. And I didn't say anything about anyone cheating.'

I decided to drop my accusatory tone. 'Just a general question, chalk it up to idle curiosity. Do you think most guys cheat on their wives or girlfriends?'

'Some women inspire it,' he said.

Snobby and mean, I decided. Leave it to me to find a total stranger to play right into my current haze-induced paranoia.

'Do you see Mimi as one of those?'

'How would I know?'

I knew he meant yes. I knew he didn't get Mimi. Probably thought of her as some uncultured L.A. girl who was not, in the parlance of guys like himself, 'a keeper.' She was someone you might have an affair with and then move on.

'Mimi's great,' I declared.

'Great,' he echoed, as if he was humoring some dimwit.

'You know what's great about her? She's kind. An undervalued virtue, don't you think?'

He knew I was not only extolling Mimi, I was challenging him.

'Absolutely.'

'Not polite, though she can be that too – in her own way. But kind. With an open, giving heart.'

Suddenly this guy looked as uncomfortable as an atheist who has stumbled into a church.

'Hey,' he said, 'I'm convinced.' And then he took his brandy and cigar and walked away.

*

There was one thing I knew I could do at the wedding that Mimi's other girlfriends couldn't – or wouldn't.

'You don't have to,' she'd said when I first brought up the idea.

'No, no. I want to,' I insisted. And I did, even though I'm not good in front of crowds. Until that moment I had never willingly spoken in front of one. A public-speaking class in the seventh grade was as close as I got, and I was lucky to rate a C-. But you can't promise someone something on her wedding day and not come through.

First I checked around to make sure Evan was back beside *his wife*. Then I refilled my champagne glass and went up to the bandleader.

'Uh . . . I've got to make a toast,' I said.

'Now?' The band was only halfway through its set.

I didn't have enough momentum to negotiate. If I debated the issue I'd lose my courage – or my guilt-driven nerve, which I was calling courage.

'Now,' I said, not budging.

What was he going to do? He stepped up to the mike. 'Can I have your attention, everybody?' About half the room looked up. 'Everybody, can I have your attention? A young lady has something she wants to say to our bride and groom.' Remembering their names, he added, 'Mimi and Evan, where are you?'

Mimi stood and pulled Evan up with her. The bandleader turned the mike over to me.

I looked out at all those people looking back at me. Scary moment. I'd once written a wedding scene for a script (that never got made) that included a timid guest giving a toast to the newlyweds. The studio said it was too long and I should cut it to six lines or I'd lose the audience. If they were right, I had good reason to be worried about what I was about to do.

INT: BILTMORE HOTEL – RECEPTION ROOM: DAY

A wedding reception in progress. Dinner has been served and cleared. The bandleader hands the microphone to Elizabeth, a guest and a good friend of the bride.

She holds the mike for a moment and says nothing, gathering courage. Finally . . .

ELIZABETH
I have a story I want to tell you which will help
explain what's so special about Mimi. Two days
ago, I went into Gucci in Beverly Hills to buy a pair
of stilettos for this occasion. Turns out they didn't
have my size. But they called the San Francisco
store and found out they did. So the salesgirl
promised to FedEx them to me the next day. Fine,
I said.

ELIZABETH pauses, checking out the audience. Are they
listening? Are they bored? The bride's grandmother nods
encouragingly. ELIZABETH's friend ANDREW smiles
approvingly.

Elizabeth (cont'd)
The next morning I'm looking out the window and I
see a FedEx truck drive down my street. It doesn't
stop. *Hmm*, I thought. *That's interesting*. So I call the
Beverly Hills store and tell them what happened. The
salesgirl says, 'Let me check on it.' She puts me on
hold. A few minutes later she gets back on and says,
'There's been a mistake and the shoes are still in
San Francisco, but we'll send them out on Monday.'
And I say, 'No, you don't understand. That's not
going to work. I bought them to wear to my friend
Mimi Lane's wedding on Saturday.'

A few girls in the audience giggle. An acknowledgment of the importance of shoes? Too much champagne? Either? Both? Doesn't matter. ELIZABETH just got her first laugh and it felt good. She's really getting into the story now.

> ELIZABETH (cont'd)
> Frustrated, I told her to forget it, and hung up. Five minutes later, *five minutes*, the phone rings. It's the manager of Gucci, calling to say that because I'm a good friend of Mimi Lane's, there's a courier at the San Francisco store, *as we speak*. The shoes will be put in the next plane to L.A. and delivered to my door by five P.M. that day.

She pauses dramatically.

> ELIZABETH (cont'd)
> And they were.

The audience loves the story. They raise their glasses as ELIZABETH holds hers up to the bride and groom.

> ELIZABETH (cont'd)
> And so, Mimi, I want you to know that because I'm your friend I get to stand in front of everyone here today . . . three inches taller. Which is appropriate, because being your friend always makes me feel taller and better and smarter than I am.

MIMI is teary. EVAN is proud. People sigh, satisfied with the emotional punch.

ELIZABETH (cont'd)
And because of that and dozens of other reasons, I
wish you and Evan every happiness in the world.

People cheer, applaud. A wave of good feeling washes over
the room. ELIZABETH stands there, seemingly stunned by
the moment and *ALL THE ATTENTION*. The bandleader
takes the microphone out of her hand.

BANDLEADER
Good job.

ELIZABETH
Now I get it.

BANDLEADER
Get what?

ELIZABETH
This is why people get hooked on acting.

CUT TO:

When I stepped off the stage, I went to find
Andrew. I wanted to thank him for being so encouraging. For smiling and nodding through my toast. I
reconsidered my previous suspicions. Maybe he's not
back on drugs or alcohol. Maybe he's just been
having a bad week. Or a bad month. Or even a bad
season. Who hasn't?

I watched him cut out of the room and head for the lobby. I followed, hoping I could talk him into a walk down to the beach. Maybe, if he needed it, I could have self-esteem for *him* for a change. I'd just faced a room full of people and hadn't crumbled. For the moment I felt as if I had a little juice, and I was glad to pass it along. Sometimes it felt as if Andrew and I were partners in a relay race with an unmarked finish line. And now I was the one ready to sprint.

The lobby was crowded. But crowds don't seem to matter when it comes to a certain blonde ponytail. Whether at a Lakers game or in a crowded hotel lobby in Santa Barbara – where there are lots of blonde ponytails – I still spotted her. Blaze was becoming my bête noir. There she was – alone – at the check-in desk.

'What are you doing here? Don't tell me you're getting married!' Jake spun me around and stood before me with a big grin. I could read that grin. It meant he was getting laid a lot, and loving it.

'Does this look like a wedding dress?'

He checked out my sexy bronze-colored dress, which I'd bought on impulse, thinking how much Jake would love the slit up the back.

'Definitely. It definitely looks like it could be your wedding dress.'

'Would I get married at the Biltmore?'

'Okay. So what are you doing here?'

'A friend got married.'

'I fucking hate weddings,' Jake said. 'I even fucking hate coming to a hotel that *allows* weddings.'

'Three today,' I pointed out. '''Tis the season. What are you doing here?'

'Blaze wanted to get away for the weekend.'

'Is this a new Jake? Living with someone. Coming up to Santa Barbara for a weekend. Pretty soon you'll be driving a Volvo.'

He laughed and gave me a hug. 'Who are you here with?'

'Uh . . .' I noted that he didn't ask if David was there. That would imply he saw us as some kind of couple.

'You've got to think about who you're here with?'

'Uh . . . a friend. A girlfriend,' I added quickly. 'Why?'

'I'm just checking up on you,' he said.

'Oh, are you?' We sounded like a couple of amateur flirts, but I was loving it anyway. Until the blonde ponytail joined us.

'It's the screenwriter.' Blaze made this pronouncement as if she was describing some service person. It's the mailman. It's the cable guy. It's the plumber.

'It's the girlfriend,' I replied. I knew that'd get her. Blaze only wants to be the girlfriend if being the girlfriend will help her to be something else.

'Hi,' she said curtly.

273

'Hi,' I echoed.

This is the advantage of being in the haze. I didn't blink first. She looked away, looked to Jake.

'Do you want to go up to the room?' She was playing the sex card. That was fine. Why not? It *is* the card to play with Jake.

'Yeah, let's.' He smiled. And then turning back to me . . . 'You staying till Sunday?'

'Leaving tonight.'

Where did that come from? I was supposed to stay till Sunday. I had plans. Brunch. An afternoon at the beach. But now I just wanted to get out of there as soon as possible. Running away, but not running toward anything. *Lovely, just lovely*, I thought. Is this what it's come to? My car is my oasis. Typical L.A. girl. Happiest in transit.

'Guess I should go back inside,' I said.

'Going to try to catch the bouquet?' Blaze smiled.

'Yeah, *there's* a tradition that make's sense to me,' I said. 'Who thought up that one? Get a pack of desperate women to fight over a handful of wilting flowers. Yup, that'll make some guy pop the question. I got to have *her*. The one who just pushed and shoved her way to some secondhand roses. Very attractive.'

I said that for Jake's sake. He loves when I get sassy. And since Blaze held the sex card, sassy was the closest thing I had to an ace. But, as it turned out, not close enough.

'You don't have to bring me flowers, baby,' Blaze said to Jake as her hand slid across the front of his jeans, lingering over his dick.

What could I say to that? To her? To him? Only one thing. I looked at Jake and said the line of the day. If you can't say something nice, just say, 'See how that is?'

*

Waiting for cake at a wedding reception is basically waiting for permission to leave. Once that knife sliced into the six-tiered dessert, I was free. It was acceptable to leave. I said my good-byes, claiming a deadline. 'Got to fax pages first thing in the morning,' I explained. Mimi knew I was lying, but she also knew she'd get the full story after her honeymoon. Julie, perfect date that she is, figured I had my reasons. We didn't even have to discuss how she'd get back to L.A. That's what makes her a perfect girlfriend date. She's flexible, resourceful, and today probably had her own secret reason for wanting to stay.

I walked around the room three times trying to find Andrew and finally gave up. He'd either wandered off somewhere or had left without saying good-bye to anyone – what he and I call a French exit. Not that unusual, but if he had cut out, he had cut out fast. And a fast French exit usually means really good news – or really bad.

★

As I waited for the valet to bring my car around, I spotted Mimi and Evan at the end of the driveway. They'd stepped out for a semiprivate moment. They were facing each other, her arms around his waist, his fingers slipped inside the back of her low-cut gown.

Who knows where this marriage will lead? I thought. Maybe he'll cheat on her. Maybe she'll end up living in San Francisco. Maybe she'll end up having two babies and two stores. Or maybe she'll end up back in L.A., divorced, after having cheated on him? Impossible to call it. But right then they were looking at each other in a way, the way we all want to look and be looked at. That's what it's about, I realized. That moment, played out in a thousand movie scenes, is what we want to find in real life. This is what makes all the other stuff bearable. And though I've never been able to understand spending thousands and thousands of dollars on a wedding, to have that moment I'd spend a million.

Sixteen

There's a point in an action movie, at the beginning of act three, with time running out, when the progress the good guys had been making through act two backfires and they end up in even worse shape than when they started. Usually some evidence or a key witness gets blown up in a major action sequence designed to jack up the adrenaline of the adolescent boys (target demographic) in the audience. According to the action formula, the good guys finally piece together all the little clues that should have warned them that this might happen.

How strange to find this formula being played out in my personal life. I too should have heeded some key clues. The day of the premiere, I couldn't reach David on the phone. He'd agreed to go with me, but all afternoon, anytime I tried calling him, he was in a meeting. I got his voice mail. He'd call me back, not on my cell phone, which is where I told him to call, but at home, where there was no chance of finding me.

This is standard guy avoidance behavior. Any girl can nail it, but when it's the day of your premiere you're not in the mood to nail your date. You're in the mood to pretend that everything is terrific. You want to believe that this is reward time. It's the 'walking down the mountain time,' to quote Davenport. I'm always complaining that the myth of Sisyphus is no myth. We really are, each one of us, pushing a huge rock up a mountain every day, only to see it roll down after we get it to the top. Davenport's response is to learn to enjoy the respite of the walk back down the mountain. And in a superficial Hollywood way, one's premiere is one of those respites. A respite that's not supposed to include wondering and worrying what the fuck your quasi-boyfriend is up to.

Things got worse when one of the messages he left was that he had a problem with the contractors on a client's house and might have to meet me at the theater. *Meet me there?* He better be building the fucking Taj Mahal, I thought.

As it turned out, he did pick me up, but the evening had already begun to sour. In David's defense, it doesn't take too much to sour me on a movie premiere – even my own. Maybe if I'd written the original draft, written every word up on the screen, and my name was up there, right between the producer's and the director's, I'd feel different. I might be embarrassingly giddy with excitement. But I was the ninth writer on the project. And though Jake claimed I saved the movie, no one would be screaming 'Author, author!'

Maybe it wasn't about that at all. Maybe I was irreversibly jaded. I'd been going to premieres my whole life. There was always a client of my dad's or a customer of my mom's or a friend who got me in – though never in any kind of VIP way. After a while, premieres became nothing more than movies with free popcorn – and lately, with studio cutbacks, you couldn't even count on that. Julie was even more jaded. Because of her job, she'd gone to so many of these events they'd become a form of torture. Mention a premiere, and she'd go on and on. 'Yeah, it's so fun to stand behind the velvet ropes outside a theater and scream a celebrity's name. It's fucking vampiric.' As far as Julie is concerned, Joan Rivers has the worst job in America.

*

'Where do you want to sit?' David asked me as we walked into the theater. The room was crowded, the aisles jammed. I looked around to see if I spotted anyone I knew, mostly because I wanted them to see me with David. Our first big outing. Our public debut.

I held up my reserved-seat passes. 'And they're

even numbered. Really reserved. Not just random seating in the reserved section.'

'You're a star.' He smiled a little too forcefully.

'No, that's a star,' I said, looking in the direction of Kevin, the film's lead actor. No one who walked by him failed to either look or stop. He was it. The one with the most heat. The golden boy. Unless the movie tanked.

I checked the tickets. 'Uhh . . .'

'What?' David asked.

'We're in *Kevin's* row.' How did that happen? Writers don't get to sit in the star's row unless they've had at least one Academy Award nomination. Then I thought, This is Jake's doing. His way of rewarding me. Or was it? As I checked seat numbers, I realized the seats were already taken by the same pipsqueak studio executive who'd been at the test screening. He was there with his wife, who had settled in with her popcorn and Evian.

'Excuse me,' I said to the exec, 'I think those are our seats.'

'Kevin wants us here,' he said arrogantly.

'Is that right?' I asked calmly.

This is an interesting test, I thought. Do I challenge the movie star, challenge the studio executive, or find other seats and feel horrible that I didn't stick up for myself?

David pulled on my arm to get my attention.

'What do you want me to do?' he asked. And I knew he'd do anything. Judging by the expression on his face, I'd say his instinct was to lift the pint-size executive out of his chair and introduce him to a new seating assignment. But it was my night, and he was going to take his cues from me. At that moment all was forgiven. Even though he might not have been a good quasi-boyfriend, he was a damn good escort.

'If I start acting like a wimp, jump in,' I replied. I swung back around to the executive. 'I'm going to go find Jake. Maybe he'll let me sit in his seats, and you two can battle it out over these.'

Finally, for once in my life, my timing wasn't off. Jake and Blaze appeared, heading toward us, albeit at a slow pace. Jake too was a star and got his share of stares and handshakes.

For a moment, the executive said nothing. Not many people want to take on Jake, because Jake will take you on. In a movie theater. In a meeting. In a restaurant. He'll get into it. He'll get in your face.

The executive mumbled something to his wife, and the two of them stood and sought out seats across the aisle.

'You'll have to deal with Kevin on this one,' he said gruffly as he passed by.

'Fine,' I said. I knew the whole Kevin thing was bullshit. I'd worked with Kevin. He wasn't the kind of guy to insist on having someone sit in someone else's seat. That wasn't his style unless he was making way for a girlfriend or Marlon Brando or Bob Dylan or one of his other cultural icons.

But I'm a girl *and* just a writer, and suits, not stars, try to pull this shit on me all the time. One of the things I loved about Jake was that I believed he'd protect me. He loved protecting the underdog. That worked for me, since protection has always been on my list of aphrodisiacs.

★

As the opening credits appeared on the screen, I suddenly realized I was relieved that my name wouldn't be up there. What if it was and no one clapped? Jake's name always inspires cheers. Kevin's name would get a big response. But my name? 'Written by Elizabeth West.' Who cares? Worse than silence. I imagined a few friends applauding. As the perfect escort, David would do his part. Andrew could be counted on. But Julie, though working the premiere, wasn't guaranteed a seat. Mimi was up in San Francisco. My dad and stepmother were away in some southern state on another save-the-marriage vacation. And my mom was in a state of depression. Her relationship with the shoe mogul hadn't worked out. That's not why she said she couldn't come, but I knew that was the deal. And that was okay. Part of me thought, She's fifty, she claims to be a feminist. She should know better. But I knew better. What do age and politics have to do with a direct hit to your self-esteem?

From that I segued right to this thought. *I am not a cool girl.* A cool girl would understand that whether or not an audience claps sufficiently at the sight of your name on a movie screen is not something that should make or break your day. That neediness does nothing for your soul, your character. The applause is heard today, gone tomorrow. But uncool girl that I am, it would matter. Maybe it was better simply to cruise on the cachet I got from my relationship with Jake. I loved the roar for his credit. Of course, I understood that Jake was simply the beneficiary of the standard goodwill that an industry audience sends out before a movie starts. It's Hollywood's way of acknowledging any filmmaker who gets any movie made, because it's such a difficult thing to pull off. By the time the lights went back up, it'd be a different story. If the movie turned out to be a potential hit, much of that goodwill could turn into jealousy-inspired ill will. If the move was a dud, people would want to distance themselves from everyone involved, lest they be tainted by loserishness.

A half hour into the movie (it took me that long to relax), I allowed myself to accept the fact that the scenes I wrote worked. My jokes worked. The action beats didn't suck. So, of course, my anxiety sought out another target. And there it was, sitting right next to me. Even though David laughed in all the right places and occasionally looked at me and smiled – a little too forcefully – I was not reassured. As the movie hit the halfway mark, the anxiety had grown to a low-level panic attack. Thankfully, the film was only a hundred minutes long, because there's no telling how far this anxiety could have taken me.

When it was over, there was a respectable amount of applause and a few whistles, I think, from some of the guys who worked on the rap sound track. I looked over to get Jake's reaction so I could interpret the response. Did they *really, really* like it? But he had, as was his custom, slipped out before the end. David grabbed my arm affectionately and whispered something in my ear. I assumed it was a thoughtful compliment. I didn't hear it clearly, so I tossed out a generic reply: 'You think so?'

'Can't you tell?' he replied brightly.

There we were, two people each pretending to know what the other was saying. Fake version of me smiling at fake version of him.

*

I should explain what premiere parties do to me. They have the opposite effect of wedding receptions.

Gone is the haze; in its place is a focus that is so sharp, a clarity so relentless, that at times it feels like an acid trip – often like a bad acid trip. Don't ask me why this is. I've thought about it. The best explanation is that I don't think anything really bad will ever happen to me at a wedding reception, so a blurred state isn't dangerous. But any number of bad things can happen in an industry crowd, so I've got to be not only alert but hyperalert.

The party was set up in a tented parking lot a half-block away from the theater. A red carpet was laid out on the walkway leading to the entrance. I noticed that it was threadbare around the edges. Nothing plush. Nothing very VIP. Yet it intimidated me. Treading on that thing was like fire walking. Only by moving steadily ahead and thinking positive thoughts could I get to the end and not get burnt. Unfortunately that rarely happens. Usually there's a gridlock of people to navigate through. As for positive thoughts, it's a little tough when all non-celebrities are made to feel like, at most, a footnote in some star's biography.

The standard horde of paparazzi and journalists was lined up and jockeying for position. It was time for lights, cameras, and reactions. A soundbyte was the goal, preferably from the most famous person in attendance. I spotted Julie talking to a publicist. I waved, and she broke into a big smile. I couldn't tell if that was her way of saying 'Happy premiere' or 'David's a stud.'

'Kevin! Kevin!' the reporters screamed as the man of the night slowly made his way past the press. Kevin was the only action star with a lot of Elvis in him. He possessed the same blend of sweetness and sexiness that the King of Rock had in the early sixties. Of course girls loved him. Beyond the reporters in a cordoned-off area were hundreds of fans straining and aching for a glimpse of him or any of his high-profile posse. The fans yelled out his name from the sidelines.

'I don't get it,' I said to David. 'Why do these people drive all the way here just to wait outside a movie theater in the hopes of getting a glimpse of someone they've never met and probably never will, who has nothing to do with their lives?'

David's eyes wandered as he replied. 'You've never had an idol?'

'I don't believe in idolizing strangers.'

'It's a lot safer than idolizing someone you know,' he teased. At least I think he was teasing, but his eyes were averted. I couldn't tell you exactly who had captured his attention, but my premiere-party antenna was up, my radar was going strong, and I knew this: It was some girl.

When he finally looked me in the eye, he still seemed distracted.

'Everything okay?' I asked.

'Yes, yes. I'm fine,' he answered. And then to divert me, he added, 'Don't journalists interview the movie's writer?'

'Not this kind of movie. Not this kind of writer. Not even if your best friend's one of the journalists.'

*

Premiere parties often have themes. It's part of the film's promotional campaign and also an attempt to distinguish this week's premiere party from last week's and the one before that. Without a theme, a premiere party can feel like just another train pulling out of the station.

This one, predictably, had a Miami theme. Cuban music. Cuban food. And South Beach models – that was Jake's touch. Blaze probably felt right at home. Except as I watched her do the room with him, I could see she was already recreating herself as an L.A. girl. My guess is she'd been shopping at Fred Segal (upstairs), and Miu Miu on Melrose for the shoes. She was still beach-bunny sexy but now with a touch of trophy wife. The new image was enhanced by the gold Rolex she was wearing. A watch that even I – someone who doesn't wear jewelry and hates keeping track of time – coveted.

'What can I get you?' David asked as we approached one of the four bars that had been set up inside the tent.

'Uh . . . wine. I don't care. White wine, I guess.'

I wasn't in a very celebratory mood, even though the executive who had tried to steal my seat now sailed past me, smiling. 'Fifteen million opening weekend.' And then over his shoulder, 'Not bad for a film that only cost twenty-two!'

David handed me a glass of wine.

'It was really nice of you to come to this with me,' I said, genuinely grateful.

'I'm enjoying it,' he replied blandly.

Ouch, that hurt. I know it seems like a harmless answer, but it was so benign, it was insulting. A better answer would have been any of the following:

1. You'd do the same for me. (The expected reciprocity implies some kind of relationship.)
2. You owe me one. (Implies a future.)
3. You don't even have to ask. (Implies loyalty.)
4. It's your big night. (Implies respect.)
5. I expect you to blow me in the car on the way home. (Guarantees a good time.)

'I'm enjoying it' implies nothing and guarantees nothing. It seemed like the right moment to take a break.

★

I couldn't find Julie, so I checked out the ladies' room. Inside were all these women fixing their makeup under lighting that exaggerated every flaw, or else I'd aged five years in the last few hours.

Even though it's all girls, it still makes me self-conscious to carry on a conversation under those lights. The whole time I'm standing there looking at the person I'm talking to I'm thinking, She looked so much better than last time I saw her, and I know she's probably thinking the same about me. There was an exception. I spotted a girl who looked much better than she had the last time we met.

'Jordan, right? You work for Renée Larkin?'

'Worked. I quit three weeks ago.'

'Ah . . . that's why you look different. More relaxed.'

'No kidding.' She laughed. 'That job was like having a flesh-eating virus.'

'Amazing how many people stay in those jobs,' I replied. 'And then, after a while, they get used to it, and eventually become the virus. Victims turned victimizers.'

'Hi, I'm Laurie,' said a girl who'd suddenly appeared next to Jordan. She was young and pretty in an offbeat way. Offbeat for Hollywood. She reminded me of Natalie Imbruglia, and I could easily imagine her in some cool video, singing a heartfelt song that made it into high rotation on VH1.

'I'm Elizabeth.'

'Elizabeth wrote the movie,' Jordan explained.

'You did? You wrote this movie?' Laurie seemed unduly surprised.

'Yeah, I did. With a lot of help from the director.'

'Renée hates Jake,' Jordan suddenly announced.

'I guessed that.'

'After you left that day, she said, "Why am I meeting with one of Jake's writers? Jake would only . . ."' She stopped. 'I probably shouldn't say this.'

'No, go ahead.'

She thought about it for a second. 'Okay, but you know you can't take these things personally. Renée said Jake would only hire a female writer who was "doing him."'

I laughed. 'She said that? Well, here's the truth. I'd like to think it's because I've been writing for him that I *haven't* been able to "do him." Still I can't believe Renée admitted that.'

'What do you expect?' Jordan shrugged. 'Renée and sex. Oil and water. She once told me that she didn't understand what women got out of blow jobs.'

'She must get a lot of dates,' Laurie said with the kind of sarcastic wit that usually comes with an East Coast address. I noticed she was casually studying me, and I studied her back. I took note of her thick, curly auburn hair. Green eyes. Good body. But mostly I noted her scrutiny. Either she was curious about me, or she was trying to pick me up. While I contemplated this, I continued talking.

'How can a woman not understand blow jobs? It's the ultimate power position, and it's so much fun.'

Laurie smiled. 'This is so L.A. Three people, two of whom just met, standing around in a ladies' room, talking about sex.'

'Where you come from, people don't do that?' I asked.

'It's a little different in New York.'

'It is?'

'A little. While talking about sucking cocks they'll throw in a line about the Bonnard exhibit at the Met.'

I liked this girl, but it was a premiere party and standing near her caused a huge blip on my radar screen.

What's that about? I thought, which is not only the generic question I use for anything I don't understand but also the name of a pilot I once wrote for MTV. I knew the answer was coming whether I wanted it or not.

*

When I got back to the party, David was no longer hanging out at the bar. I wandered around, looking for Jake or Andrew or Julie. The place was pretty packed, except for the dance floor. Why, why, why do premiere parties have dance floors when no one ever dances? Including me. Since industry events are more work than play, I'd feel like I was dancing at a meeting.

The music being played by an authentic Miami salsa band, flown in for the occasion, was the kind that would have people on their feet partying till dawn in Florida. A couple of teenage girls – probably interns at some studio – braved the empty space. Only the very young dared to be uninhibited in this crowd. And even they stuck to the periphery.

As I walked past the reserved tables, I ran into Jake and Blaze, who were talking to Darian, the film's lead actress, the one who played the part of Karin. Even though they were in mid-conversation, Jake pulled me over and put his arm around me. It was a friendly gesture, nothing flirtatious, but in that setting, it was the equivalent of an anointing. Jake was notorious for his fierce loyalty, which roughly translated into 'You fuck with my friends, you fuck with me.' And he wasn't even Sicilian.

'Where's your guy?'

'David's somewhere.'

'See, what'd I tell you?'

'What?'

'In Miami. I told you I had the perfect guy for you.'

'Problem is, I don't think I'm the perfect girl for him.'

'Oh yeah, who says?'

I started to laugh.

'What?' Jake demanded.

'Sometimes you sound like the cutest thug.'

'Me? Me?' He pretended to be upset.

Blaze immediately picked up on the playfulness Jake and I had going. She might not have been a genuine scholar, but she had the equivalent of a doctorate when it came to overseeing her territory. And she was right to throw me a dirty look. I was flirting with her guy. I hate women who flirt with a guy in front of his girlfriend. It's not my style. But it was the only language Jake and I spoke. Every conversation carried a flirtatious vibe. The alternative was to stop talking – and that I'd never do. If that meant incurring the wrath of Blaze, a girl who, as they say in Hollywood, would stab you in the front to get what she wanted, then bring on her wrath.

At that particular moment, however, she wasn't as worried about my lust for her man as she was about a bigger threat – Darian. Here was someone as pretty as Blaze, as young as Blaze, smarter than Blaze, with a gigantic trump card in her deck: She was famous. And getting more so all the time. Woody Allen had cast her in his next movie, and she was up for the lead in a new Michael Douglas film.

'I loved your performance,' Blaze lied.

'Thank you,' Darian replied politely, but it was apparent she didn't give a fuck what Blaze thought. She didn't exactly turn her back on Blaze, but she angled her body in such a way as to give new meaning to the phrase 'cold shoulder.'

Blaze stood her ground, never moving more than a few inches away from Jake. All the while she kept a smile on her face. It was the kind of smile that looks like it's stuck. Like she'd have loved to wipe it off her face but didn't know how to do that without revealing her true feelings. Blaze was not happy about Darian's performance. My guess is, she was probably standing there with that smile stuck on her face thinking, It should have been me up there, not you.

When Darian finally moved on, Blaze replaced the smile with a pouty curl of her collagen–filled lips.

'I'm thirsty,' she said to Jake.

His arm dropped from my shoulder as he looked for his assistant.

'Alex!' he shouted. Alex was, as always, hovering nearby. In a flash he was at Jake's side.

'Why aren't these waiters working these tables?' Jake asked.

'What do you need?' Alex seemed happy to be given a specific task.

Jake turned to Blaze. 'What do you want, baby?'

'Orange juice.'

I should have known then. In fact, I did know then. In some dark recess of my brain. I knew there was something to this drink order. Not mineral water. Orange juice. Blaze did grow up in the orange capital of America, but she was at a premiere, and that was just a little too healthy. Especially when hanging with Jake, who liked martinis and disliked women who wouldn't take a walk on the wild side with him.

'Elizabeth, what about you?' Jake asked. He looked like an angel. When you're in bad-acid-trip mode and someone looks like an angel, you know you're really in trouble. Or really in love, which is probably the biggest trouble of all.

'Nothing,' I lied. The truth was, I wanted everything.

★

'Andrew, Andrew, Andrew,' I called out, finally spotting him at a small table in a corner. 'You're not here alone, are you?'

He pointed in the direction of a guy in his early thirties who was refueling at the bar. 'I brought Carlos.'

I recognized the name. Carlos Sanchez, a painter who was currently being shown at Andrew's gallery. Carlos was one of those guys who, though very macho, was such a pretty boy that both men and women were drawn to him. As I watched him talking to the bartender I wondered if he was gay, and suddenly a more disturbing thought struck me. Could Andrew possibly be gay? That might explain his recent strange behavior. The secret phone calls. His reluctance to share any details of his personal life with me when before we'd always told each other almost everything. Oh my God, was I so self-involved that I hadn't picked up on something this big going on with one of my best friends?

'I saw David wandering around,' he said.

'Where?'

'Near the dance floor.'

I looked in that direction, but it was almost impossible to see past the crowd of people in my immediate vicinity.

I swung my attention back to Andrew. He was eyeing a nearby display of media frenzy. A number of camera crews were circling Kevin and his entourage. It was sound-bite heaven, and Julie and her KNBC crew were the first in line at those pearly gates.

'Julie!' I shouted.

She didn't hear me over the din of the party music. 'Andrew, what do you think? Maybe we should all go get a drink after this. You. Me. David. Carlos. Julie.'

Andrew said nothing. He continued to watch the

KNBC crew get their prime-time minute with the star. I didn't disrupt his concentration. Now that I was worried about being too self-involved, I felt guilty about nagging him for an answer. So I pulled a cigarette out of my purse but didn't light it because we were in the no-smoking section. When Andrew moved to get a better view of Julie and her team, he stepped beneath an overhead light.

Looking at his face in the light, I remembered what it was like to kiss him. Yes, just friends that we were, we did kiss once. More than a year before. We both were drunk and we never mentioned it the next day or any day after that. That one kiss said a lot, though. It told me that this is a guy who likes women. It wasn't simply the way he kissed but the way his hands touched my body. This guy likes the female form. No doubt about it. On the other hand, it didn't totally rule out the possibility that he might also like men. The way I see it, sex is like a great rock and roll song. Do I care if the lyrics are sung by Bruce or Chrissie? The right note is the right note.

As soon as Julie's crew wrapped their interview and turned off their lights and camera, Andrew bolted toward them. There he was, grabbing Julie's hand and pulling her aside for what definitely seemed like the continuation of some previous discussion. They got right into it. I didn't need radar and an extra-sensory antenna to figure this one out. It was a *lover's quarrel*. With a shock, everything fell into place. Andrew was Julie's mystery guy. What surprised me the most was not that my two best friends were involved without my knowing it but how jealous I felt. Would I get less of each of them because they had each other?

'Where's Andrew?' Carlos was holding two drinks, one Andrew's diet Coke.

'Over there.' I pointed.

'Oh yeah.' He nodded knowingly.

'Wait a minute,' I said, going from shock to disbelief. 'You knew about this? About them?'

'Everybody needs somebody to talk to,' he replied.

★

I had every intention of letting it go until the next day. It wasn't the kind of conversation I could have with Julie in the middle of a party. Besides, I had to find David. But five minutes later, there I was, having the conversation with Julie, right in the middle of the party. Andrew had left, and she was in a talking mood.

'How did it end?' I asked. 'Forget that. How did it start?'

'Like most of these things start. One person opens a door, and the other person walks in.'

'I haven't really thought about you two being together. In fact I've never thought about it. Now that I am thinking about it, though, I'm thinking . . . why not? You're both great, smart, funny — and available.'

'Don't think I haven't been through this over and over again.' She glanced toward the exit as if Andrew might reappear at any moment. 'It should work. It could work . . . But it doesn't work. We like each other too much to treat it like a casual thing, but . . .' She shook her head. 'I don't know. Maybe I haven't been divorced long enough to remember how much I hated being single.'

'Does Andrew want to get serious?'

'Yes and no. Our relationship is like this cactus plant that grows around Palm Springs. It thrives only at a particular elevation. Move it up or down the mountain and it's all over.'

'What a great way to put it.'

'I'm just quoting the master.'

'Which one?'

'Davenport, of course.'

'Figures.'

★

A half hour later I was getting worried about David. I circled the party a few times. No sign of him. Oh God, I thought, he probably hates me. He agreed to come to this event, and then once we're here, I abandon him. I am hideous, I owe him many, many favors. He is definitely getting a blow job on the drive home. I wished we were already on the road. For a minute, I indulged in a break from the intense clarity I'd been operating under. Reality and truth were blocked out by the thought of the sexcapade David and I would have as soon as we got out of this circus. It was a very fast minute, and it came to a very brutal end.

There he was, in a tête à tête with – I knew it, I knew it, I knew it – Laurie, Jordan's friend. The girl from the ladies' room. The one I liked. The one with the East Coast attitude. She was it. She was the twenty-one-year-old, mature, New York-trained actress. And David was talking to her and looking at her in a way that he never talked to or looked at me.

I had reached the nadir of my so-called bad acid trip. I knew enough, had had enough therapy to know that if you can resist something like this, the pain grows. Only by accepting it can you begin to lift the two-thousand-pound, Sisyphean rock that has fallen on your heart.

I walked over to them. 'Hi, David.'

'Oh,' he replied.

Oh. Never before had that word seemed so appropriate. It was 'Oh,' as in the Webster's dictionary definition – a word to express an emotion. No further definition of what emotion, which was why it was perfect. I hadn't a clue what emotion David was expressing.

I looked at Laurie. 'The New York girl,' I stated calmly.

She looked steadily at me. 'The L.A. girl,' she replied.

I looked at David. 'The boyfriend. Problem is, whose boyfriend are you?' Not my best exit line but good enough.

David came after me and reached for my arm. 'Are you okay?'

There it was, the dreaded phrase. The one that so often makes me feel not okay.

'No,' I said, jerking my arm away from him. I didn't want him to see my tears, because the tears weren't even about him. Not really. David wasn't the bad guy here. That was the problem. I didn't know who the bad guy was. Action movies are so much easier. Eventually, you always can distinguish the good guys from the bad. Here I was in what felt like Act Three and I still had no clue. No, the tears were not over David. They were for all the things that don't work out in life. They were for all those things that start out with such great promise and joy and end up in teary flight from a bad party.

I only wanted to get outside. I had no ride home, but that was a secondary issue. I needed to get outside

— fast. You can't be seen crying at your own premiere.

As I was making a mad dash for the door, my life suddenly veered from tragic romantic scenario to surreal screwball comedy. I ran into Nigel. We hadn't seen each other or talked since Palm Springs. Yet there he was, sporting the same smile, as if nothing had happened.

'Elizabeth, I've been thinking about you.'

Since he was blocking my way, I didn't have the option of totally ignoring him. I quickly wiped away a tear that was sliding down my cheek.

'I'm in a hurry.'

'Well,' he said in that measured way he had, 'I just want to say, it's a shame we can't be friends. That we can't see each other sometime. You know, I was driving down your street the other day, and I almost stopped and rang your doorbell.'

As much as I wanted to get out of there, even more I wanted to make sure there'd be no bell-ringing in my future.

'Look, Nigel, when I was hanging out with you, I was going through a bad time. Very insecure. Very needy. I was afraid to say what I thought, or to do anything that might not please you. I'm sure that worked for you. But now, in spite of how I may look, I feel better. Stronger. Closer to the top of my game. Trust me, you don't want to hang out with the new me.'

'Does that mean that I shouldn't call you until you're feeling weak and insecure again?'

'That's right,' I said as I walked off, knowing that no matter what, I would never be that weak and insecure again.

*

The air outside felt great. But I still had to negotiate my way through the scene. There were plenty of fans lurking, hoping for another glimpse of one of the celebrities. Of course, there were no taxis around. This is L.A. So I took out my cell phone and tried calling information, but, consistent with how the night had been going, the call wouldn't go through. I walked up and down the block, hoping for better reception.

'Hi. Did you like the movie?'

The question was posed by a stranger. A guy in his mid-twenties. Right away I knew there was something off about him. His jacket didn't quite fit. His hair was just this side of crazy.

'Yes,' I replied, as I tried 411 again. No go.

'Yeah, it was good,' he agreed. 'I know the writer.'

'You know *the* writer?'

'Yeah,' he repeated with a swagger.

I decided to play it out. 'Which writer? There were a lot of them.'

'Elizabeth West.' It rolled off his tongue.

I stopped and looked at him closely. 'Really? You know her?'

'Yeah. I met her a couple of years ago when she was writing something for Paramount. We used to have lunch together at the commissary all the time.'

Oh great, I thought. What a way to wrap up the night. I guess it was possible I'd met this guy a few years ago. Who remembers everyone they meet? But I had not ever had lunch with this guy. That I was sure of.

'You did?' I said. 'That's interesting.'

'Yeah, well, she's cool. We got real close.'

'You did? You got real close with Elizabeth West. Hmmm. That's weird.'

'Why? Do you know her?'

'Do I know her? *I am her!*'

He stared at me for a second, his eyes devoid of emotion as if his brain had frozen. Synapses jammed.

Maybe I shouldn't have done that, I thought. You can't decimate a crazy person's cover and expect him to respond sanely. Typical that my one fan was a psycho.

'You're lying,' he said.

'Yes, you're right. I'm lying,' I said as I started to walk away. 'I was just kidding.'

He followed me. 'Lying is lying.'

Maybe I should try 911 instead of 411, I decided. Then, like in a Hollywood movie, without even pressing those three digits, I was saved.

'Get in.'

It was Jake, in his Porsche, alone. He threw a look at the psycho that sent the guy running for other prey.

I walked over to the passenger side of the car. The window was down. I leaned in. 'Thanks for rescuing me.'

'That's not why I'm here.'

'It isn't?'

'I saw David back there. I know what happened.'

'Forget it,' I said quickly, not ever wanting to appear like a victim, a loser, or a dumpee in front of Jake. 'I'm fine. No problem.'

'Get in,' he ordered.

'Why?' I wasn't looking for a sympathy vote.

'Don't blow this,' he said quietly. 'Just get in.'

And so I did.

Seventeen

I never considered asking where we were going. I knew this wasn't a simple lift home. Not to sound like a bad movie title, but I did feel as if I was on a 'date with destiny.' And how often do we get one of those? How often are we in an anxiety-free zone? Two times in the last ten years was my count. And those other times didn't involve an actual date. To be with a guy I was crazy about and to be anxiety-free was a whole new experience. Mimi wouldn't get it. She'd say a girl never knows. Pre-Evan, she'd been on dates with guys who flirted all night long and then, as they drove back from the movies or dinner, the guy would 'take a hard left on Beverly Boulevard' – Mimi's way of saying they dropped her off with a good-night kiss and nothing more.

'How can a girl ever be sure what a guy's thinking?' she'd ask earnestly. The answer to that is, you can't, but I did. I knew, from the minute I got into Jake's car. Sometimes things just build up momentum and, short of a forceful act of nature, nothing is going to fuck with the velocity.

I had only one question: 'Blaze?'

'Alex is taking care of her,' Jake answered as he turned east on Wilshire. 'After one of these premieres I can't go right home,' he confessed. 'I need to do something, go someplace that has nothing to do with Hollywood. My way of detoxing.'

'Does it work?'

'If it didn't, I'd never go to another premiere.'

'Not even your own?'

'Especially not my own.'

I wanted to tell him that he was my detoxer. Ten minutes in the car with him and what had felt like a bad acid trip was the faintest of memories. Jake was the antidote, my chemical balancer.

'You know what you are, Jake?'

'Don't tell me. Better I don't know.' He smiled.

'No, really. You'll like this. It's a compliment. You are a drug. A good drug.'

'I've been told that before.'

'By someone you haven't fucked?'

'No, never by someone I haven't fucked.' And then, because he never avoided the bottom line, even the harsh ones in his own life, he added, 'And never by someone who didn't need me to pay her rent.'

★

This is what I've always suspected about Jake. He understands the aesthetics of sex. I've always suspected that he is the kind of guy who understands that sex, like every other beautiful thing in life, has a rhythm and a grace. There are times when there's tremendous grace in throwing a girl up against a wall and fucking her, and other times when that move is crude and ultimately boring. He knows when to hold back and when to unzip. Though a lot of people in Hollywood write Jake off as a compulsive, an out-of-control misogynist, I've always suspected he understands the art of courtship better than anyone else in town. Not because of any chivalrous code, but because he knows, like any serious aesthete, a good setup results in a more rewarding payoff.

*

We ended up east, way east, way past La Brea, at a Mexican restaurant that, except for us, was filled with Mexicans. Jake knew Ruben, the bartender, and Elena, the hostess, who seated us at a cozy corner table. He spoke to them in Spanish, and though I couldn't understand a word, they acted as if he was one of their favorite customers.

'Where did you learn to speak Spanish?' I asked as an all-girl mariachi band took their position on a small stage in the front of the room.

'I live in L.A.,' he said.

'So do I.'

'So you should know what . . .' he rattled off something in Spanish, 'means.'

'What *does* that mean?'

He glanced toward the mariachi band. 'It's a line from one of their songs.'

'And what does that mean?'

'The literal translation is "Because of your accursed love, my soul is tossed by the wind." Which is another way of saying we're all doomed.'

'Have you always been this pessimistic and I just haven't noticed?'

'I talk tough. But you've probably figured out there's a lot of mush in me.' And then, uncomfortable with that jokey admission, he said, 'That's what's great about the Mexican culture. You can be mush and macho at the same time.'

We drank margaritas and listened to the music. The lead singer appeared to be no more than twenty years old. She sang with great passion and directed some of the lyrics at Jake.

'Tell me. Is she one of your girlfriends?' I asked playfully.

'She's Ruben's daughter. He'd have me killed if I so much as lit her cigarette.'

'I know how much you like danger. That must make her irresistible.'

He laughed as the band launched into a lively,

loud tune, one of those Mexican songs that can either make you feel like life is a fiesta or can depress you beyond belief. But we were both into it. Into all of it. The place. The people. The entertainment. And most of all, the fact that it felt as if we were thousands of miles from a Hollywood premiere.

And yet, the curse of being a writer is that even when I'm free of anxiety, and destiny is my date, I can't leave a good thing alone. I'm always trying to come up with a snappy line to describe and encourage the moment. An updated version of the kind of line Katharine Hepburn or Barbara Stanwyck might have uttered in one of those sophisticated forties films.

INT: MEXICAN RESTAURANT: NIGHT

ELIZABETH and JAKE are having a drink. They're seated near the stage, where an all-girl mariachi band is performing.

Theirs is the kind of sexual tension two people have before the first real kiss.

She nervously plays with the menu.

ELIZABETH
Here's something to consider: There are forty kinds of tequila on this menu and only seven story ideas in Hollywood.

He laughs. Their eyes lock. One step closer to that kiss. The band launches into a new tune as we . . .

CUT TO:

The thing about the lead-up to the first big kiss — in movies and in life — is that no matter what you talk about, it's all foreplay. Which is why when Jake brought up my career, I didn't panic and think *Oh no, he's having second thoughts.*

'I've got a couple of scripts I want you to look at,' he said.

'Uh . . . that's great. I'd love to work with you again, but . . .'

'There's a "but"?'

I hadn't planned on getting into this with him — or with anyone — but since he started it . . . 'I have to do something else first.'

'You're not doing the script for Renée, are you?'

'No, no, never.' I took a sip of my margarita. 'I've started to write a spec script. It'll probably never sell, and that's okay. It's just something I feel I've got to write for myself. Got to go a little deeper — if for no other reason than just to see if I can.'

He smiled. 'You . . .' he said. He was looking at me the way Mimi and Evan had looked at each other the day of their wedding. The way David had looked at his New York-actress girlfriend at the premiere.

311

'What?' I expected him maybe to tease me or say something sweet. What I never expected was that he would say something that rendered me speechless.

'I like you the way you are,' he said quietly.

You have to understand that when you grow up in Hollywood, you're constantly being measured against a fantasy ideal. Movie stars. Rock stars. Video Vixens. And off the screen – perfect bimbos, so many of them, everywhere you look. You grow up thinking that men look at you only in relation to that standard. 'Anyone ever tell you that you look a little like a young Natalie Wood?' (I don't) boosted my ego for a whole year when I was eighteen. Looking a little like someone else is what it's often about, which is why what Jake said stunned me. And if you make a writer speechless, not to mention breathless, then you know you've scored. Even a force of nature can't change that.

For a few moments nothing more was said. And then because we were both so far in, so deep into this date with destiny, I could afford to lighten things up for a second. I looked at the stage, looked back at Jake, and said, 'I think Ruben's daughter is flirting with me too.'

Eighteen

'Is this where you come on those nights when you don't want to be alone in your house?' I asked.

We were in a room on the fourth floor of a five-story hotel on the ocean side of Pacific Coast Highway. It wasn't a trendy place. I'd never heard of it or even noticed it before. But it was perfect. A simple but warm room with a big bed, a couple of dark wicker chairs, a few framed floral watercolors, and what appeared to be a working fireplace.

Jake stood at the window and stared out at the Pacific. 'I've been here a few times. Not lately.'

I joined him. 'I like that you never asked me if I wanted to come here. That you just assumed.'

'That's not confidence, just habit,' he admitted. 'Act like it's happening, and it'll happen. If that's not Hollywood's first commandment, I don't know what is.'

He twisted open a bottle of water he'd brought in from the car and took a sip before offering it to me.

I took it and stepped over to the bed and sat down. 'So here we are,' I said.

He moved toward me. 'Here we are.'

*

Later I would recall with astonishment that there had been no drugs or alcohol to keep us going all night. We didn't need it. We were already in an altered state, with more than enough adrenaline to reach sunrise. I wanted to remember everything about that night. Every feeling, thought, and action. And I think I did a pretty good job of logging in the memories. Though later when friends asked for details, I had only this to say: 'I would crawl across cut glass to suck his dick.' I know that sounds crude, but here's the thing: If I said I would crawl across cut glass to make a deal, no one would be surprised or appalled. The reaction would be, Well of course you would, you live in Hollywood. What can I say? I'd do it for a dick but not for a deal. Guess I'm not a material girl.

But don't misunderstand me. I don't literally mean I'm looking forward to a lifetime of bloody knees. It's a way of describing a certain kind of surrender. Call me an American geisha. I love the exhilaration that comes from surrendering to a man I respect but don't *need*. Being independent is the all-important American part of being an American geisha. I might occasionally be a wreck about getting another job, paying my bills, surviving, but I know, in the end, I can take care of myself. Without that, you're not surrendering, you're negotiating.

I guess the ideal is a man to whom you can surrender who also happens to be a Mr. Maybe. Not easy when you're attracted to bad boys. The authentic ones. The ones who work hard and play hard. The ones whose spirits demand diversity. The ones who seek truth and embrace ambiguity. The ones who don't pretend life isn't messy but who also believe in surprises. The ones who fuck you in such a way that it transforms your life.

I did worry a little though. After it was all over, when we were lying on the bed drenched in sweat, I had to ask, or explain, or disclaim.

'Was I hideous? I'm worried that I was too aggressive about wanting to surrender.'

'You were flawless,' he said.

And even though I wasn't, and never will be, his saying so made it a permanently flawless moment.

*

At eight A.M., I awoke to him dressed and ready to leave. It could have been high noon and I'd still have been in a dreamy state. Dreamy like something out of an Elvis movie.

'Okay,' I said. 'Where should I build a temple to thank the gods for bringing you into my life?'

'I've got to leave,' he said softly.

'That's all right. They still deserve the temple.'

He sat on the edge of the bed, his hand gently running up and down the inside of my leg. 'I'm going to suggest something which could make me sound like an asshole.'

'I doubt it,' I said. 'Once there's been penetration, there's no such thing as objectivity.'

He smiled and playfully gripped my thigh. 'I'm counting on that.'

In spite of the levity and the leg massage, I braced myself for his announcement.

'I'm going home now,' he said. 'That means home to Blaze, who I guess is my . . . girlfriend.' He stumbled over the word before continuing. 'I mean, she *is* my girlfriend.' He paused. 'Look, the thing is she's pregnant and . . .'

He got up and walked over to the window. 'Did I ever tell you I have a ten-year-old daughter?'

'You do? Here in L.A.?'

'No. In Maryland. I've seen her twice. Her mother hates me. And how about this? Always did. She was just one of those women who wanted to have a kid more than anything. We went out a couple of times, no big deal, then she calls and says, "I'm pregnant, I'm having the kid, and you have to support it."'

Jake shook his head, as if he still couldn't believe

it. A guy who always recognized the bottom line had missed that one ten years before, but he had it right this time. 'You know what women like that are? They're sperm trappers.'

I had to laugh. It was typical Jake. Truth, pain, and humor all rolled together in one sentence.

He laughed too. 'But this time,' he said, 'this time it's different.'

'Are you getting married?'

He moved back to the bed. 'I don't know. Maybe eventually. Maybe never.'

'At the risk of asking every cliché question in the book, Are you in love?'

He waited a moment before answering. 'When I was growing up there was a girl in my high school I always wanted to go out with. The night before she left for college, three thousand miles away, we had a date. The date turned out to be a disaster, but this is what I'll always remember. I'll always remember how excited I was as I walked out the door and got into my car. I'll never forget how great it felt driving to her house to pick her up.'

I knew exactly what Jake was talking about. Mimi would have looked at him like he was crazy, but I got it thanks to Norman Mailer. '*The Deer Park*,' I said.

'What?' Jake seemed bewildered.

'Did you ever read it?'

'Should I?'

'Yes, for a lot of reasons, but mostly because of this line: "The only faithfulness people have is towards emotions they're trying to recreate."'

'That's brilliant.'

For a few moments we remained silent. I understood the situation. I knew what hooked him to Blaze. And it was possible it could all turn out okay. Better than okay. This child could forge a bond between them that would keep them together, and maybe even happy, for a long time. Or Blaze could turn out to be another woman who was simply a fetal envelope looking for financial security. If I had to bet, I'd bet on its working, only because it isn't in my best interest to bet on anyone's failure. It may not be a Hollywood commandment, but it should be. By wishing failure on someone else you forfeit your right to divine protection. It's pragmatic spiritualism.

'So far you haven't said anything that made you sound like an asshole,' I said.

'I want to keep seeing you. I want to do this again and again.'

'Sounds good to me.' I was beaming.

'It could get complicated.'

'It doesn't have to.'

'No, but somehow these things always do. On the other hand, some forms of love come with no blueprint.'

'What's that a line from?'

'From my life,' he said with a smile.

★

When he left, my first thought was that I would never be able to fuck anyone but him: Who could follow in those footsteps? But that was just the first thought. I decided to stay around for a while. I didn't want to go home just yet. I decided to stay right where I was and look at the ocean. I moved a wicker chair onto the terrace and all afternoon sat there and thought and thought and thought. And this is what I came up with. If this were a movie, someone might sum up the plotline like this: Girl in the zone falls in love with a man who is seriously involved with another woman who at any minute could become his wife and in seven more months will definitely be the mother of his child.

Though that was true, it wasn't the whole story. Sure, conventional wisdom, which my experience has shown me isn't all that wise, would say that Jake was in this 'just for sex.' Even if that were the case, I've never understood the negative connotations of the phrase. 'Just for sex' is a lot – if the sex is good. It's no small thing to be getting fabulous sex. Same deal with the phrase 'just friends,' as if having a friend is insignificant. Friendship is gigantic. Where do the naysayers who go around saying 'just for sex' and 'just friends' get their attitude?

319

Being 'just friends' with Jake or having him call me 'just for sex' were two situations I could live with and enjoy. That thought shook me up as much as any third-act blow-up finale. How could any girl in the zone think such a thing? Ah . . . and then it grabbed me. This second explosion was the one the audience wasn't expecting. The surprise payoff. This was the first time in months that I felt free of the zone – which is another way of saying happy.

Mimi wouldn't get it. She'd never understand the big smile on my face. 'Are you insane? Where's this going to get you?'

Julie would be her usual nonjudgmental self. 'Sounds like you've got to play it out,' she'd conclude.

I'm living dangerously, I'd say. *I'm starting from hope.*

And then I realized there was only one person I could talk to, had to talk to, right then. And it had to be in person.

I picked up the phone and dialed. I knew his number as well as I know my own. 'Yes, yes, yes, you're there!' I practically screamed with excitement when he answered.

'What's wrong?' he asked.

'I've got to see you. What would you think of meeting me at the beach?'

I knew he'd say yes.

Nineteen

There weren't too many people on the beach at this time of day. But even if there'd been a crowd, I'd still have been able to pick out Andrew from a distance. I knew that walk of his, the body language, hands in pockets, shoulders slightly slumped, head slightly down. As he got closer and I could see his face clearly, I was relieved to see he looked fine.

'I'm back,' he said.

And he was back. We were back. Back to being best friends. We talked about Julie. Jake. Julie. Jake. Julie. Jake. Him. Julie. Me. Jake. Him. Julie. Him. Jake. Him. Me. Julie. Me. Him. Julie. Jake. Julie. Jake. Me. Him. Me and him? Hmmm. And, of course, the zone.

'I'm supposed to think happiness is about a guy, a baby, a family. But what if happiness can also be about a guy and no kids? Or a baby without a guy? Or a guy and someone else's kids? Or no guy? Or lots of guys? Or a friend and a kid? Or friends-plus and no kids? Why are all my girlfriends and I in a frenzy thinking there's only one way to live this life? Who wrote this fucking rule book?'

'Don't go Norma Rae on me,' Andrew joked.

'And why don't they want us to know that there are other books, other rules?'

Andrew dropped his arm around me. 'Don't go Oliver Stone on me.'

'What if there are lots of options in life?' I continued. 'At this moment, I think anything is possible.'

'You've changed the trajectory,' he said.

'Don't go technical on me,' I teased.

'It's a science. The angle of incidence. Alter an angle by half a degree and your target range can increase by an extra two miles. Shift your perspective slightly and the whole picture changes.'

The sun had just hit the water, and for a second it was as if a horizontal band of green light was drawn across the horizon.

'Live dangerously,' I said. I was about to add *Always start from hope*, but Andrew interrupted.

'Choose to be happy.'

'What?'

'Live dangerously, choose to be happy.'

There I was, speechless for the second time in twenty-four hours. Andrew had taken my motto to a higher level.

'Once you decide to go for what really makes you

happy,' he explained, 'a lot of the things you thought you wanted, or had to have just . . .'

'Go?'

'Gone.'

'That really is dangerous.' I said.

'Are you worried?'

'Not at all,' I said. 'Not yet.'